SANAAQ

CONTEMPORARY STUDIES ON THE NORTH
Series editor: Chris Trott

4 *Sanaaq*
An Inuit Novel
MITIARJUK NAPPAALUK

3 *Stories in a New Skin*
Approaches to Inuit Literature
KEAVY MARTIN

2 *Settlement, Subsistence, and Change among the Labrador Inuit*
The Nunatsiavummiut Experience
EDITED BY DAVID C. NATCHER, LAWRENCE FELT, AND ANDREA PROCTER

1 *Like the Sound of a Drum*
Aboriginal Cultural Politics in Denendeh and Nunavut
PETER KULCHYSKI

SANAAQ

An Inuit Novel

MITIARJUK NAPPAALUK

Transliterated and translated from Inuktitut to French by
Bernard Saladin d'Anglure
Translated from French by Peter Frost

ᓄᓇᕕᒻᒥ ᐊᑐᐊᒐᓐᖕᒍᑎᑕᐅᑎᑦᓯᕕᒃ
Publications Nunavik

UMP
University of Manitoba Press

University of Manitoba Press
Winnipeg, Manitoba
Canada R3T 2M5
uofmpress.ca

Publications Nunavik
Avataq Cultural Institute
Inukjuak, Quebec
Canada J0M 1M0
publicationsnunavik.com

Printed in Canada
Text printed on chlorine-free, 100% post-consumer recycled paper

18 17 16 15 14 1 2 3 4 5

Cover and interior design: Marvin Harder
Cover photo by Yaaka Markusie Yaaka, taken at Wakeham River near Kangiqsujuaq, Quebec, 2004.

Library and Archives Canada Cataloguing in Publication

Nappaaluk, Mitiarjuk
[Sanaaq. English]
Sanaaq : an Inuit novel / by Mitiarjuk Nappaaluk ; transliterated and translated from Inuktitut to French by Bernard Saladin d'Anglure, translated from French by Peter Frost.

Includes bibliographical references and index.
Issued also in electronic formats.
ISBN 978-0-88755-748-4 (pbk.)
ISBN 978-0-88755-446-9 (PDF e-book)
ISBN 978-0-88755-447-6 (epub e-book)

I. Frost, Peter, translator II. Saladin d'Anglure, Bernard, 1936-, translator III. Avataq Cultural Institute, issuing body IV. Title. V. Title: Sanaaq. English.

PS8576.I8873S3513 2014 C897'.1243 C2013-903755-1
C2013-903756-X

The University of Manitoba Press gratefully acknowledges the financial support for its publication program provided by the Government of Canada through the Canada Book Fund, the Canada Council for the Arts, the Manitoba Department of Culture, Heritage, Tourism, the Manitoba Arts Council, and the Manitoba Book Publishing Tax Credit.

CONTENTS

FOREWORD

Sanaaq is an atypical novel. Atypical like its author Mitiarjuk, an Inuk[1] from Nunavik (Arctic Quebec) who was illiterate in the sense of being unable to read or write the Roman letters that European languages use and that have recently been adopted for her language. Yet she is deservedly called a writer. She wrote over a thousand pages in syllabics—a kind of shorthand that Wesleyan missionaries created in the late nineteenth century to advance the conversion of the Canadian Cree Indians, who had no writing system of their own. The syllabic alphabet was then adapted by other missionaries to the Inuit language of present-day Nunavik and Nunavut. As new prayer books came into use, it spread quickly through imitation and learning.

Mitiarjuk never went to school. She nevertheless earned a PhD from McGill University in June 2000 for helping advance the teaching of Nunavik's Inuit language and culture. Her school was the world of her mother and related female elders, who taught the many tasks of women's traditional work. Less traditionally, her father taught her the secrets of hunting and other male tasks, having no sons and she being his oldest daughter. He was in poor health and often had to let her hunt wild game alone. Culturally and socially, she belonged to a "third sex"[2] (or gender), neither male nor female, which gradually made her a mediator between the men and women

1 Out of respect for the Inuit language and in keeping with the practice of the journal over the past forty years, I refer to one Inuit person as an "Inuk" and more than one as "Inuit." The adjective "Inuit" is invariable, e.g., the Inuit language, the Inuit culture. All authors who speak the Inuit language use this form of writing.

2 Bernard Saladin d'Anglure, "Le 'troisième sexe,'" July–August 1992, 836–844.

of her people and between different generations. Perhaps this explains her renowned creativity, as evidenced by the stone carvings that have earned her prestigious awards.

While not shirking the role of a devoted mother (later a grandmother) and wife, she always enjoyed taking part in the political and social debates of her community and even in academic debates, such as at several conferences organized by *Inuit Studies*. Occasionally, at seasonal camps she always enjoyed rounding out her diet by hunting seals or birds. She was valued by everyone in her home village, men and women alike, and became known far beyond the borders of Quebec and Canada. In 1977, Radio-Canada featured her in the TV series *Femmes d'aujourd'hui*. In 1999, the National Aboriginal Achievement Foundation awarded her its national prize for excellence and, in 2001, UNESCO honoured her literary works at an international conference of Indigenous writers in Paris.

At the age of sixteen, she was courted by the best hunters of the local bands, being admired for her personal qualities and hunting prowess. The successful suitor was the youngest one. He agreed to live with her parents and take her place as the family's provider—contrary to the Inuit custom of the wife moving in with the husband's parents. She devoted the first years of her marriage to her children and husband, at times missing the hunting life. Yet she quickly came to the attention of the local Catholic missionaries, who were studying the Inuit language and translating their prayer books. Her dynamism and familiarity with the local culture made her a valuable assistant. She initially assisted Father Lucien Schneider, O.M.I., in producing his Inuit/French dictionary. She then worked with Father Robert Lechat, O.M.I., who wanted to improve his proficiency in the native language. He provided lined notebooks and asked her to write down sentences, in syllabics, that contained as many terms as possible from daily life. She started writing in her igloo or tent, while the children slept or when free from household chores. But this task grew wearisome. Letting her imagination roam, she created characters and described their fortunes and misfortunes over the different seasons. In short, she recounted the life of a small group of semi-nomadic Inuit families just before the first

(Europeans) became established in the region. At twenty-two years of age, Mitiarjuk reinvented the novel, even though she had never read one.

This novel is atypical in more than one way. First, it reflects the author's initial task of transcribing as many terms and grammatical structures from her language as possible. The vocabulary is thus large (nearly 3,000 words) and highly redundant, as may be seen in the frequent use of synonyms. Second, the novel took almost twenty years to write, for several reasons. The first part covered a little over half of the final manuscript. It stopped at the beginning of episode 24 (The Legend of Lumaajuq) because the author had to leave for a long stay at a hospital in the South and then because Father Lechat had been transferred to Kuujjuaq (Fort Chimo). Father Joseph Méeus, O.M.I., took over supervision of her work and about forty new pages were written, i.e., episodes 25 to 37. The novel continued to remain unfinished with her return to hospital and the transfer of Father Méeus to another village. Mitiarjuk stopped writing for several years.

I met Father Lechat in January 1956 during my first stay in Arctic Quebec. He welcomed me to Kuujjuaq, offering the hospitality of his mission, and told me about the novel *Sanaaq*. In his hands was the first part, written in pencil with almost nothing crossed out or added. It had been transliterated into Roman letters, with the author's help, before he had left Kangirsujuaq, and had also been partially translated. But the spelling of the Inuit language had not yet been standardized and the imprecision of syllabic writing, the lack of punctuation, and the distance from the author made the job impossible for him to pursue. He read me some of the translation and my interest was aroused right away. It was not until 1961 that I finally met Mitiarjuk, during anthropological fieldwork at Kangirsujuaq. I convinced her to start writing again. The next year Father Lechat gave me his manuscript of *Sanaaq* so that I could work on it with Mitiarjuk. This literary work was now the focus of my PhD, the challenge being to make it available to the public. When Father Méeus provided the other part of the manuscript, everything fell into place for what became the final novel.

With the support of Claude Lévi-Strauss, who had been supervising my research from his Laboratoire d'anthropologie sociale in Paris, I was given funding for an eighteen-month mission by the Centre national de la Recherche scientifique (France). I went to Kangirsujuaq in the spring of 1965 with a heavy agenda:

- record Mitiarjuk reading the syllabic version of her manuscript, in order to transliterate it as precisely as possible into standard alphabetical spelling;
- punctuate the text with her help;
- work with her on a line-by-line translation;
- check the transliteration and the translation with the village's new missionary, Father Jules Dion, O.M.I., who had offered me his assistance;
- ask Mitiarjuk about any difficult passages we might come across;
- record, transcribe, and translate her comments on the text;
- go through the different activities in the novel and observe them in day-to-day Inuit life, to gain a better understanding;
- photograph (or even shoot on 16-mm colour film) the technical operations described in the manuscript; and
- identify the animal and plant species mentioned in the novel, etc.

These activities took me six years, including the time spent working with the author during the summers of 1967, 1968, and 1969. She completed episodes 24 and 38, and added six new ones, nearly sixty new pages, not to mention a sequel to the novel, now being transliterated and translated. In addition, nearly 500 pages of ethnographic commentary were written, transcribed, and translated and now await publication. Father Schneider agreed to read and revise my translations and transcriptions before retiring to Europe. Finally, in 1983 a publishing contract was signed with Mitiarjuk, who asked me to make the necessary arrangements for publication of her work, then in my hands. The first draft of *Sanaaq* was published by the Association Inuksiutiit

(Quebec) with funding from Quebec's Ministère des Affaires culturelles. It had been rewritten in standard syllabics from my alphabetical transliteration and was lavishly illustrated. While visiting Mitiarjuk in the spring of 1999, I was quite surprised to see the fifty author's copies she had received in 1984 carefully kept in a cupboard. She intended to have them passed on to her many descendants after her death.

This version may be found in all Inuit schools across northern Canada. It is now out of print.

Much remained to translate the manuscript for non-Inuit readers. There were many additions and the whole text needed the form and flow of a novel written for the average person. I again got to work and, with the assistance of the Avataq Cultural Institute and Canada's Department of Indian and Northern Affairs, this task dominated my life for much of the years 2000 to 2002. The enthusiasm of publisher Alain Stanké and his publishing team brought everything to fruition, and fifty years after being first written my French translation of this unique work was published (2002) and soon became a Canadian bestseller. This English edition of *Sanaaq* was translated by Peter Frost from the French version.

This novel lets us share the daily lives of Mitiarjuk's characters, with their seasonal activities and also the joys and pains of their life cycle. But it seems appropriate to inform the reader about certain aspects of this life story, using the very numerous comments that the author made to me during our many years of working closely together. I will thus deal with the form, the content, the historical and cultural context and, finally, the characters of this striking work of literature.

FORM AND STYLE

Mitiarjuk's style is brisk, fluid, and lively, with precise, detailed descriptions. This is all the more remarkable because she seldom reread her work and hardly ever corrected what she wrote. It must be said that the syllabic writing system, in its simplest form—the one used in *Sanaaq*'s manuscript—is really a kind of shorthand that can be written almost as fast as it can be read aloud. This fact, together with the oral manner of passing on traditional knowledge among the Inuit, may account for the great spontaneity of her writing and the importance given to direct speech. There are virtually no pages without at least one sentence in direct speech. This makes the writing so vivid that the novel seems at times to read like a film script. On another note, the sensorial intelligence of the Inuit is more developed than that of Western peoples. For them, the senses of hearing, sight, touch, and smell, combined with taste, are invaluable tools for hunting, sewing, and food preparation. Mitiarjuk has strewn her novel with expressions that evoke sounds: the crackling of a flame in an oil lamp or the dripping of water falling to the ground. One also comes across onomatopoeia: words like *tikkuu* for a gun going off or *sarvaq* for an object plunking into the water. There are many interjections to express feelings or the calls of animals. Finally, much use is made of children's language with its reduplication of syllables: *apaapa* (food), *uquuqu* (bird or sea animal), and *utuutu* (land animal).

Content and Implicit Surrounding Details

This novel may be read on several levels. First, one can focus on the action, the feelings, and the relationships between the characters, thereby gaining a mass of details on the Inuit culture and life of the past—and also on Inuit psychology, which is so inaccessible when one does not speak the language and does not know the sociocultural milieu. On this first level, too, slight variations are noticeable in the content of the episodes, depending on whether they were written for the missionaries or for the anthropologist. Some self-censorship by the author may be detected in the first two manuscripts collected by the Oblates, i.e., the first thirty-seven episodes. Mitiarjuk was a practising Catholic and in these episodes, through the utterances of Sanaaq, her heroine, she expresses moralizing judgments on the old beliefs, such as omens. She avoids any allusions to sex or to invisible beings, which appear in the rest of the novel. In episode 27, when describing the bone game, the author wrote after listing the different little bones: "There is still one whose name I don't dare give." Questioned in 1965 about this omission, she confessed that the bone was an *utsulutuq* (figurine of a vulva), which she then added to her list. The second part of episode 24, interrupted by the author's hospitalization and completed later for the anthropologist, clearly shows a change in attitude, with a long development on mythology and beliefs. Furthermore, the last ten episodes address themes that are absent from the initial manuscripts, such as conjugal violence, sexual possession by incubus and succubus spirits, and sexual relations with *Qallunaat*.

On a second level of textual understanding, which requires good knowledge of the Inuit milieu, there is a mass of implicit information that fleshes out the meaning of the text and that appears in the author's comments. It would have doubled the novel's volume had it been included.

A third level of interpretation of *Sanaaq* is harder to grasp. On the one hand, it deals with Mitiarjuk's personal life, i.e., the events and experiences that inspired or influenced her literary creation. On the other, it deals with the symbolism that is present in Inuit culture. This symbolism may be detected in the form of day-to-day objects, in the way different aspects of the human body and the natural environment are perceived, and in the Inuit terms that designate them. I will confine myself here to one example. When Mitiarjuk began to read aloud the first few lines of episode 9 of her manuscript, where Qalingu is coming back from hunting in his *qajaq*, I was surprised to see her smile while reading the following passage: "Arnatuinnaq hauled the *qajaq* out of the water by pulling on its *usuujaq* (bow)." This term, as mentioned in the glossary, literally means "what looks like a penis." I interrupted her and asked what was making her smile. She burst out laughing and told me the following story:

> Fifteen years ago, my cousin Nutaraaluk was sleeping in the family igloo. She shared the same skin blanket as her young brother, an adolescent about ten years old. All of a sudden, in the middle of the night, the whole family was awoken by the cries of the young boy, still asleep, like his sister. The mother raised the skin blanket and saw that the young girl was pulling with both hands on her brother's penis... Awakened by her mother, Nutaraaluk recounted that she dreamed that her brother was coming back from hunting in his *qajaq* and that she was helping him come ashore by pulling on its bow.

Historical and Cultural Context

The novel has many historical references:

- arrival of the first Whites by boat and establishment of the first traders [episode 8];
- visit of the first Anglican and Catholic missionaries, and establishment of a Catholic mission [ep. 25];
- landing of the first airplane [ep. 23];
- first evacuation by air to a hospital in the South [ep. 39];
- first intervention by the police and threat of imprisonment for beating and injuries [ep. 40];
- first visit by a Northern Affairs agent, first payment of family allowances and old age pensions, and first paid employment offered to the Inuit outside the village [ep. 43];
- first medical visit by a nurse, and sending of young patients to a hospital in the South [ep. 45]; and
- first Catholic baptism, and conflicts with the Anglican pastor [ep. 46].

One must not, however, look for a rigorous historical framework in this novel. Although Mitiarjuk had direct knowledge of the region's events since she was born in the early 1930s, events further back are known from what the elders told her and were thus, in her memory, condensed into a shorter time-frame. Her parents told her about the establishment of the first trading post (Révillon Frères) at Kangirsujuaq, in 1910, followed by the Hudson's Bay Company post four years later. As early as 1884, however, an ice-observing station had been established and it operated for two years on Stupart Bay. It was the first sustained contact with *Qallunaat* for most of the local Inuit. Only a few heads of family had previously had the opportunity to meet any while fur trading—first on the Labrador Coast, then in the Great Whale region and, finally, from the 1860s on, at Fort Chimo on Ungava Bay. When the story begins, the Inuit were already using tobacco, matches, and guns. They had old coal bags, old tin cans, and fabrics. With regard to Christianity, the first attested visits by Inuit-speaking missionaries were those of Rev. Peck, who went to Kangirsujuaq by boat from Baffin Island in the early 1920s and baptized some Inuit. So many would eventually be evangelized that when Catholic missionaries established the first permanent mission, in 1936, the Anglicans had already baptized the entire population. Mitiarjuk's father was one of the catechists for the community. Nonetheless, Mitiarjuk enthusiastically joined the new Christian faith in the 1940s. It was a personal choice and she stuck by it. This has not been so for many other Anglican and Catholic families who have chosen to join the Pentecostal church in recent years.

Although the last shamans passed away in the late 1920s, taking with them the great shamanistic rituals, many traditional beliefs and practices have persisted while being intermixed with Christian beliefs and practices. The belief in the invisible world's influence on human behaviour has even been strengthened with the rise of Christian fundamentalism in the Arctic.

The cultural context in which the first part of the manuscript was conceived and written was that of the early 1950s, when the Inuit of Kangirsujuaq spent winter in their igloos, in five or six camps, and spring and summer in their tents, in a dozen or so small hunting camps. This way of life was a false archaism, to borrow an expression from Lévi-Strauss, for it was an impoverished form of the life from before the coming of the *Qallunaat*. The combined effects of the Great Depression of the 1930s, the plummeting prices for Arctic fox pelts, and the Second World War had brought about the closing of the two trading posts that had operated there since 1914. The caribou, so important to the traditional economy, had gone, as had the *umiat* (large multi-passenger boats covered with sealskins) which were used to move families over long distances in summer and autumn. The few owners of Peterheads (wooden boats with a sail and motor) purchased when Arctic fox prices were at their height, had left the territory for other communities that still had trading posts.

In 1950, the Inuit of Kangirsujuaq received their first family allowance and old age pension cheques. In 1961, they had their first small prefab homes, their first school, and their first motor boats. Then came snowmobiles, electricity from generators, housing developments, and the sedentarization of families around establishments (missions, stores, schools, and nursing stations). What makes this novel interesting is that it covers the pre- and early transitional period, i.e., Mitiarjuk's childhood from the early 1930s to the aftermath of the Second World War.

Characters

There are about thirty characters in the book, fifteen or so of whom play an active role. The active ones are those close to Sanaaq—the young widow at the centre of the story—and a few *Qallunaat*. In many ways, the heroine resembles the author, while differing from her in other ways. Like Mitiarjuk, she is responsible for a young sister and marries a young, inexperienced man who often has to seek advice from his older sister and her old husband. Like Mitiarjuk, Sanaaq has a strong will that impresses her husband. She is nonetheless tender toward her children and compassionate toward people in need. She is also capable of self-criticism when her emotions get the better of her reason.

The novel gives women major roles in all generations: Sanaaq's old relative, Ningiukuluk—with her bad character—who is nonetheless loved and respected; Aqiarulaaq, Sanaaq's friend, partner, and rather scatterbrained stepsister; Arnatuinnaq, the young, active, and sentimental sister; and Qumaq, the little daughter who single-mindedly does what she wants but thinks over her mistakes and tries to correct them. All of these female characters, through their weaknesses, set off Sanaaq's rich personality.

Except for old Taqriasuk, the most elderly man in the camp, whose knowledge and advice are appreciated, the male characters appear to be lightweights. They try to perform their role of provider, while plagued by numerous blunders and gaffes (Irsutualuk is rejected by Sanaaq, who stands up to Qalingu, her husband), by tragedies (Jiimialuk's death), by fears (panic of Maatiusi and Ilaijja), and by distress (possession of Maatiusi by a succubus after he suffers disappointment in love). The White men hardly fare any better with their rather futile religious quarrels, their maladjustment to the cold and to the North, and their loose relations with Inuit women (harassment of Arnatuinnaq by store employees).

In all this we have an original female viewpoint on Inuit life and psychology—too often described by men and by people from outside Inuit culture who have underestimated the contribution of women and ignored their viewpoint.

To conclude, I will say that Mitiarjuk always attached much importance to her language and its proper usage. Instead of getting by with a kind of pidgin English when seeking to be understood by *Qallunaat,* like many fellow Inuit, she always insisted on correcting mistakes and giving the exact term or the correct grammatical form. *Sanaaq* attests to this rigour, as well as to a lively imagination without limits. It will always be a reference book for coming generations of Aboriginal men and women. For non-Aboriginals, it will be an invaluable introduction to a culture that is so captivating and has changed so much.

On May 14, 2004, Mitiarjuk received her investiture as a Member of the Order of Canada from the Right Honourable Adrienne Clarkson, Governor General of Canada, with the following citation:

> One of the most respected elders in Nunavik, Mitiarjuk Attasie Nappaaluk is committed to sharing her knowledge and to preserving the Inuit culture. As a young woman, she taught missionaries her language and, in return, she was taught to write syllabic script. Thus, her life as a writer and teacher began. Since then, she has authored twenty-two books that have served as teaching tools, has overseen teacher training and has helped develop a curriculum for the Kativik School Board. As well, she wrote *Sanaaq,* the first novel written in Inuktitut. Also involved in municipal and health issues, she is the recipient of a National Aboriginal Achievement Award.

She was now in poor health. Back in her community and surrounded by her beloved family, she passed away in May 2007, one year after I had last visited her.

Thanks go to two of my old friends: Peter Frost, PhD, my former student at Laval University, for his professional translation into English, and Christopher Trott, PhD, Warden and Vice-Chancellor, St. John's College, University of Manitoba, for his enthusiastic efforts with the University of Manitoba Press and with Avataq Cultural Institute to promote this English edition and unique piece of Inuit literature. A thousand new pages were written in syllabics by Mitiarjuk at my request and are waiting to be published for the benefit of the Inuit people and the rest of the world. This should be an exciting challenge...

Bernard Saladin d'Anglure, CM, PhD
Professor emeritus
Centre interuniversitaire d'études et de recherches autochtones (CIÉRA) University Laval, Quebec City

SANAAQ

I

GATHERING DWARF BIRCH

A woman, Sanaaq, was getting ready to go and gather branches for mat-making. This is what she did. Before leaving, she assembled a tumpline to carry the load, her ulu to cut the shrubs, and a glove to yank them out of the ground. She also filled a small bag with provisions: tea, meat, and blubber, as well as her pipe, matches, and chewing tobacco.

Sanaaq set off across a wide plain and then through a long stretch of foothills. She kept walking further and further from home, followed by her two dogs, Kajualuk and Qirniq. On the way she saw some *aqiggiit* and prepared to kill them with a few well-aimed stones. But the dogs ran after the birds. Sanaaq tried her best to stop the dogs, yelling at the top of her voice, "*Hau! Hau!* Kajualuk *hau! hau!*"

Her shouting was to no avail and the dogs continued to give chase. The ptarmigans flew off. Very much annoyed, she continued on her way and came to the end of her journey.

There, she busied herself preparing an *ullugummitaaq* and making a fire. Her teapot was a small metal bucket and the water came from a small pool. She placed a few stones around the fireplace for shelter from the wind and gathered some heather to keep the fire going. She now waited for the tea to boil, eating some meat and blubber. The dogs, no longer asleep and rolled up into furry balls, were foraging for her scraps of meat and bone. Suddenly one of them, Kajualuk, started choking on a bone. Sanaaq was panic-stricken. What to do? Thinking fast, she remembered the leftover pieces of blubber: "If I can make it swallow some large chunks of blubber, that might help it get rid of the bone."

She gave the poor animal what she still had. The chunks of blubber did the job, helping the bone slide down the dog's throat and letting it breathe freely again. At last she could drink her tea, straight from the small teapot for want of a cup. Soot smudged her hands and mouth, even her cheeks. Unaware (how could she see herself?), she went to gather branches for mat-making. Some dwarf birches looked suitable and she started yanking them out of the ground, using her ulu to cut the more stubborn ones. When one patch of ground had been stripped bare, she moved to the next, leaving behind piles of pulled-up birches. She pulled up more and more, one after another, the sweat streaming down her face… Then she stopped. Stretching her tumpline out on the ground, she bundled the branches for the trip home. There was much to take back and the load would be a heavy one. After tying the bundle up, she lit her pipe and puffed repeatedly, inhaling deep breaths. The provisions were all gone and she was very hungry. She strapped the tumpline around her chest and, laying the bundle on a large rock, finished fastening it to her body to carry in front of her. The load was indeed heavy. She could barely stand up.

She began the long trip home, foraging for anything edible on the way, although it was now twilight. The route was uphill and so tiring that it was often necessary to stop for rest. Several times she found some wild berries. She picked them as a gift for her daughter, who was minding their home, and dropped them into the improvised teapot.

The little girl was waiting at home and was increasingly in Sanaaq's thoughts as home drew nearer. Sanaaq was almost there but the two dogs were the first to arrive. She trailed behind, within eyesight.

Her daughter saw her and shouted, "It's Mother! It's Mother!"

The little girl ran out so eagerly that she fell several times, even hitting her face on a rock. Finally the two were together. The mother cuddled her little girl—no wonder, she had just hit her face on a rock—and offered the small berries she had picked for her. She then gave her a *kuni,* murmuring a *mmm...* of affection and taking her by the hand. Arriving outside their home and exhausted, Sanaaq put her burden down and crawled in headfirst, pushing the bundle in front of her.

"It's yours to take inside!" she said.

It was taken inside and she was finally home.

A quick arrival meal was made ready. She ate some of the boiled seal—a shoulder blade and a rib—that had been saved on a plate for her return. Her daughter Qumaq—that was her name—sat beside her. Helping herself to the food, Sanaaq exclaimed, "My ulu, Qumaq, pass me my ulu!"

The little girl passed it to her and had some of the boiled meat. Sanaaq recounted how their dog had choked on a bone.

"Kajualuk was choking and I tried to get the bone out by getting it to gulp down the pieces of blubber I still had... That was all I had left of my provisions... A bit longer and the dog would've been a goner. For a long time after, it would whimper while I was making tea, because of the bone that had been stuck in its throat."

Her daughter was curious. "Mother, was it our big dog?"

"Yes!"

Qumaq began to chatter "*Taka taka taka...*" while playing on the sleeping platform. Her mother knew it was bedtime.

"Daughter, I'll help you undress and you'll go to bed. It's now quite late... I'll take your boots off. *Iii!* My, my, they're soaking wet! My girl is really getting around! She just got those boots! I'll soak a piece of leather for you to make a new sole. I'll let it soak overnight."

She put a piece in a plate to soak. Qumaq undressed for bed, talking all the while. "Mother *ai! Apaapa!* I'd like to eat some black crowberries!"

"Take a few, but that's all for today. I don't want you getting sick to your stomach!"

"Yes! By the way, Mother, I don't have a daddy, do I?"

Being just a child, she said whatever crossed her mind. Her mother answered, "No, it's true, you don't. Long ago your father died, a very long time ago. We'll see him only in the hereafter... Long ago he fell into the water while travelling far away... He often told us to behave properly. So you too will try to behave yourself!"

"*Ai!* He died when I was very little!"

Mother and daughter had finished talking to each other and tried to go to sleep. But no sooner had Qumaq fallen asleep than she began to sleepwalk. She stood up and walked, sobbing, "Mother, carry me on your back... Let's both go walking..."

Sanaaq reached out and pulled her daughter close, to put her back to sleep.

2

IRSUTUALUK AND THE FISHING DAY THAT WASN'T

Irsutualuk and his son Angutikallaaluk were going fishing for *iqaluppik* in the river. The time was ideal because the char were swimming upstream to the lakes. They set out on their way, intending to camp overnight by the river and taking a dog as a pack animal. As they left, the father said, "If there are any *iqaluppik,* we won't be back tomorrow. We'll try to fill several stone caches."

They began walking. The son led their dog, Taqulik, on a leash. After a while they stopped to rest. The father heard something like a willow ptarmigan: "*Irrr!...*"

"Listen!" whispered the father. "A ptarmigan is calling from up there!"

"Where?"

"Up there!"

"I'll go look... Listen to it calling! There it is, up there! I'm going to shoot... Missed! It flew off."

"Let's go! Time to get on our way again."

They came to the river and set their net. One of them waded across and the other stayed on the bank. They stretched the net from one bank to the other but there was not the slightest sign of any Arctic char.

"Looks like there aren't any," said Irsutualuk. "Let's make sure by throwing some blubber into the water upstream. The wind is making the surface quite dark."

"Don't seem to be any around!" concluded Angutikallaaluk. "Just to be sure, *ai!*, I'll pitch some stones into the water and see if I can flush any of them out... Now I'm sure! None at all... I really feel like heading back. So what if we go home the same day... They probably haven't got this far upstream."

His father agreed. "Let's head off! Time to go home! But first let's make a cache and stash away our provisions. We'll be coming by here later."

They both headed back to their camp. As they walked, the father began thinking, "I'd really like to have Sanaaq as a wife, even though I'm a bit old..."

They soon arrived back at the camp. There were others: Sanaaq's family, Irsutualuk's family, and the family of Ningiukuluk, who was Sanaaq's relative.

3

A DAY IN THE TENT

We are now back with Qumaq and her mother. Their sleep had again been disturbed, this time by several visitors. Sanaaq lived with Arnatuinnaq, her younger sister. All three had been outside for some time when they saw the men come back from fishing for *iqaluppik*. Sanaaq shouted, "Look, they're back from fishing for *iqaluppik*. They probably caught some!"

Hearing this, Qumaq asked, "Mother, those men out there, what have they been doing?"

"They've been fishing for Arctic char!"

Qumaq went back to her games, saying, "I'll draw something! I'll draw little dog teams, Mommy!"

"Daughter," said her mother, "come and I'll wash your dress, because the water I put in to heat is almost boiling. I'll give it a good wash... Sister, get busy. Tomorrow you'll be sewing some *sulluniit*. So start cutting some seal skin to make them!"

She poured the water she had been heating and began her wash.

"*Aa! Aaah!* I scalded myself! *Aa! Aatataa!* I must have a burn. My hand's throbbing with pain. Qumaq! Daughter! Cool this water down a bit, so I can wash your filthy dress... Now I've got it clean. But where's my shirt? I'd like to wash it too while I'm at it."

"It's up there," replied Arnatuinnaq, "in the *kilu.*"

"Go get it if you see it! I really feel like some tea but it takes too long to prepare. I'll make some when I'm done washing this. Here we go, time to wring it dry... *Uuppaa!*" She was squeezing hard. "It's probably not as dry as I'd like."

"Mother," said Qumaq. "I'm hungry! *Apaapa!*"

"I hear you. Fetch my ulu! It's in the *aki*... You're going to eat some *nikku.*"

She cut off a chunk of *nikku.*

"There you are! Dip it in the *misiraq*... Be careful not to spill any down the front of your shirt."

"I won't!" replied Qumaq.

"And sit down!" added her mother.

Just then Ningiukuluk walked in.

"*Ai!* Ningiukuluk *ai!*" exclaimed Sanaaq.

Her daughter cried out, "*Anaanatsiaq ai!* Look! I'm eating some *apaapait.*"

"*Iii!* There's oil running down all over her hands," said Ningiukuluk indignantly. "Sanaaq! Lick them clean and give her only solid food to eat! I'll get you eating right, little girl!"

"I'm done. I don't want any more!" said Qumaq.

"Clean your hands with this willow ptarmigan skin," said her mother.

Qumaq responded by wailing, "No! *Ii Iiii! Ia-a!*"

She was afraid, the poor little girl, of this big feathery thing she had been given for a hand towel. Her mother added, "Well then, I'll clean your hands with this piece of a coal bag. No feathers on it. Otherwise you won't clean your hands properly... Ningiukuluk! You and I let's play cards while the tea heats over the oil lamp!

We'll then melt some blubber over the lamp... Sister! Get the pieces of blubber we're going to melt. Pound the oil out of them, there, in the little bowl. Let's go! Ningiukuluk, let's play cards. You're dealing! We'll each put five matches into the pot. Is it my turn to throw away a card?"

"Yes!"

"I beat you! *Iii!*" She burst into laughter. "It's mine!"

"Let's call it a night. I've got to go home!" said Ningiukuluk.

Qumaq called out, "Come to me, Mother, I'm sleepy!"

"Go lie down on the sleeping platform. I'll put you to sleep. Take your boots off!"

The little girl was soon asleep. It was evening and time for Sanaaq to fetch some water. She took a dipper with her. When she got to the nearest stretch of water, she began filling the dipper.

"It's full of insects! There are even diving beetles... I'll draw my water elsewhere, preferably from a pool higher up."

She began filling her dipper again. When it was full, she noticed some clouds and thought, "That big one is a rain cloud. Even dark enough to be a storm cloud."

She walked back. When she got home, she said, "Looks like we're going to have thunder. The clouds are really dark now."

"*Ai!*" said her younger sister. "If it thunders overnight, it's going to be all the more scary... I wish there were more of us!"

They tried to fall asleep, everyone except Arnatuinnaq. She remained fully dressed and stretched out on the bed, for fear of thunder. It did thunder during the night and loud claps rocked the air.

"It's thundering something awful!" cried out Arnatuinnaq, awaking her older sister.

The rain became a downpour, so much so that a steady stream of water dripped through the tent lining.

4

FISHING ON THE FORESHORE

Everyone awoke at daybreak. Arnatuinnaq said to her niece, "Qumaq! Let's go fishing, the two of us, on the foreshore. Tomorrow we'll be moving to Ujararjuaq for good. Let's go fishing on the foreshore here one last time! *Ai!* Qumaq! It'd be a good thing to bring along a digging tool, in case we come across any *ammuumajuit.*"

Sanaaq spoke up. "Daughter, take this little pail to put them in. Sister, you can dig with a *kiliutaq.*"

"Let's go! Let's go to the foreshore!" said Arnatuinnaq.

They began walking. Qumaq shouted, "Auntie! Wait for me! Give me your hand!"

When they came to the foreshore, the aunt said to her niece, "Qumaq! This pool is probably full of *kanajuit.* It has a lot of stones that can be lifted up. Let's have a look! I'll start with this one!" She lifted it. "Yes, look! A sculpin! It's slipping out from under. There it goes... I'll catch it!"

"Auntie, did you catch a sculpin?"

"Yes, I caught one, but there goes another. It's sliding underneath the big stone. Wait a bit *ai!* I'll force it out with a stick. Watch to see if it swims that way!"

"Yes, the water's swarming with all kinds of *uquuqu!* I'm going to catch a big *uquuqu!*"

"Get a good grip on it with your hand! There's nothing to be afraid of!"

"Oh! It got away!"

Many swam away from Arnatuinnaq but she still caught quite a few. Inside the pail, the captured sculpins were flipping their tails and thumping against each other. The two had stopped looking for sculpins and were now in search of clams.

"It's full of clams! Their holes are everywhere," said Arnatuinnaq. "I'll dig this one up. It's just under the mud. Over there is another clam squirting water. I'll dig it up..." After a while she spoke again. "We've gathered a lot of clams and it's time to go home. The water's rising now. I'm done filling my pail, let's go! We're going home!"

"Sure!"

They headed home. Arnatuinnaq exclaimed, "Look at all the *kaugaliat,* Qumaq! Let's eat some limpets!"

"Yes!"

"I've got a stone to break them open... *Uu!* I just love sucking the innards out of a clam! *Uu!* Are they ever good! What a great taste! Look, the water's really rising now. Let's go home. Your mother's minding the tent all by herself."

So they went home. After all, they had to move the next day. When they arrived, Qumaq's mother was overcome by affection for her daughter. "Daughter! *U! Aalummi!* Come to me, my little one! Did you learn all the tricks of fishing on the foreshore? *Aalummi!* Have some tea, both of you... I have some ready for you. Let's eat clams! Pass me a plate. I'll put them on..."

Kuu kuu kuu! One by one the clams clunked down onto the plate.

"Let's also get a container for the juice dripping out of them and another for the empty shells," added Sanaaq. "Daughter! I'll crack your clams open and you'll collect the juice. That's how you're going to eat them. Do as I say... Take this one. Enough! I don't want any more!"

"Me neither!" chimed in Arnatuinnaq, followed by Qumaq.

Sanaaq said to her sister, "Put these aside. As for the empty shells, toss them onto the rubbish heap!"

No sooner had Arnatuinnaq taken them out than the dogs came bounding after her, yelping, "*Muu muu muu!*"

They began to yap and fight amongst themselves. It was too much for poor Arnatuinnaq. "*Uai!* Look at all those dogs! Scram, you filthy creatures! If only I had something to throw at them!"

She went back in. Night was falling.

"The water has stopped rising!" she announced.

"*Ai!*" said her older sister. "We'll probably be moving tomorrow to our camp mates' place over on the other side of the bay. We'll take our stuff there on our backs."

Then they undressed for bed, for night had fallen, and went to sleep.

5

MOVING DAY AND SANAAQ'S REMARRIAGE

Day broke and Sanaaq was already awake. She called out, "It's high time that both of you got up. We're well into the morning! We'll start getting things ready right away. Have some tea. It's going to be a long trip."

Her sister had been shaken out of a sound sleep.

"You said it! I really don't feel like getting up. Eating those clams has left me feeling hot all over."

She was now wide awake and starting to put her clothes on. Sanaaq spoke again. "Daughter! Get dressed. Time to get going!"

They got everything ready. Sanaaq and her sister stuffed their things into a big bag while chattering away. Arnatuinnaq said, "I'll put the tent on my back, a dog will carry the tent poles, and I'll take my bedspread as well."

"Since we're ready, let's go! Let's get walking!" said Qumaq.

Arnatuinnaq was less sure. "Hold on! We're not at all done getting things ready! Take this stuff out. The mats can be left in a cache."

Sanaaq added, "We'll come back for them today, the two of us. Come on, let's take the tent down!"

"Sure!" replied Arnatuinnaq. "Which way should it fall?"

"To the left!"

Little Qumaq sang softly beside them, as they made their preparations.

"*Lalaa lalaa lalaa!*"

"*Uai!*" shrieked Arnatuinnaq. "Those dirty dogs are wolfing down our food, bunch of good-for-nothings! They're helping themselves to the provisions we stored in the *aki*. Throw some stones at them!"

A stone struck one of the dogs in its paw. It ran off yelping, "*Maa maa maa!*"

"I got that no-good Ukiliriaq. I pitched a stone right in its paw and it can't stand on it anymore. Those dirty animals are now fighting amongst themselves!"

"*Maa maa maa!*" The dogs were leaping back and forth as they fought over the provisions from the *aki*.

Sanaaq shouted, "Daughter, stay out of harm's way! Come here!"

Qumaq was growing into a young girl who increasingly knew the ways of the world. She spoke up. "Mother! The two of us can go ahead. Auntie can follow with the rest of the stuff."

"Yes, let's go! Let's get walking, the two of us... *Hau hau!* Kajualuk! *Hau!*"

She was calling for her packdog. Mother and daughter set out on their way, up a slope. Soon Arnatuinnaq left too. Although they were taking a shortcut, the route proved to be long and tiring. Qumaq cried out to her mother, "Mother! Let's stop awhile. I'm very tired."

"No need to stop now. We're almost right where we're going to pitch our tent. Aren't we almost there? Yes, we are! This nice stretch of gravel seems to be a good spot for a tent!"

They pitched their tent. They had arrived at the Ujararjuaq campsite and its inhabitants came out to welcome them. Among them were

Aqiarulaaq, the wife, and Taqriasuk, her husband, with their grown son, Jiimialuk.

"*Ai!* Sanaaq *ai!*" said Aqiarulaaq. "Let's shake hands! So you made it safe and sound?"

"Yes! We got here early because we had to leave some of our stuff behind at the other campsite."

"*Ai! Suvakkualuk!* But don't you have anyone to help you? *Ai!* Let's shake hands! But who is this girl?"

"It's Qumaq, my daughter... And here comes my sister. You can see her over there, in the distance."

"*A ii!* Is she ever loaded down! Come, have an arrival meal with us."

"Sure, let's go. We're very hungry. We didn't have any tea on the way because we thought it would take too long."

So they ate together while telling each other about the latest happenings.

Aqiarulaaq recounted: "My son killed a seal today, right in front of our place... He simply wounded it, so his father went after the animal in an old, broken-down *qajaq*. He harpooned it, only to discover it was a skinny little seal, a little *siiqrulik* that had lost its mother."

It was now Sanaaq's turn to talk. "*Ai!* Am I ever lucky! Irsutualuk has fallen in love with me. As soon as I found out, we moved away. I don't want him. He really looks old and I won't settle for just any wretched man who comes along."

"*Ai! Qatannguuk ai!*" said Aqiarulaaq. "I'll fix you up with my brother in no time at all. You need a man to help you out. Not right now, of course. First, get your tent up!"

"Yes, let's pitch our tent! We'll get some stones to anchor the bottom, then we'll raise it!"

"Yes. We're here to help!" exclaimed Aqiarulaaq.

Qumaq held one of the tent poles upright. They attached the guy ropes and anchored the base of the tent with stones. Scarcely had they finished raising the tent when they saw old Irsutualuk coming. He called out, "*Ai!* Sanaaq *ai!* I've been following you, trying to catch up. I'll no longer take no for an answer. You're going to be mine!"

"*Suvakkualuk!* But I don't want you... You're getting very old... You don't even have your front teeth anymore... And we got no help from you today, when we could have used it. You also won't be my husband because I'm afraid my daughter will be abused. As long as it's in my power, no one but me will lay a hand on her. You'll not be my husband because you're very old. Old men don't please me at all. Don't stay here! Go away!"

"What a shame! Being old is disgusting to you! I'm ready to do anything to have you. I'm going to undress and sleep here. I have no intention at all of laying my hands on Qumaq."

"You're really very old! *Aaq!* You smell old! Get out and stay out! I don't want an old man's smell rubbing off on me!"

So he went off, completely disheartened, and Sanaaq made her feelings even clearer. "The man I'll choose to be my husband isn't an old man. He's even a handsome man. He is Qalingu, the brother of my *qatanngut.*"

As planned, the marriage proposal was made while Sanaaq was being visited by her new camp mates.

Qalingu walked in.

"I wish to stay here and have you for my wife, but I'm afraid you'll be taken by another."

Sanaaq accepted. "Good thing I didn't accept the proposal from that old man!"

Everyone now undressed again for bed. As usual, her daughter began to sing, "*Ali ali ali taka taka a!*"

The new stepfather did not intimidate her at all, for Qalingu was very likeable. They all crawled into bed and drifted off to sleep right away.

6

A QAJAQ FOR QALINGU

Qalingu, the brother of Aqiarulaaq, had no *qajaq*. At daybreak, the two *qatannguuk*, now sisters-in-law, went to prepare the *amiksait*. The skins had been left to soak in a stone cache. Aqiarulaaq said to her brother, "Brother, Qalingu! Get these skins ready. Take them out of the stone cache."

"Yes, I'll pull them out of the stone cache. We'll carry them away with one person holding each side. They're bundled up in a laced skin bag... Let's get going! They're very heavy, so hold onto them on each side!"

They went to the *avvik* and started preparing the skins on that late summer day.

"I'll put the *avvik* into place," said Sanaaq. "We'll stretch a skin over it... With this sharpening stone I'll first hone my ulu, which is under the baseboard of the sleeping platform. There's no longer any cutting edge on it."

"I sharpened my ulu today," said Aqiarulaaq, "but it doesn't seem to be cutting properly. The edge isn't quite right. It'll do the job only if we break it in on some leather first."

They went to work on the raw hides. They first stripped off the blubber layer under the skins while chatting amongst themselves. Suddenly Aqiarulaaq yelled, "A *puiji* down there!"

She ran off shouting, "Son! Son! A *puiji* down there! It's swimming to the hunting lookout!"

"I've got to hurry up and finish removing the *mami,*" said Sanaaq. "It's getting dark out... *Ii!* There I go, I just sliced off a bit of my skin while my mind was on that dirty little *puiji* over there... Arnatuinnaq! Get cooking. You're going to make some boiled meat!"

"OK, I'm going! But first I'll watch that guy go after the *puiji.* Look at the two of them. He seems to be taking aim... Listen for the gun going off. I can hear it go off, *Tikkuu! A – Ii!* There it is down below. It's starting to float, near the area where the water looks darker because of the wind."

Sanaaq could now see it. "Yes, there it is! *Ii!* Will it sink?"

"No! He's right by it," answered Arnatuinnaq.

The man down below, Jiimialuk, seemed to be shouting for something: "A line! A line!"

"What?" said Arnatuinnaq.

"A line!"

Only Aqiarulaaq understood.

"He's saying: A line! Take him this leather line, the one in the *uati,* just across from my place!"

Arnatuinnaq hurried away with the line. When she got to him, she asked, "Did you catch a *puttajiaq?* I'm late because it took us a while to figure out what you were calling for... Your mother was the first to understand what you were shouting."

"*Ai!*" replied Jiimialuk. "I'm going to try and get a hold on it. *Ai!*"

"Yes!" said Arnatuinnaq.

He was trying to throw the line around the animal. "*Ii!*"

With each throw, the stone at the end hit the surface and threw up a spray of water. *Sarvaq!* was the sound it made.

"*Ii!* I can't get hold of it! Let's try one more time... *Ii!* Got it, it's mine!" Jiimialuk had lassoed the line around the seal. "It's a lot fatter than the last one I caught... Let's go! We'll haul it away... Or rather I'll carry it off on my back, *ai!* I don't want to scrape its fur off!"

Back at his tent, Jiimialuk began skinning the animal. He removed its small intestines and cleaned them out to make *nikku*. Then he strung them out to dry, forming a hose stretching from one side of the tent top to the other. While skinning the animal, he avidly licked the blood that dripped from his fingers. "*Am! Am!*" he said. He cut off a lumbar vertebra and ate all the meat while continuing with his work. "*U! Uu!* Is it ever good! Is it ever good! *Uu!*"

He stopped. He had finished eating and his mouth was smeared with blood. He went to rinse the sealskin in the water and also rinsed his hands and mouth. By now the *qajaq* skins were ready.

Sanaaq and Aqiarulaaq had completed their work. With night falling, Sanaaq shouted, "Come and help us. We're done! The skins need to be carried away to the tent with someone on each side."

So Sanaaq, Qalingu, Aqiarulaaq, and Jiimialuk started to carry them off, with two people on each side. They were straining.

"*Uuppaa! Uuppaa!* Not heavy at all!" said Jiimialuk. "Let's go that way!"

They now stopped. They had come to their tent.

"Mother *ai!*" said Qumaq. "Let's drink some tea!"

"Let's have tea!" replied Sanaaq. "Arnatuinnaq! Has any tea been put in the teapot?"

"Yes, I put some tea in. Help yourself!"

"Go ahead. Let's have tea! Where's my daughter's cup? There it is down there, on the other side of the trunk... Qumaq! Drink your tea without spilling!"

"OK!"

"*Iii!*"

"She's spilled all her tea down the front of her shirt… Is the teapot empty? She's spilled all her tea!"

"Will we be double-stitching everything tomorrow?" asked Arnatuinnaq. "I'm going out for a short visit."

She went to visit Aqiarulaaq, who told her, "*Ai!* Arnatuinnaq *ai!* Take home some of the meat. Here, take this shoulder."

"Sure!" said Arnatuinnaq. "The sea is very calm. Once we start sewing, we should work as fast as possible, to get it all done in a single day."

"You're right! We'll try to get up early and do it all in one shot."

Arnatuinnaq now went home. She undressed for bed because it was nighttime. Everyone went to bed and drifted off to sleep. Qalingu was snoring loud and hard.

"*Qaa! Qaa!*" This was the sound of his snoring.

7

JIIMIALUK LOSES AN EYE

They had all planned to wake up early that morning. Around five o'clock, Aqiarulaaq entered the home of her camp mates and said, "My kinfolk! Wake up, it's high time you got up!"

"Yes!" answered Sanaaq. "We're up!"

Arnatuinnaq awoke too and dressed after having some tea. They were going to cover Qalingu's *qajaq*. For this, Qalingu started cutting the skins to fit the frame. He stretched the *utjuk* skins over the *qajaq* with Jiimialuk's help while the others—the elderly and the women—looked on and told them how to do the job.

"Jiimialuk! You hold while I cut," said Qalingu. "But how are they supposed to be cut?"

Aqiarulaaq explained. "You cut the skin along a line from the big hoof of the front foot to the corner of the lips and then along another line from the hind foot to the udder. That's how we usually cut it... Try to remember that this is how we cut skins for a *qajaq!*"

"Yes," said Qalingu. "I'll try. Jiimialuk! Attach the skin with a leather strap."

Once this was done, the three women went to work inside the tent. They double-stitched the skins together while talking and chatting.

"*Irtuu!*" said Sanaaq. "I should first make some *qitirsirait* with this old caribou skin. Only with *qitirsirait* can we hold the thread right while sewing... Let's get to it! Let's get sewing!"

They began to sew. Qumaq was playing. She knew more and more about the world around her and talked incessantly while playing with the husky pups. There were five of them. She often opened the door and the draft from the strong wind outside caused the oil lamp's flame, which was heating the tea, to waver this way and that.

Sanaaq scolded her daughter. "Stop opening the door all the time. The oil lamp is exposed to the draft and its flame is being blown about by the wind! *Ii! Iii!* Dirty pups! They're running into the tent one after another!"

"*Uai!*" shouted Arnatuinnaq. "Bunch of good-for-nothing mutts! What a pack of useless bums." She went after them, giving one pup after another a good kick. "*Uai* bums! Look at all these pups!"

"*Maa maa maa!*" whimpered the pups as they scampered away.

The women had finished sewing. The entire team would now fasten the covering of skin to the frame. While the men rinsed the stitched skins in the sea, Taqriasuk daubed the *qajaq* frame with oil to make it slippery, using a piece of sealskin. The men then came back and the women began stretching the skin over the frame. Meanwhile, Jiimialuk was preparing boiled meat in a large pot and filling it with whatever could go in. As he cut the meat into morsels, he said, "I'll set up a windbreak because the wind is blowing hard and the meat is really going to take too long to cook."

He erected a windbreak using a large *mangittaq* of old *qajaq* skins. He could now go ahead with the cooking... The flames were already high. When the meat morsels began to boil, he turned them over with a long metal pick. But as he was turning them over, he splashed himself in the face with the boiling hot water. He screamed, "*Aatataa!* I've scalded myself something awful... My eye has been burned open! *Aa! Aatataa!* All I've got is my left eye now... There's fluid spilling out of my burned eyeball. It's stinging really bad."

"*Ii!*" exclaimed Aqiarulaaq. "My son has lost an eye. His eye is wide open. It's been burned open by boiling liquid! Who will provide for us now that our only provider has lost an eye?"

"Mother! I'm probably going to die. My eye was burned open when the boiled meat I was preparing was almost done. I've lost my lens... *Ii!* There it is, a tiny little lens! Look! That used to be my lens! But what's to be done with it now? It may end up being eaten by the dogs..."

They knew nothing about the existence of doctors or even big ships. When the women working on the *qajaq* had finished their work, they got down to eating some of the boiled meat.

"Come and have some boiled meat!" shouted Sanaaq to her companions. "Have some!"

"I will!" answered Aqiarulaaq, "but my son can no longer have any. He's burned himself very badly... Look at this. It used to be his lens!"

"*Ii! Autualu!*" said Sanaaq.

Qumaq was beside her. She saw the lens and, still not knowing many things about life, said, "Mother, I want to eat that eye!"

"*Ii!* It's just not done. You can't eat an eye like that. It's a man's eye. It was your little cousin's. It was his eye!"

"I want it! Give it to me!"

"But I told you it was a man's eye! It is said that the eyes of people who eat human flesh turn completely white... We'll throw it away because your eyes would turn white."

"Yes!" said Qumaq, who seemed to understand.

Night had fallen. They undressed for bed. Jiimialuk soaked a cloth compress in water and placed it over his eye. Unable to fall asleep, he tossed and turned because of his burn. Everyone else went to sleep, leaving him alone with his pain.

8

THE FIRST QALLUNAAT ARRIVE

While they slept, at daybreak, a very large boat arrived. Arnatuinnaq was taken aback when she left the tent that morning. It was the first time she had ever seen such a thing. She shouted to her kinfolk, "*Ilakka!* Wake up! What's this thing standing still in front of us?"

Just as her last words trailed off, the ship made a loud booming sound and, coming nearer and nearer, made several more. The strange sight filled everyone with fear, and they made frenzied efforts to hide behind tent covers. Some, like Arnatuinnaq and Qumaq, even began to cry. Finally, a large outboard full of *Qallunaat* headed to shore. These beings were clearly human, and the camp's inhabitants, though still surprised, were no longer afraid. The *Qallunaat* had come to visit.

Once they were ashore, Aqiarulaaq shouted to the Big Eyebrows, "*Ai!*"

They failed to understand, not making the slightest response. They began to talk among themselves. The Inuit were astonished to hear them speak and greatly appreciated the many gifts that they handed out, even the empty tin cans.

Sanaaq left to go visiting. She had heard about the *Qallunaat* and told everyone, "People say the Big Eyebrows are really nice! Don't be afraid. It's even said that they have doctors."

Qumaq was not at all intimidated by the *Qallunaat*. They were soon well liked because of all the gifts they handed out.

The *Qallunaat* went back to their big boat, to get things ready for moving ashore. Once they were inside, a loud clanging and banging could be heard. The Inuit were filled with astonishment and cried out, "Listen to that! There's an awful racket going on!"

"You said it!" said Aqiarulaaq. "But what can they be up to? Look over there, that little boat is full of stuff!"

The outboard landed on the shore again and the Inuit went to meet the newcomers, who began unloading large wooden crates. The Inuit watched with amazement.

"It'll be nice to have them in our country," said Sanaaq. "There'll now be Big Eyebrows here!"

Jiimialuk hardly felt any pain in his eye anymore. He accompanied those who welcomed the newcomers. He shouted, "Isn't it great that the pain has almost gone from my eye?" He even began to sing, "*Laa laa laa*. Isn't it just great? What does it matter that I'm now one-eyed? Who cares, the pain's going away!"

The newcomers continued to unload. They picked things up and laid them on the shore while the others worked at building a large house.

9

QALINGU TRIES OUT THE *QAJAQ*

Qalingu had returned from hunting in his *qajaq*. His sister-in-law, Arnatuinnaq, and his stepdaughter, Qumaq, came to meet him by the shore. His load was a very heavy one: an *utjuk* and also two *natsiik* that he had killed. Arnatuinnaq hauled the *qajaq* out of the water by pulling on its *usuujaq*. She was dragging it by the bow to dry land.

Seeing her pull it all by herself, Qalingu spoke up. "Hold on! It's really loaded... I'll get out first. I've just killed an *ujjuk!* I had to chase it a long time before I finally caught it. It came up for air. I fired and shot it. It was wounded so I had to keep chasing and whenever it broke the surface I shouted '*ua! ua!*' while firing my rifle. *Tikkuu!* That made it dive. I paddled ahead as fast as I could while it was still under water. And when it reappeared at the surface, I kept on yelling and trying to make it dive again right away. After a while it was running out of breath and coming to the surface more often. I got closer and closer. I fired and finally shot it again when it was just alongside. It almost sank, but its back rose to the surface twice and I rushed ahead to grab it before it could sink."

Qalingu had finished his story. The two began to carry part of the animal away, each taking a chunk of meat they had carved off. Their folks, Sanaaq and Aqiarulaaq, came to help. When all four were together, Sanaaq said, "*Qatannguuk ai!* Once we're done carrying all of this away, we'll have a feast with the *kujapiit* of the *utjuk.*"

They hauled the meat away two by two. The *qatannguuk* were carrying off a haunch between the two of them, chatting all the while. Sanaaq said, "*Qatannguuk!* Let's take a break. I'm really tired."

"Yes," said Aqiarulaaq. "But let's rest up there *ai!* Where there's no sand!"

"Sure! I'm really tired... *i i i i.*" She burst into laughter. "Don't you think I'm tired? Just look: my hand has gone all white... Let's go! Time to get back to work. We've almost reached our tent."

The two of them started carrying the meat again. Suddenly the part that Aqiarulaaq had been hanging onto ripped away.

"*Iirq!* My handle has ripped off *ai!* There it goes. My handle has ripped off!"

"*Ii! Autualu! Qatannguuk,* did you get grease on you?"

The dogs were now assailing them and they tried to get into the tent.

"*Uai! Uai! Ii!*" exclaimed Sanaaq. "They're biting into the meat we've been carrying, those dirty dogs! They're really starving. *Ii!* That dog bit into the heart I was holding... *Uai!* Dirty no-good mutt!" Sanaaq grabbed a rock and threw it. "*Ii!* Missed ... My aim must have been off!"

They finally got in. The other two, Qalingu and Arnatuinnaq, were together carrying a shoulder and the adjoining head. They had left behind the other shoulder, a haunch, the two ringed seals, the skin of the *utjuk,* and the viscera. Those remaining pieces were being guarded by Qumaq on the shore.

Before leaving her, Qalingu had said to Qumaq, "Don't stop throwing stones at those dirty dogs *ai!*"

"I won't!"

Now left to herself, she was beginning to feel very afraid. She yelled, "*Uai!* Dirty no-good dogs!"

Qumaq had some stones in her hands to throw at the dogs but was very afraid. "*Iaa iaa a a a!*"

The poor girl started to cry, letting her guard down. Immediately, the dogs descended on what she had been guarding. They fought amongst themselves and devoured almost whole the haunch and shoulder they had torn off. Qumaq wailed, "Mother! Come!"

Her mother saw her trembling with fright and came running right away. She was now by her side and showering her daughter with affection.

"*Umm!* Cry no more, my poor little child... *Aalummi!*"

Qalingu also came running to chase the plunderers away. He pitched some stones and the dogs he hit ran off yelping, "*Maa maa!*" The pillage was over. The shredded pieces of meat no longer mattered much to Qalingu.

"There's no point in guarding those two pieces of *utjuk* anymore. They've been bitten into all over!"

He began to drag the *utjuk* skin to a stone cache. After stashing it away in the cache, he went home and started eating some boiled chunks of meat for his arrival meal. He dipped them in *misiraq*.

The women, meanwhile, were making preparations for a *kujapiit* feast. On the ground they stretched a *mangittaq* on which they laid the *kujapiit* as well as the *utjuk* heart and some pieces of blubber. Sanaaq shouted to her camp mates, "Come and get some *kujapiit!*"

"Yes!" agreed Aqiarulaaq, adding, "but where's my ulu?"

"Behind your oil lamp," replied Jiimialuk.

"There it is!" she said. "I'm going to get my ulu too and join in the feast!"

When she entered the tent, Sanaaq said, "*Ai!* Come and eat some *kujapiit. Ai! Qatannguuk!*"

"Go ahead!" she replied.

Aqiarulaaq tried to cut one of them off, slicing away at the tendons holding them together. This was no easy job, as she admitted good-naturedly. "I'm a big liar because I can't cut through these joints... *Ia ia ia!*" she laughed.

She began to eat, holding a *kujapik* with blubber in one hand and her ulu in the other. As she ate, Aqiarulaaq talked about her plans.

"By the way, I'm planning to visit Ningiukuluk tomorrow to adopt her daughter, the middle one... Ningiukuluk once told me in so many words that I could have her... I'll go tomorrow. We'll both go, my old man and I."

"If you're going," replied Arnatuinnaq, "I'll go too... And I'll sew something to the soles of my boots. I might wear holes through both of them, while we're walking tomorrow... Qumaq and I will follow if it doesn't rain... Little niece! I'll get what you'll need for your trip tomorrow. We'll take something to carry you on my back with and a strap to hold you in place."

She was busy sewing patches to her soles and heels... She was soon done. As dusk darkened the sky, large snowflakes started to come down. The freshly fallen snow was wet. Arnatuinnaq exclaimed, "It's snowing big snowflakes and here I was planning to go on a visit tomorrow... Our things are too close to the side of the tent. They're going to get ruined!"

Night had fallen. They undressed for bed and, knowing they had to leave early the next day, went to sleep.

10

A DAUGHTER IS ADOPTED

They awoke with the rising sun, had some tea, and prepared to leave. Aqiarulaaq came in and said, "*Qatannguuk ai!* I'm going to look for a girl to adopt and I'm not coming back empty-handed."

"Good for you!" said Sanaaq. "You're lucky she was promised to you!"

They set off, all three of them. A few dogs tagged along, the same ones. On the way they saw some *ukpiit*. A male and its mate came very close... One of the two sank its claws into a dog while letting out a shriek.

"*Au!*"

It swooped down on the women several times. They were terrified, not having even a rifle. Seeing it prepare to dive again, they flipped their hoods over their heads... Arnatuinnaq tried her best to hit it with a stone but missed. Qumaq clung to her aunt's skirt for dear life, so much so that she ripped it off.

"Qumaq!" exclaimed Arnatuinnaq. "You've made a big rip in my skirt by hanging on so tightly! It's torn to pieces now and we're almost at our hosts' place!"

Just then, the two snowy owls dive-bombed the dogs again. One even stripped some fur off one of them. The Inuit started walking again to get away from the owls. As they walked, Arnatuinnaq said to Aqiarulaaq, "Look at the rip that Qumaq made. When one of the owls went after us, she clung to me for protection, even though I too was very afraid..."

They came within sight of Ningiukuluk's home. The oldest of Ningiukuluk's daughters spotted them and cried out, "Over there I can see people coming. They've got a child with them. It's probably Qumaq!"

"*Ai!*" shouted back Ningiukuluk.

"They're close. They're arriving. They're coming in."

Aqiarulaaq entered first and said, "We're paying a visit, Ningiukuluk! *Ai!* Let's shake hands!"

"*Ai!* You've just got here? Let's shake hands! Qumaq! And your mother?"

"She's at home!"

All three of her daughters were eager to play with Qumaq. There was Akutsiaq, the oldest, Aanikallak, the younger one, and Tajarak, the youngest.

"Let's play, Qumaq!" exclaimed Aanikallak.

But no sooner had her daughter spoken than Ningiukuluk broke in, "First have something to eat!"

"Have some of this *ai!* Qumaq!" said Aanikallak. "Over there, eat some *mattaq*. Use the knife!"

"Sure!"

Aqiarulaaq spoke again. "Ningiukuluk! I wish to talk to you. I've come on this visit to adopt one of your daughters, Aanikallak, because I really want to have her... I don't have a daughter of my own."

"*Ai!* On the one hand, I'd rather not give her away. On the other, I'm not so fond of her because she often wets her bed and I'm ashamed of her."

"I truly wish to have her. Some time ago you sort of promised her to me. So now I'm insisting. I want her to help me out, Ningiukuluk!"

"I no longer really care for her, but the other ones, her two sisters, I certainly can't give them away... Go ahead! Take her!"

Aqiarulaaq started recounting the latest news. "We saw some Big Eyebrows arrive. They've even begun to build a home for themselves on our land... That's all I have to say for now. We're going back this very day... Aanikallak! I've adopted you, so you'll be following us!"

"No! No! *Aaa!*" The poor little girl began to cry.

Qumaq looked her straight in the eyes and even tried to offer her some *mattaq,* hoping to console her. She kissed her again and again.

"Don't cry, little girl!" She added, "Look! There's a little willow ptarmigan on the ground... Let's play, just the two of us. Let's have fun looking around outside!"

"No! No!" Aanikallak was still weeping.

Her new mother nonetheless prepared for the trip home.

"Qumaq, come here!" said Arnatuinnaq. "I'll carry you on my back. *Iirq!* My skirt has been ripped apart on this side... I'll have to sew it together first. Hand me a needle and some sinew. There we are, all done! Here's your needle."

"Thanks!" said Ningiukuluk.

They were now ready to leave. Aqiarulaaq took her new daughter by the hand but could not make her budge. The little girl stood her ground and stamped her feet while weeping and wailing. Her new family finally set off on the walk home, yet she still resisted despite efforts to console her. At long last, after many efforts, she calmed down.

They all arrived at their destination and Aqiarulaaq was questioned by Taqriasuk.

"Did you get a new daughter? She'll try to go to sleep. Get her undressed for bed... She can have a place under my bedspread... And give her some tea."

"Here you are. Aanikallak, drink some tea. Put a shirt on and try to sleep."

She undressed her and slipped another shirt on.

"*Ii! Autualu!* It's infested with fleas! Oh, it's just crawling with those dirty fleas... Just look! *Ii!* This filthy shirt should be thrown away!"

It was tossed outside. The dogs came running and even started to fight over it. Kajualuk sank its teeth into the old shirt, making a popping sound as it crunched one flea after another.

Aqiarulaaq was now outside the tent.

"*Uai!* Dirty no-good mutt! It'll probably have blocked intestines after eating that old rag."

Everyone now tried to fall asleep. It was late autumn. A frosty slush was spreading over the shoreline and the calm ocean surface had a thin layer of frazil.

11

AN UNSUCCESSFUL HUNT IN THE *QAJAQ*

When they awoke early the next morning, it seemed impossible to go out in the *qajaq* because a thin layer of ice covered the sea near the shore. Qalingu, however, had found a small channel of open water, having been up and about very early. He took the *qajaq* down to the water's edge with Jiimialuk's help, also taking along a float and a harpoon. But he had forgotten something and yelled from the shore, "Bring me the harpoon line!"

Arnatuinnaq came running but fell headlong into the soft ice and sank into it. Trying to pull herself out, she said, "It'd be nice to have something I could grab hold of because I'm really stuck in this soft ice!"

Qalingu was now leaving in his *qajaq* across the thin ice. He saw a *puiji* and fired his rifle.

"*Ii!* Didn't get it! I shot too far to the right and missed! Just like the last time!"

He then paddled away in his *qajaq* and thought about how to get home.

"Maybe I could go ashore on this point of land... Seems to be the best place."

The women in his family were becoming very anxious. They watched from a hilltop.

"He probably won't be able to land now," said Sanaaq, "because there's thin ice everywhere... But where's the *qajaq?*"

"There it is! Over there," said Arnatuinnaq. "Just off the small point, looks like a *qajaq* coming... And the water over there doesn't have any of that icy slush."

He was still taking a long time to land. His folks, Sanaaq, Jiimialuk, and Arnatuinnaq, walked down to the stretch of shoreline where he would land and waited. When he came near them, Sanaaq shouted to her husband, "Do you think it might be impossible to land?"

"It's this awful thin ice!" answered Qalingu. "All the same, as hard as it may be, I should be able to get ashore."

And so he landed, with the rising tide, on a small point jutting out from the foot of the hill. They now all walked up to the camp, dragging the *qajaq* behind them.

"We should drag the *qajaq* with the paddle underneath," said Qalingu. "Let's go! Pull on each side by the *taqrait.* I'll pull the *usuujaq!*"

They began jerking the *qajaq* forward.

"It's really heavy!" groaned Arnatuinnaq. "Is it heavy because it's soaked up a lot of water? *Uuppaa! Uuppaa!* Just a moment! Let's rest a little. I'm very tired!"

"Off in the distance, that patch of still water looks like it's icing over," said Sanaaq. "Or is it already a sheet of thin ice? Let's go! We need to get pulling again. We're almost there."

They were now on dry land.

"I barely managed to get ashore!" confessed Qalingu. "I really thought I'd not make it, being so tired from paddling and so cold. The cold made the outside of my upper lip all swollen and my hands completely numb... I certainly won't be going kayaking any more! Tomorrow I'll build a snow house."

They went to their tents.

"Let's go! Let's get moving!" said Sanaaq. "Tonight I'll look for the brushwood I stashed away for fuel. It's starting to get really cold at our place... Let's go!"

They were now on their way. They walked along the *qainnguq* because it was becoming quite hard. After a while they arrived. Qalingu was carrying the equipment from his *qajaq:* the float, the harpoon line with the *ipiraq,* the guns, and the ammunition. Once inside, he placed them in the tent's *uati.* He sat down. His clothes were soaked through and through with seawater. He took them off, his boots too. Qumaq was playing once more on the sleeping platform. She frolicked back and forth, snuggling under the bedspread several times. That evening, she asked her mother, "Mother, make me a doll!"

"Get undressed for bed," answered her mother. "It's late and we're probably going to move to a new place."

"I will!" agreed Qumaq.

When they were in bed, Sanaaq turned the wick of the oil lamp down and said, "It's probably going to smoke during the night. I haven't turned the wick down far enough."

They tried to go to sleep. As feared, the oil lamp began to smoke as they slept. The remainder of the wick and the blubber started to burn for lack of oil... Qalingu awoke with a start and shouted, "The one over there is smoking!"

"Autualu! Ii!" shouted back Sanaaq. "We're completely engulfed in smoke!"

She added some oil, which started to crackle loudly. *Qiiii...* That was the sound of it crackling. Once she had finished adding oil, she went back to sleep because morning was still far off.

12

SANAAQ MEETS A POLAR BEAR

Dawn roused the people at the camp from their slumber. Arnatuinnaq stood up, shivering with cold as frost crystals fell from the tent ceiling. A coating of hoarfrost had formed overnight on the tent's inner surface. The girl was so cold that her teeth were chattering.

"I can barely get my boots on!" she said. "They're frozen rock-hard."

She hurried to light some brushwood in the small stove cut out from a barrel. The water pail had frozen to the bottom and offered only a trickle of water. No one felt like sleeping anymore and they all got dressed. Qalingu went out for some good snow. In his hand was a snow knife and on his arms *airqavaak*. As for Sanaaq, she had been too busy yesterday to do all she had wanted to do.

"I'll go fetch the brushwood I stored away," she announced. "We'll need it because we probably won't be able to move today."

She left, taking with her the skin of a young *utjuk* to use as a sled, a leather strap to tow her load, and a stick to knock the snow off the wood.

Arnatuinnaq told her, "I'm going to stop up the cracks on the outside of the igloo. Qumaq will stay at someone else's place while I plug the holes because I'm afraid she'll get cold."

Qalingu dug a hole in the snow, but it was not good snow. He said, "It isn't any good, so I'll make the igloo out of packed snow... We'll trample it today to pack it together. It will harden overnight."

He cut out a large number of blocks that he broke up with his snow knife. Arnatuinnaq then used her feet to pack the snow. Qalingu told her, "We're going to be very cold tonight. I probably won't be able to start building our igloo before tomorrow."

"The snow is very powdery. It will take long to harden," replied Arnatuinnaq. "There's some wet snow a bit further away..."

"It should harden with this cold," said Qalingu. "It's going to get really cold."

Sanaaq was walking up the hill, a snow stick in her hand. Once she arrived at her woodpile, she removed the covering of vegetation she had placed over the brush. A few dwarf willows had been left exposed, however, and were covered with icicles. She beat them with the snow stick and piled them onto the *utjuk* skin. She stacked her load, tied it up, slipped the snow stick under the *utjuk* skin, and began pulling the make-do sled home, laden with firewood.

An idea crossed her mind. She hitched her dog to the sled and called out, "*Uit! Uit!*" to make it go forward. The dog jumped to its feet and started off. And so she pressed on, alone with her dog. Suddenly, however, she spotted a polar bear. She was not far from home and, though terrified, fought back the urge to scream. The polar bear being still unaware of her presence, she tried to make her way home by the other side of the hill, while abandoning the dog and the load of wood... She ran ahead, stifling the slightest cry of panic.

Her dog came to the bear tracks and, without showing any sign of fear, bounded off in hot pursuit. The dog, Kajualuk, was barking loudly and sniffing the ground with its snout. "*Muu muu!*" was its muffled grunting.

Meanwhile its master was running silently, as fast as she could, holding back her fear. A short distance from home, she yelled, "*Nanualuk!* A big polar bear! My kinfolk!"

Qalingu heard.

"Listen!" He went outside to look. "Listen! She says there's a polar bear!"

"Yes!" said Arnatuinnaq. "She says there's a big polar bear. Up there, look at her run... *Ii!*"

Qalingu grabbed his rifle and rushed to meet her. The "old woman" and her "old man" finally caught up to each other. Sanaaq explained what had happened. "I saw a big polar bear... The only reason it didn't kill me is because I went by the other side of the hill... But Kajualuk ran after the bear and has probably caught up to it."

With his rifle in hand, Qalingu hurried to the bear and the dog. He soon saw them and drew closer. The bear was cornered, the dog nipping the back of its knees whenever it tried to move away. The bear was growling loudly but could not bite the dog, which nimbly ducked every swipe of the bear's claws and teeth. The dog had not been hurt in the slightest.

Qalingu stopped to take aim. *Tikkuu!*—the gun went off. He fired several times but failed to reach his target. He was still too far away. *Tikkuu! Tikkuu!* He fired repeatedly and, despite his poor aim, finally heard a bullet strike home. Though hurt, the bear was not dead. It tried to nurse its wound, nibbling on the flesh. Qalingu drew nearer and shot again, this time fatally. Sanaaq's dog lapped the blood oozing from the wound. Once he knew the bear was dead, Qalingu went home for a sled and for help with skinning. The sun was still out when he arrived home and walked in. He said, "I killed the bear... Almost ran out of bullets because I missed it so many times... I've come for a sled and for help with skinning."

"That's great news!" said Sanaaq. "We're going to have plenty of bear meat! We've got to let our camp mates know. I'll go myself and tell them!"

Arnatuinnaq was rummaging around for the harness.

"I have to hurry up and get the dogs harnessed! But where's the *nuvviti?*"

"Over there," said Qalingu. "I'm finishing my tea!"

Two of the dogs were missing and Arnatuinnaq called out, "*Hau! Hau! Hau!*" But both had gone running after Qalingu.

Meanwhile Sanaaq was going from one tent to another. "Jiimialuk! We need your help. Qalingu has killed a polar bear!"

"I'll help!" answered Jiimialuk.

"Oh! *Suvakkualuk!*" exclaimed Aqiarulaaq. "*Qatannguuk!* Were you almost devoured by the bear?"

"Yes! Barely got away... I left my firewood behind while the dog I had with me went after it... I was so afraid, I didn't utter a single word... Qumaq was all I could think about. I told myself, 'If I am eaten by the bear, she'll no longer be properly taken care of. Her boots will be in poor shape and, when she feels down, people will make her cry for no good reason. She'll also be scolded often and neglected... When hungry, she'll not be given food like the others.' That's what I thought, *qatannguuk!*"

"*Suvakkualuk!* To think that you went there alone, when I should have gone with you, *qatannguuk ai!* Have a little tea! It's a bit weak because we're almost out... You're really lucky not to have been eaten by the bear. Without you, Qalingu wouldn't have been able to kill the bear!"

"It's really the first time in my life I've been so afraid. I thought I was done for!"

"*Uit! uit!*" shouted Jiimialuk and Qalingu. They were getting their dog team going again.

Jiimialuk was pulling on the *nuvviti* to help the dogs climb the hill.

"*Uuppaa! Uuppaa!*" he yelled, throwing a rock at the dogs to quicken their pace. He remarked, "*Ai!* I got burned just a short time ago and here I am going to get some bear meat... Good thing I didn't die back then!" he said jokingly. "I lost an eye while boiling some meat and though missing a lens I'm still alive!"

He came to the dead bear and prepared to help with the skinning.

"Jiimialuk *ai!*" said Qalingu. "Let's start skinning!"

While they were skinning the bear, their dogs, still tied up, grew restless. Five of the dogs harassed them as they worked. Jiimialuk had a piece of the bear's heart snatched away. As soon as one dog bit into it, the others became even more restless. They were wild with hunger.

"*Uai!*" screamed Jiimialuk. "Pack of no-good mutts! Should I feed them the viscera *ai,* after removing the stomach and setting it aside?"

"Yes, do that," answered Qalingu. "They shouldn't eat too much, or else they won't feel like pulling very hard!"

"Right! Only some of the viscera then, *ai?*"

"You've got it!"

They skinned the bear by cutting its joints apart and dismembering it. When they were done, they loaded the pieces onto the sled. Their hands were very dirty now, so they cleaned them off in the damp, slushy snow. They then tied the load down with a strap. They were stretching the *naqitarvik* when it snapped. Jiimialuk, who had been stretching with all his might, was suddenly thrown to the ground and hit his tailbone on a stone.

"*Iirq! Autualu! Aatataa!* I've hurt my tailbone... How am I going to make this strap longer?"

"Make a knot, after loosening it a little here!"

Once he had knotted it together, they continued to tie down the load. Qalingu unfastened the tuglines from the sled. The dogs had been running back and forth while the bear was being skinned and had made a complete mess of their tuglines. He untangled the lines while talking to the dogs.

"*Au!* Stop moving around! I can't unravel your lines because you've tangled them all together!"

Jiimialuk came to help. The dogs were keen to get going and, once untangled, raced off. Jiimialuk ran after them, shouting "*Hau! Hau!*" but in his haste fell head over heels into a patch of marshy ground.

"*Iikikii!* I tripped and fell... My knees are soaking wet! *Iikikii!*"

He stood up and began to run again. "*Hau! hau!*" He caught up to the dogs, pulled them back by their tuglines, and slid the loops of the lines onto the *nuvviti.* Then the two of them got the dog team moving. The load was heavy, forcing them to push the sled on both sides, for the snow had melted away in many places.

They were almost home when Qumaq came running out to them. She caught her feet in the tuglines, however, and was dragged along the ground by the dogs. Jiimialuk used his feet to brake the sled with all his strength.

Now Qalingu came running out. He was shouting. "*Hau!* They're going way too fast!"

Qumaq was crying. No wonder, she had scraped her cheeks while being dragged on the ground.

"*Aatataa! Aatataa!*" She was crying in Qalingu's arms. "*Aappuu!*" And screaming too. "*Aatataa! Aappuu!*" She wanted to be made *aappuu.* She wished to be consoled as one would console a child. They finally arrived home.

"Who hurt my daughter?" shouted Sanaaq.

"She got caught in the tuglines," answered Qalingu. "She was dragged on the ground when those dirty dogs picked up speed!"

"But why hasn't anyone taken care of her?"

13

ARNATUINNAQ CATCHES HER FIRST GULL

The sea had not completely frozen over yet. This provided Arnatuinnaq with a chance to hunt gulls on the water with an *ii.* She recited the following charm: "My *ii,* my *ii,* swallow it, make a mouthful of it, stuff your beak with it, even if you have begun to spit it out! Stick into the inside of its throat, stick into it!"

This is what the Inuit recite when they hunt gulls with an *ii.* They say they want to make it swallow the *ii.*

"I got a big gull to swallow the *ii!*" said Arnatuinnaq to herself. "Several times it tried to fly away, but it was firmly hooked to my *ii!*"

Here is how an *ii* is used. It is set down on the foreshore and attached to a long line anchored by a stone. A little piece of wood will keep it afloat and the hook is a metal nail smeared with blubber.

Arnatuinnaq headed to the big gull and took it back to shore. When she came home, Sanaaq said to her, "Arnatuinnaq! Is it really the first gull you've caught?"

"Yes! It's the first gull I've caught!"

Sanaaq exclaimed, "We'll quarter it! Let's go!"

Qalingu went outside holding the gull in his hand and shouting to his camp mates, "Come and quarter!"

"Yes, we're coming right away!" replied Aqiarulaaq.

And she added, speaking to her old man, "He's asking that we come and quarter!"

"Yes, with great pleasure!" answered Taqriasuk

All the people were outside and they began to quarter the bird: Taqriasuk and Jiimialuk each held down one of its feet, Aqiarulaaq grabbed a wing and Sanaaq the other wing, Qalingu held its tail, and Arnatuinnaq its head. Arnatuinnaq shouted, "Let's go! Everyone pull on our side! This is really fun! *i i i i i!* But I haven't got anything! It's a really tough one to quarter, *i i i!*"

All the participants laughed heartily. Taqriasuk, the oldest of the group, got a foot and started to eat it raw while boasting, "I'm eating raw foot... *uumm!* Is it ever good!"

But no sooner had he eaten some of it than he felt sickened by the gull's taste and began to throw up uncontrollably.

"*Ua! ua! Ua! ua!* Water! I really feel sick to my stomach... I threw up something that's got an awful gull taste... It's really not meant to be eaten raw!"

Once they were done, the participants went home and undressed for bed.

At that moment Ningiukuluk's family arrived within view of the camp, having been overtaken by nightfall during their move to the campsite.

In her tent, Aqiarulaaq was scolding her adopted child, Aanikallak, who, though already a big girl, frequently wet her bed and still had fleas. "Aanikallak! Undress for bed and, since you often wet your bed, take this dog skin to put under yourself!"

They all undressed for bed. As they were falling asleep, their dogs began to howl in the black night, "*Muu, muu, miuu, miuu!*"... disturbed as they were by the arrival of strangers. Ningiukuluk's family was approaching. Qalingu heard something and said, "Listen! There are dogs barking loudly. Sounds like harnessed dogs pulling on their lines!"

The members of Ningiukuluk's family were pitching camp in the dead of night. They were erecting their tent, for the snow had melted in spots following a rise in temperature. Ningiukuluk said, "The moon is bright! Let's put the tent up quickly. We'll get our things in order tomorrow at daylight!"

Akutsiak and her younger sister were shivering with cold, having travelled at night. After raising the tent, they took their things in. Irsutualuk, their old man, was there too. They unharnessed their dogs, settled in, and undressed for bed, but not before having the tea they had made over a small fireplace for want of a camp stove.

At daylight, they were visited by Aqiarulaaq, who exclaimed, "Why did you do that? Why didn't you come and have an arrival meal? You arrived without my even noticing!"

"We refrained from having one so as not to wake you up!" answered Ningiukuluk.

Meanwhile, everyone having left Aqiarulaaq's tent, it was now being invaded by the dogs.

"Listen!" said Aqiarulaaq. "Sounds like the dogs have gone into someone's tent... Yes! It's mine they've gone into! Our home is full of dogs!" She chased the plunderers away. "*Uuit!* Pack of no-good mutts!"

She hit the dogs with a stick, seriously hurting one of them in the spine, one of Irsutualuk's dogs. She was very embarrassed about the injury and did not dare talk about it. Irsutualuk went to Aqiarulaaq's place in a fit of anger.

"Who hurt our dog? Our only good dog... Someone had better get me another one! Were you the one who hurt it?"

"I hurt it, but not on purpose, when I was chasing away the dogs that had invaded my home!"

14

FROM TENT TO IGLOO

Qalingu, Taqriasuk, and Irsutualuk were going to move from a tent to an igloo. It was very cold and they were going to look for good snow, near the foot of the hill. They each had their snow knife. Qalingu said, "The foot of the hill, up there, often has lots of snow!"

"Yes," replied Taqriasuk, "but I'll probably have trouble building an igloo because of my advanced age, and because Jiimialuk, my son, hurt himself while fetching some bear meat... He got thrown onto a big stone, his behind is all swollen!"

The snow was indeed very good and they began to cut a large number of snow blocks to build their igloos. Qalingu did not feel cold at all while cutting the blocks out. Once enough had been cut, he laid the first circle of blocks for the base. He plugged the outside cracks and packed snow around the base to keep the blocks from sliding or turning. Once the base was done, he cut new blocks out and laid the spiral of the snow dome. He then took a break from work to have some tea at home. To get out of the igloo under construction, he made an opening in the wall and emerged covered with snow. He told his companions, "I'm taking off for a short while to have some tea and to get a box that I'll use as a stepladder. I can no longer reach the top of my igloo."

"Makes sense," said Taqriasuk, "but I haven't finished the base yet."

"I'll go for some tea, too," said Irsutualuk. "I'm really thirsty!"

They went to join their wives, at home minding the tents. Qumaq, who was often darting in and out, spotted them. "*Aa!* My *ataataksaq* is coming! I'll go meet him!"

She ran to him and Qalingu called to her, "Are you coming to meet me? Watch out for the dogs!"

Qalingu walked into the tent. Arnatuinnaq was trying to light the stove. She added some fuel, which she ignited after spitting a mouthful of oil onto it. She then started to heat some tea. Qalingu was eating half-frozen meat that he had taken from the *aki*. Dipping it in rancid seal oil that tasted a bit piquant, he exclaimed, "This *misiraq* is really good. It's got a fairly sharp taste because it's rancid. *Iirq!* We'll soon be able to start moving!"

When he had finished eating, he said, "Hand towel!"

Sanaaq poured him some tea, saying, "The bannock to be used for our moving-out meal is completely frozen. Arnatuinnaq! You'll make bannock while I go and pack the snow by trampling it."

"Yes!" said Arnatuinnaq.

Qalingu left again for his igloo under construction. For use as a stepladder, he took along the case that he usually kept his camp stove in.

Arnatuinnaq was getting ready to make bannock. "Flour!" she called out. "And also baking powder!" After adding baking powder, she scooped out a hole in the middle of the flour and spat oil into it. The cold, however, had congealed the oil, making it painful to sink her teeth into. Even her mouth felt the freezing pain. "*Aatataa!*" she shrieked. "My mouth has been burned by the cold!"

After spitting the oil, she went for salt water on the foreshore and told Qumaq, "Qumaq *ai!* Mind the tent for a moment. I'm going to get a dipper-full of salt water!" She went to fetch some water and began to draw it. "*Ii!* It's full of *kinguit*. Nothing but scuds!"

Qumaq was calling for her, and weeping. "Come! Hurry! *A a a!*"

Arnatuinnaq came, bringing not only salt water but also *qiqruat* because she felt like eating. Now home, she laughed and poked fun at Qumaq.

"Qumaq *ai! iii!* Have you been crying again?"

"It's because you were taking so long to come!" answered Qumaq.

Arnatuinnaq was hard at work making dough. She used an ulu to cut a piece of blubber from the *aki*. She crushed it with her teeth and spat the oil out. Qumaq, who was beside her, took the remaining bits of blubber and, in turn, tried to extract oil from them with her teeth. But in the process she completely stained her *manu* with oil. Arnatuinnaq shouted at her, "*Ii!* Qumaq! Don't spit oil. You're dribbling a lot of it away. Your *manu* is all stained with oil now!"

When Arnatuinnaq had finished spitting oil, she poured a little salt water into the flour and kneaded her dough. She said, "Bring me a bit more flour. I've put in too much water!"

As soon as the flour was added, she kneaded the dough and made it consistent. She then adjusted the flame of the oil lamp with a *tarquti* cut from a dwarf willow branch. She started to bake the bannock for their moving-out meal. She turned it over and flattened it several times.

Now, back to the igloo builders. The domes were almost done. With the top of her igloo almost completed, Sanaaq, who was on the outside, shouted, "I can no longer reach the top! To plug the holes I'll have to climb up on top!" She tried to clamber on top. "*Ii!* I'm slipping… I'm scared!"

On the inside, Qalingu had now finished building the dome. He installed the *igliti* and built the *aki* with snow blocks. He next made an opening in the *kilu*. Sanaaq could now get in to trample and pack the snow while Qalingu brought in the snow blocks needed inside. Sanaaq cut them into thin slices with her knife. From the outside, Qalingu shouted towards the interior, "Is it packed?"

"Just about! It's almost ready!" answered Sanaaq.

Qalingu crawled in and helped her flatten the sleeping platform's surface properly. The two of them packed the snow with their feet. Finally, when it was well packed, they crawled out and Qalingu plugged the opening with a snow block. They headed back to their tent, to prepare for the move.

"The wind's blowing the powder snow, up there on the hilltop!" said Sanaaq. "Good thing we're ready to move into the igloo!"

They both arrived home. Qalingu told Qumaq, "Qumaq *ai!* We're going to move. The igloo is finished!"

And so they busied themselves with moving. Sanaaq and Arnatuinnaq, the two women of the family, would put the belongings into bags. Sanaaq said, "Arnatuinnaq! Let's get all the stuff together. Just roll the fur bedspreads up and bag any odds and ends you find around the bed."

They filled the bags while Qalingu took the full ones out and loaded them onto the sled. Arnatuinnaq hurried to get everything packed. She would say, "*Uuppaa! Uuppaa!*" while filling a bag and stuffing it with all her might. Because the door remained open for Qalingu to take the baggage out, the dogs came in and rooted around everywhere. Sanaaq shouted, "*Uit!* Pack of good-for-nothings! A piece of wood to hit them with! Those bums! They've invaded our tent!"

She hit one dog and it began to whimper, "*Maa maa!*" Qumaq, for her part, was very happy to be in the midst of these preparations. She put on her mittens and a scarf while singing softly, "*Taka taka taka!* I'm so happy! Mother, let's go riding off on the sled!"

"Yes, we're going to leave!" said Sanaaq.

When all the pieces of baggage had been taken out, Sanaaq and Qalingu lashed them solidly with leather straps to the sled while Arnatuinnaq went to harness the dogs. "*Hau! Hau! Hau!*" she called to them. They came running to be harnessed. Arnatuinnaq slid each dog's head through the neck of a harness, and its forelegs through the shoulder straps. She then slipped the loops of their tuglines onto the *nuvviti.* They were now set to go. Qalingu ordered a rightward turn by shouting, "*Uit uit! Auk!*" When all the dogs had fully stretched their lines, Qalingu rearranged the ones that were poorly placed, and the dog team was on its way and soon pushing ahead at a good speed. Sanaaq and Qumaq were on foot. Sanaaq told her daughter, "Daughter! Let's walk hand in hand."

"Yes, yes, yes, Mother! Give me your hand!"

They kept walking and soon arrived at their future snow house. Meanwhile, the dog team was climbing uphill slowly, with the help of Arnatuinnaq, who pulled on the *nuvviti.* Sanaaq turned around, walking back to the dog team and calling her dog, "*Hau Hau!* Kajualuk! *Hau!*"

Qalingu pushed the sled to the igloo. They could now move in. Arnatuinnaq, Sanaaq, and Qumaq crawled into the igloo through the *kilu* opening and Qalingu handed them the pieces of baggage. Arnatuinnaq took them while Sanaaq set them down inside. On the sleeping platform she laid the dwarf-birch mats and fur mattresses, leaving the fur bedspreads in their bags. Now that he had finished bringing everything in, Qalingu closed the *kilu* opening completely. He said, "I'm plugging it because I'm going to make an entranceway."

"Plug it!" replied Sanaaq.

She now began to install the *paugusiit.* With a knife, she made a hole in the wall of the igloo and said, "Pass me something to hit with. Something I can use as a hammer. Even a simple piece of wood."

She pounded away. *Tak tak!* Once the first *paugusiq* had been driven in, she made a second hole with the snow knife and inserted another rod, which she likewise hammered in. Next, she installed the vertical supporting post, also called a *paugusiq.* As soon as it was secure, she attached the first two rods to it and hung a strap from this rack with a hook at the end for the cooking pot. Finally, underneath, she placed her oil lamp. It was set on a base consisting of four wooden rods stuck into a piece of board. An old tin can would collect any oil dribbling down from the lamp. She also installed a shelf and tidied up her *ungati*. This being done, she filled the lamp with oil from the blubber pieces crushed by Arnatuinnaq and lit it after adding some moss as a wick. Once the lamp was lit, she adjusted the flame with her wooden poker. She then said to her daughter, "Qumaq! Bring the drying rack in because I'm going to be melting snow for tea... Arnatuinnaq! Put some snow to be melted *ai!* And my lamp will tend to smoke because it burns seal oil and that kind of oil won't heat well."

Qalingu was building the entranceway. He asked the people inside, "Is there any tea?"

"No," answered Arnatuinnaq. "It's not boiling yet because it's snow that had to melt... It's already melted though!"

She made tea despite the lack of water. Outside, night was falling and little Qumaq was having fun sliding. She was sliding with Aanikallak. Just then, Qumaq tumbled into the hole where the snow blocks had been cut out. She began to wail, "*Aatataa! Ataa!*" And she began to weep.

Aanikallak took her by the hand and led the girl to her mother's home, saying, "Qumaq! I'm going to lead you to your mother's place because you've hurt yourself, poor little girl... Cry no more, little one! Let me make you *aappuu!*"

"*Aatataa! Ataa!*" continued Qumaq, louder than ever.

The two of them entered.

"*Ii!* What's wrong with you?" exclaimed her mother.

Aanikallak recounted what had happened. "While sliding down the hill, she tumbled into the hole where the snow blocks were cut out."

"*Ii!*" said Sanaaq. "*Ii! Aiguuq!* Come quick! She's really hurt herself... Her head is all swollen! She must have hit her head on her little sled!"

Having finished the dome for the entranceway, without having taken time to plug the cracks, Qalingu immediately rushed in and said, "*Ii! Autualu!* But what did she do that with?"

"She says she banged her head on her little sled!" answered Sanaaq. "Is it serious?"

Aanikallak went home to tell what had happened. She told her adoptive mother, "Mother! Little Qumaq had a nasty tumble while sliding!"

Aqiarulaaq, thus alerted, ran over to Sanaaq's place. She entered, saying, "*Ii! Autualu!* Did she hurt herself very badly?"

"She doesn't really appear to be very hurt," answered Sanaaq. "But she's got a bump and bruises on her head!"

Qalingu ran to the trading post to ask the White employees for help. They were the only Whites around. He told them, "There's someone at our place who's hurt! I've come looking for an ointment to treat her with."

The chief factor answered, "I'll come. I'll go see her."

They left together but the White man felt very cold coming over. He was blue from cold when he came in, his face completely numb. Sanaaq saw him and said, "Poor thing! He's completely frozen! Even his face has been numbed by the cold... Arnatuinnaq! Give him something really hot to warm him up. He's been chilled through and through."

Arnatuinnaq poured him some tea and offered it. "Here you are *ai!*" she told him.

He declined and began to rub Qumaq with an ointment. Qumaq did not wish to cooperate.

"*A! A!* No! No! *Aa!*" she screamed, weeping.

"Don't cry!" said her mother. "You'll be healed fast!"

"Yes," said Qumaq.

After rubbing the ointment onto her, the chief factor went home. He stumbled many times because night had fallen. He continually bumped into hummocks of snow, tripping again and again. He even fell into hollows several times. And then, with all his stumbling, the dogs came yelping from behind. "*Muu! Muu! Muu!*" He tried to fend them off by throwing snow at them but, although they would slip away, they always came back. He finally arrived home and staggered in completely out of breath. "*A a a*"—this was the sound of his breathing, after keeping the dogs at bay.

Everyone in the snow house went to bed now, and to sleep. But because their dwelling let in more light than the tent had, and because the howling of the wind was harder to hear, Qalingu and his family had trouble falling asleep. During the night, holes began to form in the wall behind each of the two drying racks and, while everyone slept, the holes grew larger.

The people in the snow house awoke and had breakfast. They were short of bannock and had to make do with tea. But this just made Arnatuinnaq and Sanaaq feel sick because they were not used to doing without solid food in the morning. Qumaq began to weep and wail, "*Apaapa!* Something to eat! Mother! *Apaapa!*"

"Don't cry," said Sanaaq. "There's nothing. You'll get some later."

Arnatuinnaq stayed in bed under the covers, for the tea made her feel nauseous. She cried out, "*Irq!* I'm about to throw up! Pass me the chamber pot! I'm about to throw up! *Ua! Ua!*"

Qalingu very much felt like laughing. He passed her the *qurvik,* saying, "Here's the *qurvik!*" He began to laugh. "*I i i!*"

Arnatuinnaq decided to get dressed and said, "I'm getting dressed for fear of the cold. I'm less and less inclined to move around... I can no longer put my boots on. They're frozen stiff! I'll let them thaw out first on the drying rack."

Because many holes had formed in the snow wall overnight, Qalingu got to work plugging them from the outside. Meanwhile, Sanaaq was laying out a sealskin, to be traded at the trading post, to catch any bits of falling snow. Qalingu asked from the outside, "Have you laid down something to protect against the bits of snow?"

"Yes, go ahead!" answered Sanaaq.

Qalingu cut out some pieces of hard snow, for use as plugs. He asked, "Where should they go?"

"Put one of them a bit lower," said Sanaaq. "That's enough. *Irq!* You brought down quite a few bits of snow! Over here too! But it's not a hole. It's a cavity made by the heat... Will you plug it? Wait a little and let me pierce it!"

"Yes, there it is! Go ahead! Lay down the protection against the bits of snow!"

"You can plug it," replied Sanaaq. "It's protected on my side!"

Qalingu came in to examine the wall and said, "*Ii! Autualu!* There sure are a lot of cavities from the heat. They can't be seen from the outside."

"Leave them be!" said Sanaaq.

15

JIIMIALUK'S FATAL ACCIDENT

Qalingu and Jiimialuk wanted to go hunting on the fresh sea ice. Jiimialuk went to the home of Qalingu, who told him, "*Ai!* Jiimialuk *ai!* Let's get ready!"

"The ice looks dangerous to me!"

"It should be safe enough to walk on. It was very cold overnight."

The two headed out to the new sea ice. They were carrying their rifles, tied to their backs with *ipiraq*. In their hands were their cutting knives and harpoons. They waited for the tide to go out, the water having risen very high and partly covering the ice. Now they tried to make their way to the pack ice.

"We could get there by this small point of land," said Qalingu.

"That's right. Let's go *ai!*"

"OK!"

They walked out to the pack ice, which the ebbing waters had left fairly high and dry. In places, however, the sea was still partly open with cakes of floating ice. They crossed these cakes while talking.

"There are a lot of ice cakes," said Qalingu, "and they're separated from each other. Hope we don't fall in!"

"I'm scared," answered Jiimialuk. "I want to go back to dry land. I'm scared! I'm scared! There I go, I'm starting to fall into the water! I'm telling the truth. I want to go home!"

Qalingu smiled to hear such words from his companion, who really was very afraid. But Jiimialuk persisted in wanting to turn back and said, "Let's go home!"

"Why?" retorted Qalingu. "We'll get to the solid pack ice by steering the floating ice cake we're on now!" He took the opportunity to lecture him. "Jiimialuk! You must always remember that you are a hunter and that at all times you will face danger and live through unpleasant moments. You should act in such a way that your loved ones will never suffer from hunger and you should think more about them than about yourself. You should never sit still and do nothing when an opportunity comes to provide for their needs, *ai!*"

Jiimialuk complied. They began to steer the ice cake, a tiny floating slab, by rowing with their harpoons. They navigated their way to the pack ice, even though the slab tipped dangerously back and forth. Jiimialuk could no longer hold back his fear and panicked.

"I'm scared! I'm scared! We're capsizing! I'm falling in! I'm telling the truth, the honest truth!"

"You really think so? You're telling me the truth? What a fearful person you are!"

They finally made it to the solid pack ice and began walking on it to small stretches of open water. When they got to one, they several times saw *puiji*. Jiimialuk shouted, "*Ai!* Look! A *puiji!*"

But the animal would not let itself be easily approached and, after Jiimialuk whistled at it several times, it quickly slipped away. They soon saw another one, not at all shy, which began to swim in their direction upon seeing them. It even came quite close. Qalingu fired a bullet into the animal but failed to kill it.

"*Ii!* I didn't kill it! I just hit it. It's lightly wounded... I'll try to get to wherever it's swimming to!"

He went to where his prey, pushed by the wind, would land. He stayed put, immobile, and waited. Then he fired once more but missed again, and the seal simply swam away. Although they saw many *puiji*, they failed to kill any. It was now late in the day, and they were both hungry.

Just then Jiimialuk again saw a *puiji* in a small stretch of open water. He whistled at it several times, and suddenly the seal headed toward him, coming very close. Jiimialuk grabbed his rifle, aimed, and fired. *Tikkuu!* He killed it. Being quite far from his companion, he started thinking, "*Aa!* My stomach is just aching... As soon as the animal gets to the edge of the ice, I'll eat it, for my stomach is really growling. I'm hungry for seal meat."

He began shouting and waving to his faraway companion. "Come quick! I've killed a seal. It's floating!"

Qalingu came hurrying over. When he arrived, he said, "I never did get the one I wounded! You really ought to be thanked for killing one that floats... But it doesn't look like it's coming to the edge... I'll steer an ice cake over there and fetch it!"

"But it does look like it's getting closer," replied Jiimialuk.

"*Ai!* Never mind, *ai!* We'll try to catch it by tossing a weighted line."

"It's floated to the edge! I'll get it," said Jiimialuk.

The animal had indeed come closer but was stuck against a few small pieces of floating ice, and Jiimialuk was unable to grab hold. He nonetheless tried to reach it by stretching his arm further and further. Then he cried out, "*Ii!* I'm falling in!"

Trying to grab his prey, Jiimialuk had fallen into the sea. Qalingu rushed over. He saw a Jiimialuk's head poke out of the water, then disappear and, despite his efforts to look under the ice, saw nothing more... His companion had been swept under the ice by a strong current and was gone... Yet Jiimialuk's seal was still afloat. Qalingu caught it. The one who had killed it had drowned, the very man who had said he would eat the seal...

Qalingu was now all alone on the ice, with night falling and his companion dead. He had to go home and Jiimialuk's seal had to be dragged there. To do this, he tied a leather strap to one of its rear flippers as well as to its lower jaw, by means of a slipknot. He set off, obsessed by the memory of his drowned companion. He was very unhappy thinking about the man's kinfolk, whom he would have to tell the news. The prospect filled him with some apprehension. He thought, "I'll soon arrive alone... Our companions still think that Jiimialuk is out hunting... They'll be very unhappy about Aqiarulaaq's only son dying while still young... He was saying not long ago he was going to eat, not thinking that death was close at hand... He had no idea he was going to die..."

Qalingu stood still a long moment, as if in a daze, thinking, "And what about me, when will I die? I have no idea! And Jiimialuk, where has he gone? If he's gone to *kappianartuvik,* it'd be because death had taken him unexpectedly, but if he's been sent to *quvianartuvik,* he'll already be very happy... And what about me, what will become of me? I too will die like him, even though it doesn't seem like I'll be dying soon... Death may take me by surprise the same way..."

Such were Qalingu's thoughts as he plodded home. Even though he had not been instructed yet about Christianity, he could still ponder these matters.

Back home, their folks were hoping to see the two arrive soon. Night having fallen, nothing more could be seen. They listened keenly for the sound of footsteps. Arnatuinnaq, after going out to listen, entered the igloo of Aqiarulaaq, who asked her, "Have you heard anything yet?"

"No! I haven't heard anything!"

It was a time of night when one trips while walking, for the moon had not yet appeared in the sky. It was a time of year when the moon was taking longer and longer to show itself. Arnatuinnaq, who had gone out again, heard a voice, crying from afar. As soon as she heard it, she ran inside and cried out, "Listen, there's shouting from far away!"

All the members of Aqiarulaaq's family went outside, that late autumn night, and heard the voice crying from afar. They did not understand the words because of the wind. Aqiarulaaq hurried over to the homes of her camp mates and shouted, "Sanaaq! We hear a voice! It sounds like the voice of someone in despair!"

They rushed out as the moon gradually rose over the horizon.

"*Ii!* Listen!" said Sanaaq. "But what can he be saying? Arnatuinnaq! Go out to them, and take Maatiusi with you. Little Qumaq is asleep, so she can be left alone."

The two went to meet the hunters. But Qalingu was alone. When they reached him, he told them, "*Ajurnamat!* I'm by myself because my companion fell into the water. I couldn't do anything to help because of a powerful sea current!"

"*Ai!*" said Arnatuinnaq.

Two of them got to work dragging the seal across the land-fast ice and arrived almost at the shore. Arnatuinnaq was trying her hardest.

"*Uuppaa! Uuppaa!...* I've just stepped into a big hole!"

They finally arrived at camp and were joined by Aqiarulaaq's and Sanaaq's families, to whom they told the sad news about the death of Aqiarulaaq's only son. When Aqiarulaaq learned the news straight from her brother Qalingu, she was horrified, for she would never even see her son's remains. She went back to her home in tears. Once inside, she told her old man, "I've just learned about my son's death. I was told the news of his death!"

"*Suvakkualuk!*" said Taqriasuk. "He was taken away unexpectedly. He died very young, while really trying to tackle the risks of life!"

The little girl and her adoptive parents were now the only three left in their snow house: Aqiarulaaq, Taqriasuk, and Aanikallak. It would be the last time that their igloo would receive a seal killed by Jiimialuk.

During this time, Qalingu and his family were together in their snow house. Qumaq had awoken during the evening. She was starting to grow up now but did not have the slightest inkling that they had lost a family member. She spoke up, "Mother, let's both go to Grandmother's place!"

"We'll go tomorrow. It's getting late."

They undressed for bed. Sanaaq exclaimed, "*Ii!* Water's dripping on the bed! It's dripping there... Is it ever! Frost crystals will also be falling... Pass me an ulu with something to put those dripping knobs of ice in!"

Arnatuinnaq gave her an ulu and a plate for the broken icy knobs dripping with water... This was the sound they made as they fell down: *Tak tak!* Sanaaq added, "*Ii!* It's also dribbling on the *kilu* down there. That's been happening without making the slightest sound. There's already a small pool! Put a pad of snow here. It doesn't seem that cutting those icy knobs off has changed much!"

She put a pad of snow under the dripping knob of ice.

16

A HARSH WINTER IN THE IGLOO

Arnatuinnaq was busy drying Qalingu's boots. They were waterproof, made of dehaired sealskin, for use at sea. She removed the boot socks and softened the soles with a *kiliutaq*. After softening the soles and removing the stockings and boot socks, she turned the socks inside out and hung them on the drying rack, saying, "I'm going to fill my oil lamp with oil residues because we'll soon be short of fuel… But with oil residues, we might not get much of a flame and it will flicker without good fuel, or even go out… And we'll no longer be able to dry any boots!"

They now tried to sleep and, as predicted, the oil lamp went out, because it had been filled with oil residues.

Sanaaq and her entire family awoke the next morning, at daybreak. As soon as Qumaq was awake, she began to tell her dream. "Mother! I dreamed I had been given a little brother, a poor little thing with no eyes who cried because he had tumbled..."

Sanaaq started to laugh, "*I i i i i!*" She could not hold back her laughter...

Because they would be running out of oil, Akutsiaq came early that morning from the igloo next door to offer some in an old tin can. Sanaaq thanked her warmly, saying, "Akutsiaq *ai!* Thank you so much! Dry your hands on this gull skin."

"Sure!" said Akutsiaq.

Sanaaq then said to her sister, "Arnatuinnaq! Pour this oil into the lamp and try to light it. If the lamp won't light, it's probably because it ran out of fuel and had water in it... Just a moment *ai!* Let me take the residues out first. Then I'll try to light it."

She removed the residues with a spoon, put them onto a small plate, and threw them to the dogs. But the dogs were already harnessed because Qalingu was going to look for oil in his reserve. They rushed to devour this meagre offering of food and eagerly fought amongst themselves.

"*Uai!*" exclaimed Arnatuinnaq. "Filthy creatures!"

Arnatuinnaq clubbed them one after another with a stick as they whimpered, "*A a ma a maa!*" She went back in and said, "Dirty dogs! They all went after it."

Qalingu's dogs had moved around a lot and their tuglines were completely tangled. He had to unravel them before leaving to go for oil. Finally, he shouted, "*Uit!*"

Sanaaq, Arnatuinnaq, Qumaq, and Akutsiaq—who was visiting—were in the igloo with frost crystals falling and the temperature becoming ever colder for want of lamp oil. Qumaq was penetrated through and through by the cold and was almost turning blue. She played on the floor and on the sleeping platform, humming, "*Siu siu siu si si siu!*" Because she was right next to the edge of the platform, her mother told her, "*Ii!* Qumaq, don't fall!"

She complied and moved a little further into the *kilu*. In some spots the packed snow had melted and turned into ice. So Sanaaq decided to go looking for some fresh snow and pack it with her feet. She said to her daughter, "Qumaq! Put your boots on. I'm going to pack some fresh snow!"

She chewed on Qumaq's boots, which were on the drying rack, and turned them inside out. She began to soften them with the *qauliut* that she had hung there. Then she said to her daughter, "Let's go! Come, I'll put your boots on."

She slipped the boots onto the child's feet, straining, "*Uuppaa! Uuppaa!*" After Sanaaq had put the boots on and tied the bootlaces, Qumaq stood up on the floor and almost slipped and fell several times.

"*Ii!*" shouted Sanaaq. "Take care not to slide! Oh, she won't stop sliding!"

Sanaaq packed the snow with her feet while Arnatuinnaq went for some fresh water. This is what Sanaaq did: she moved her things off to the side; she lifted the dwarf-birch mats and held them up with a snow stick that she stuck into the base of the platform; she went out and cut some blocks of soft snow, which she crushed and packed in the igloo.

Qumaq was very talkative. "Should I bring this snow block inside?"

"Wait a little!" answered her mother. "I'll first cut it in two because it's too big... Take that one in."

"Sure!" answered Qumaq.

The two of them brought the snow blocks inside. When Sanaaq had finished placing the blocks on the sleeping platform, she cut them into thin slices with her knife and packed them down with her feet. She then said, "There's still a little missing here. Qumaq, go and get me a little more snow!"

"Sure!" answered Qumaq. "Here's some snow. Should I put it here?"

Sanaaq now put her things back into place. She unrolled the dwarf-birch mats and laid out the fur mattresses and bedspreads. When she was done, she made some tea. She adjusted the flame and wick of the oil lamp with her poker.

Meanwhile, Arnatuinnaq had gone for fresh water, taking along an axe and a bag in which to put the pieces of ice and carry them away on her back. She went to the frozen lake where people usually got ice and began to hack away at the edge of an ice crack to split pieces off, putting them in the bag one by one. When she was done, she headed home. She was tired, though, and found her load heavy. She said, "*Uu!* Am I ever tired!"

But she kept on walking, intent as she was on providing her folks with fresh water. On arriving, she tried to enter and, speaking to those inside, said, "Take that in!"

"You really deserve to be thanked!" said Sanaaq, grabbing hold of the bag.

She began melting the ice in a bucket, breaking it up into small pieces with a knife, but the coldness of the ice burned her fingers. She screamed, "*Aatataa!* I've burned myself! *Ai!* A mitten!"

Arnatuinnaq gave her one.

"Here *ai!*"

Sanaaq pounded away again at the pieces and filled a pot with ice in order to make water. She then melted the ice by hanging the pot over the lamp.

Qalingu had gone looking for oil, as well as food for the dogs. He now arrived at his oil reserve. With his knife, he scooped congealed oil out of the wooden barrel he had kept it in and filled a large tin that he used as a jerry-can. He also added the hard blubber rinds. In doing so, however, he stained the front of his shirt and the cuffs of his sleeves. Once his can was full of *misiraq,* he covered the barrel again with a piece of beluga skin on which he placed stones and pieces of wood. He told himself, "Even the dogs won't be able to undo that... So it should be safe from predators..."

He headed to one of his stone caches and tried to open it, but the stones were completely stuck together by the cold. He had to pry them apart before he could open the cache. In this way, he came across a food bag that had once contained oil and gamy meat, but it had not been full for a long while... It had been eaten into by voles and no longer contained any liquid at all. There was not even a drop of *misiraq* anymore, for the bag had been pierced by many holes. With a leather strap, Qalingu tied a slipknot around the end of the bag and tried to draw it towards himself by pulling with all his might.

"*Uuppaa! Uuppaa!*" he said while pulling. "It no longer contains any liquid at all. Yet it had been prepared for oil storage!"

He then began loading his sled for the trip home. He tied his load down and untangled the tuglines while shouting at the dogs, "*Au! Au!*" When he was done, he counted the tugline loops as he slipped each one over the *nuvviti,* to make sure none were missed... All were accounted for. "*Uit! Uit!*" he shouted to the dog team, to urge them forward and up the slope. He himself pulled on the *nuvviti,* for he had a heavy load of dog food—a load of gamy meat.

The people minding the igloo had almost no flame left. Qumaq remained on the sleeping platform with her boots off because it was so cold. Sanaaq was sewing. She was making boot socks. Ningiukuluk came to visit Sanaaq, who told her, "*Ai!* Ningiukuluk *ai!* Sit down!"

"Yes!" said the other, complying. "I can no longer do anything because I'm an old woman. My feet are cold." She talked non-stop, also speaking to Qumaq. "*Umm!*" but not as an *mmm...* of affection. "*Umm!* My little girl *ai!* Let me tell you a story."

"First have some tea," said Sanaaq.

Ningiukuluk agreed and said, "Arnatuinnaq! Cool it off with some ice. It's very hot!"

Ningiukuluk drank abundantly and began telling a story from the old times.

"A very long time ago, it's said, there once was a man, an Inlander, who was alone, without even a dog, in a tiny snow house whose floor was covered with large trout he had caught with a hook and fishing line. During the time of the long winter nights, he was awakened one night by sounds of footsteps on the snow. Right away, his snow house seemed to be surrounded by a galloping noise, by creatures that had come without warning. The man began to think to himself, and to talk to himself, for he knew full well that they were wolves, and that there was no way for him to escape. 'Let it be! Let them enter like humans! Let them eat some trout!' And then, so it is told, they entered. The she-wolf had taken human form and pushed inward the snow block that plugged the doorway. She said, 'Let's enter like humans! Let's eat some trout!' During the night, the pack of human-looking wolves—the old male, who was with them and also his many offspring—ate trout. The she-wolf munched on trout all night long and told stories. This is what the she-wolf told the man, who had no fire. She often chased caribou, so she said, while her folks trailed far behind and only caught up after she had killed the animals whose tracks she had been following. She said she was the fastest one. When the wolves caught up to her and began to eat, the old male left her offspring with very little to eat. For that reason, she said, she was very angry with him, describing him—the one always last to arrive—as a selfish brute.... They ate trout during the night. They crunched away in the darkness. The Inuk began thinking once again, 'Given that the wolves haven't stopped eating, they'll probably use up my supply of trout during the night.' The she-wolf further recounted that, as soon as she had caught a caribou, she took out its tongue, which was delicious. The female that had taken human form and was a very good person again told her host, 'Tomorrow you'll follow our tracks!' At that point, all the wolves left and no sooner had they gone out than they began to race away. When the Inuk awoke, at daybreak, the trout that had been eaten overnight were intact. He then remembered the she-wolf's advice and followed the wolf pack. He walked a very long time, following the tracks until he saw before him two cadavers, one of a wolf and one of a caribou, lying side by side. They were the gifts of the she-wolf. The dead wolf was her old male, gnashed to death by his own female. She hated him because he left their offspring with so little to eat. The man felt grateful for the caribou and for the wolf..."

Ningiukuluk's story was over. But Qumaq wanted more. "*Aalaalaala!*" she hummed. "Grandmother *ai!* More!"

"It's over for now because I'll be going home!" answered Ningiukuluk.

"Do you have tea at home?" asked Sanaaq.

Ningiukuluk indicated a "No" by grimacing and raising her nostrils. She said, "We get by, thanks to gifts. Just this morning we breakfasted on food from others."

"*Suvakkualuk!*" said Sanaaq.

She then prepared some tea leaves to offer her, wrapped in a small piece of cloth. She tied them up with a leftover bit of sinew and said, "Take this! Here's something to make tea with!"

Ningiukuluk stood up and said, "Yes! My back really aches. Where are my mittens?"

"Grandmother! There they are, up there, on the drying rack!" said Qumaq.

Ningiukuluk left.

As night fell, Arnatuinnaq played a guessing game on the ice window, as Qumaq looked on. If enough marks were made, it meant that visitors would arrive... She played *aakut-tuasi* by scratching the frost on the ice window, with the aim of making the right number of marks. She said, "*Aakut-tuasi nikut-tuasi* the big wolf that I meet says *ai!* Yes!"

This is what the marks looked like:

It was now the height of winter. Qalingu had come back and was busy putting away the harnesses, his load, and his sled. He had removed the harnesses from the dogs and was starting to coil up their tuglines. His dogs were very warm but covered with frost. They were nosing around in the refuse heap by scraping the ground with their feet. Arnatuinnaq went out just then and said, "*Ai!* Pack of no-good mutts!"

She coiled up the tuglines, after Qalingu had unravelled them. He then took the dog food in by rolling the meat bag and the blubber into the igloo. Qalingu cautioned, "*Uuppaa! Uuppaa! Irq!* Qumaq! Make sure you don't get clobbered by the meat bag!"

"I won't! I'm in no danger," replied Qumaq.

"Step aside a bit," said Qalingu. "This big thing might hurt you!"

"Really, I'm in no danger!" she asserted.

But, always wanting to have the last word, she was hit by the bag. She wailed, "*A! Aataata!*" Feeling greatly distressed, she began to cry, because she had really been clobbered.

Qalingu said, "Listen! Sounds like she was bowled over."

Sanaaq heard something and said, "Listen! But what's with her?"

She seemed to lose all self-control because her child had been hurt. She was panic-stricken because her daughter's feet had been run over—her daughter who had been thinking, just a short while ago, that there was no danger. Sanaaq cried out, "Qumaq will probably die. She's just been hit by Qalingu!"

She seemed to share her wounded child's pain, even though it had not been caused on purpose. But there was nothing wrong with Qumaq's feet. Sanaaq removed her footwear and examined them.

"Let me see! Qumaq! Let me take your boots off!"

Qalingu looked and said, "Didn't I tell her to make sure she didn't get clobbered?"

Sanaaq began thinking to herself, "She'll probably want to be spoiled more and more. I'm clearly wrong in coming to her defence... I'll be very careful not to come to her defence the next time. If she gets used to being defended too frequently, she may often start crying, even for no reason..."

Qalingu crawled into his home. He said that after his arrival meal he would feed his dogs. He had five dogs that were named Kajualuk (the same one and now very old), Sinarnaaluk, Kuutsiq (his dog with the longest tugline, his lead dog), Nuilaq, and Itigaittualuk. These were his dogs. Because night was falling, he went to feed them, saying, "My sealskin mittens! I'll use them because I'm afraid my hands will get cold."

He took the snow knife to cut the gamy meat into pieces while Arnatuinnaq prevented the dogs from coming in. Arnatuinnaq went out, holding the snow stick to keep the dogs back. Qalingu said, "Go ahead! Let one of them in!"

"OK! Kajualuk! Kajualuk! *Ii! Uit!* Bunch of good-for-nothings!"

With all of them rushing forward, she whacked Kuutsiq, who began to whimper, "*Maa! Maa!*" Qalingu fed the first dog and called out to his wife, "Sanaaq! Get me some blubber rinds, *ai!* Let me give them a taste of blubber!"

"Here are some that have hardened in the sun. They're leftovers we can no longer pound any more oil out of."

After feeding all of them, he used a *kiliutaq* to scrape away the bits of gamy meat on the ground in the two entranceways.

Arnatuinnaq came in, saying, "*Aa!* Are my feet ever cold! There are a lot of northern lights outside and it's starting to blow really hard."

When she had finished speaking, Qalingu said, "Listen! Sounds like dogs yelping in the distance and pulling on their tuglines."

"*Aaa!*" said Qumaq. "That's great!"

She was happy, the little one, to hear the travellers arrive. Qalingu went out and could clearly recognize the yelping of dogs pulling on their tuglines and parked on the land-fast ice. There were four dog teams out there despite the biting cold and wind. Arnatuinnaq also went out to look and immediately came back in, saying, "But who could be on those four sleds?"

"Hurry up and fill the teapot with water!" said Sanaaq. "They must be completely frozen!"

A lot of people had arrived with many children. On each sled was a child all bundled up and tied down. Two women were each carrying a baby in the back pouch of her coat. a boy and a girl. One of the children tied to a sled was let free by untying the leather strap. His name was Irsutuguluk. He exclaimed, "*Aaa!* Am I ever cold!" and he began to cry.

Qalingu lifted him up and brought him into the igloo. The child was shivering with cold. The women who had just arrived came into Sanaaq's home one after another.

"*Ai!*" said Sanaaq. "Are you arriving? You're travelling in very cold weather! Be our guests! Arnatuinnaq! Is the tea ready?"

"Yes!"

The arrivals were warmed up with a hot drink.

"But who is this?" asked someone.

"It's Aanaqatak!" answered one of the arrivals.

The others brought their belongings in. They put some of their things in the entranceway and the bags and fur bedspreads in the snow house. Arnatuinnaq tried to scrape the snow off their belongings with the snow stick and said, "I can't manage to get this snow off. It's sticking really hard... The blizzard has glued it on!"

The others in turn entered and knocked the snow off their clothes with the snow stick. They undressed, beat their mittens, and put them on the drying rack. They were then offered tea by Arnatuinnaq.

"Here's some tea!"

"Sure! Thank you so much!"

"Here's some bannock," added Arnatuinnaq.

Qumaq hid behind her mother's back. She felt very shy, she who had previously shown so much joy on hearing them arrive.

The man of the group of travellers, Ittusaq, finally entered and talked non-stop while having tea. He said, "I'm so thankful to have arrived among people who have tea! We came here because we're completely out of tea... Several times we even had to drink decoctions of *kakillanaquti* and *kallaquti!*"

"*Ai! Suvakkualuk!*" replied Qalingu. "I'm getting ready to go inland tomorrow, before we completely run out of dog food."

"Good thing," said Ittusaq. "Let's hope you won't get bogged down in the soft snow. It's starting to snow and the wind is shifting to the east. As for me, I'm going to build a snow house tomorrow, even though the days are getting longer."

17

SANAAQ GIVES BIRTH TO A SON

It was evening and Sanaaq was sewing. She was making mittens out of sealskin that still had its fur. With her ulu she cut out the two pieces for the back of the hands, the pieces for the upper part of the palms and, finally, the pieces for the lower part of the palms. She then chewed on a piece of sinew, softening it and removing the remaining bits of meat. She pulled out a fibre, which she smeared with blubber and threaded through the eye of a glover's needle. She could now pierce the leather and sew the pieces together.

Having sewn all day, she said, "*Aa!* Am I ever tired! I no longer have any strength at all in my back. My back is really sore. I'm going to undress for bed. Arnatuinnaq! You'll finish the job."

"Sure!" answered her younger sister.

The time had come for Sanaaq to give birth. Aqiarulaaq acted as the midwife, with Qalingu's assistance... It was soon over. Aqiarulaaq had helped bring into the world her *angusiaq*. She said his name would be Qalliutuq, the name of Sanaaq's dead brother.

Aqiarulaaq called for Qumaq to come and see the baby. She said, "Qumaq! Look! You've got a little brother!"

But Qumaq still knew little about these things and did not understand very well. She said, "Let me see! Yes! That little one, give him to me!"

She grabbed the baby and smiled broadly, her face reddening and her body quivering with joy and gratitude.

"Take care not to hurt him!" she was told.

"I won't hurt him!" she replied.

Then, once again, she acted without thinking and hit the baby on the head... He began to cry, "*Ungaa! Ungaa! Ungaa!*"

Sanaaq shouted straightaway, "Give him to me! The baby's very fragile because he's so little!"

Qalingu laid the baby down on the *kilu,* but Qumaq approached the child again. She not only refused to believe in his fragility, but also immediately lay down on top of him.

Arnatuinnaq said, "Qumaq! Get undressed for bed. We're both going to sleep under the same blanket."

They undressed for bed. The night was pitch-black, but everyone had trouble sleeping, as if something were keeping them awake. This was the case with Qumaq, who was anxious about the newborn baby.

Sanaaq tried to breastfeed the child, but he could not suckle properly yet, having just been born. She changed his diaper and unwrapped his swaddling clothes... he was still quite skinny. She wrapped him up again and laid him on his side. He began to cry, "*Ungaa! Ungaa!*"

18

TRIP INLAND

Day had dawned and Qalingu got dressed. He went out to coat his sled's runners with wet snow. As he put the slushy snow on, he said, "*Aa!* My hands are frozen!" He was coating the *sirmit* of the runners with wet snow to keep them from getting worn. He was going to travel across the pack ice, over the frozen sea.

Arnatuinnaq in turn got dressed. She put on her newly washed dress and her furskin boots whose soles had been bleached in brine. She had made the boots herself. She now pierced eyelet holes for the laces she would thread through.

After she was dressed, she stood up on the floor of the igloo. "*Aa!* I'm sliding! My boots are really slippery!"

She slid several times, falling on her rump and hurting her behind. She then went out with the chamber pot to empty it. Once outside, she was harassed by the dogs again.

"*Uai!* Pack of bums!" Angry, she splashed some urine on one of the dogs and smiled...

Qalingu was getting ready to leave. For the trip, his provisions would be flour, tea, tobacco, and salt. He was also taking some gamy meat and blubber. His travelling companion was Ilaijja, from Ningiukuluk's family. His companion harnessed the dogs and then tied the load down, the two men helping each other from opposite sides of the sled. They then slid the loops of the dogs' tuglines onto the *nuvviti.* After completing their preparations, they entered Qalingu's igloo for their going-away meal. They ate some gamy meat and frozen meat, dipping it into an old tin full of oil thickened by the cold. They had some tea and were now ready to go. As Arnatuinnaq's family looked on, they left and called out to the dogs, "*Uit! Hra!*"

The dog team took off down the sloping shoreline to the pack ice. Because of the incline, the sled raced so far ahead of the dogs that one of them was dragged along after the sled's runners passed over its tugline. The runners hit and crushed another dog, causing serious injury. It began to whimper, "*Maa! Maa!*" Because he was badly hurt, the dog was simply unharnessed. They were leaving on *Alliriirtuni,* the day when their camp mates used to greet many new arrivals, and heading inland because their families were short of food, even though a little meat remained.

At the camp, Akutsiak paid a visit to Sanaaq's home in the hope of being offered a bit of gamy meat to eat. She crawled into the igloo and drew her head down completely between her shoulders, after pulling her hood as far as it would go over her head. Qumaq was glad to see her.

"Akutsiak! Let's play together!"

"In a moment," she replied. "My hands are very cold!"

Having not eaten, Akutsiak had nothing to heat her body with. She was cold, all the more so because the igloo was not at all warm. There were even frost crystals falling from the ceiling. She drew her head firmly down between her hunched shoulders.

Sanaaq said, "Arnatuinnaq! Feed her some gamy meat from the meat bag in the entranceway... and get her something hot to drink."

Arnatuinnaq obeyed and went to the entranceway with an iron hook. She pulled out the pieces of meat and put them on a plate, for they were dripping with *misiraq*. She covered the meat bag with a piece of skin. Even in the entranceway, flecks of frost were falling from the ceiling. She said to Akutsiak, "Eat this gamy meat."

Akutsiak slipped her arms out from under her *atigi* and slid them into her sleeves. She grabbed an ulu and began to eat some of the gamy meat. As might be expected, she devoured the food, wolfing it down. She started to cough and choke—"*U u uaq!*"—almost throwing up as she choked. When she finished eating, she said, "Hand towel!"

She wiped her hands and mouth and then began to play with Qumaq. While chattering together, they played who-can-make-the-highest-mark-possible-on-the-ice-window. Qumaq called out, "We'll make our marks while standing with arms stretched up. Then we'll make our marks standing on tiptoe. Akutsiak! Because you're much taller we'll make our marks while jumping!"

"Sure! Here I go," answered Akutsiak, who had started jumping. "Go ahead, Qumaq! Match my record!"

"Since I can't match you," replied Qumaq, "let me make a mark with a piece of wood!"

"No! Only with our hands!"

Both of them stopped playing. Akutsiak went home to her family. She crawled in and told them how happy she was to have been so well treated.

"I had tea and ate some gamy meat!"

"Good for you!" replied Ningiukuluk. "Since you got some, it's as if I got some!"

Sanaaq's baby was beginning to get plump. He started to cry, "*Ungaa! Ungaa!*" Sanaaq wanted to change his diaper and said to her sister, "Housemate! Turn the flame up. The baby has no more dry diapers!"

She wrapped him in swaddling clothes and, because he continued to cry, she stood him up on his little feet.

"Oh! He's smiling for the first time! Qumaq, look! Your little brother is smiling!"

"Yes! Let me see!" replied her daughter, feeling very affectionate. "Let me take him and have fun with him!" Qumaq was eager to devour her brother with affection. She even ground her teeth and started to act more and more recklessly.

Sanaaq said, "Give me the baby. He could easily get hurt!"

"Not at all. He won't get hurt!"

"Give him to me. He could bump his head!"

"In a moment! I'll hold him right!"

As could have been predicted, at that very moment she bumped the baby's head against the baseboard of the sleeping platform. "*Ungaa! Ungaa!*" he cried, apparently inconsolable because the bump had been a hard one.

Sanaaq acted as if she felt her child's pain. She seemed to lose all self-control out of affection for her baby.

Qumaq was frightened by her mother and began to ponder things a bit. She had again hurt her little brother while believing herself to be right and her mother wrong. She said to herself, "A while ago, I too bumped myself because I'd do only what I wanted to do, despite being warned by my mother to pay attention... And now here I've hurt my little brother, because once again I thought I knew better... Clearly I don't know more than my mother does. So the next time I'm told to pay attention, I will..."

19

HUNTERS CAUGHT IN A BLIZZARD

Qalingu and his hunting companion were travelling, with spring drawing nearer. It was the day of their departure and they now stopped for their daily meal. The wind was blowing about the powder snow that covered the ground and the sky was somewhat hazy on the side from which the wind was blowing. Qalingu's companion built a windbreak with his snow knife. He dug a hole in the snow, cutting out snow blocks that he laid in a row to break the wind. He then plugged the cracks. Next he untied the case that contained the camp stove and which, placed at the front of the sled, had been his seat for driving the dog team. He set the camp stove behind the windbreak, lit it, and on it placed the teapot, which he filled with snow to get water. He stirred the water constantly, to keep it from getting a burnt taste. Once all the snow had melted, he added a little more snow and then some tea. He and Qalingu got ready then to have their daily meal.

While his companion was busy making tea, Qalingu took a walk and saw two migrating willow ptarmigans in a little willow grove, apparently resting there after having eaten. Qalingu ran back the way he had come as fast as he could. He shouted to Ilaijja, "Bring me my rifle and ammunition! Get them out of the satchel!"

His companion darted off to the sled and then ran back to him, bringing the rifle and ammunition. Qalingu told him, "I just saw some ptarmigans but wasn't able to shoot at them."

"*Ai!* Will you run out of ammo?" asked his companion.

"No, that should be enough. There are only two of them."

He went back, keeping his head down to avoid being seen. Then he began to fire: *Tikkuu!* Too far to the right... He tried again. This time too far to the left. He tried again: *Tikkuu!* He had hit short of the target and missed the birds... *Tikkuu!* He had hit beyond the target. All of his ammunition was used up. He could no longer do anything, although he had said there would be enough bullets... He returned to get some more ammunition and said, "They got away on me. I couldn't get them with the gun!"

He went back to where the ptarmigans had been, but they were no longer there.

"*Autualu!*" he said, disheartened.

His disappointment was understandable. He quickened his pace and again saw ptarmigan tracks. He followed them but found nothing, except the birds' still fresh droppings... Qalingu was beginning to feel his empty stomach. Not seeing any more prey, he thought, "I'm going to turn back. I probably won't see them any more."

He was about to head back when suddenly he shouted, "*Aa!* That gave me a start! What's that thing that scampered away?"

It was an Arctic hare that he had seen and scared off. He called out to the animal, "*Itingit, itingit!*"

The hare stopped and sat down, as if ashamed to be seen with its many anuses. It is said to have seven. While it sat, Qalingu aimed his rifle, cradling it on a stone for fear of missing his target. The sound of the bullet hitting home could be readily heard. The hare had been struck but was only wounded. Qalingu fired once more and hit again. He ran to the animal and grabbed it. But Qalingu jumped with fright. "*Ii!*" The Arctic hare had begun to cry like a baby, "*Ungaa! Ungaa! Ungaa!*" He smothered it by standing on it... The hare died. Qalingu returned to his companion for the daily meal. Everything was ready when he arrived and he recounted what had happened.

"I killed the hare on my way back. I was lucky to run into it because the two ptarmigans had flown off... That hare was probably what made them fly away!"

"*Ai!* What a nice stroke of luck! It will fetch a good price."

"I'm not going to sell it!"

They set off with their dog team, up a slope.

"*Uit!*" shouted Qalingu. The dogs stretched their tuglines and he unravelled the tangled harnesses. He then ordered a change in direction: "*Hra! Hra!*" Qalingu was walking ahead and yelling, "*Hau! Hau!*" while dragging a piece of gamy meat at the end of a leather strap. His dogs, pulling with all their strength, suddenly bolted up the hill.

Taken off-guard, and about to climb onto the sled, Ilaijja clung to it with one hand and was dragged in the snow for some distance. "*Aatataa! Aa!* Pack of big stomachs!" he yelled at the dogs. He was hurting badly, for the snow had scraped his face.

Once the sled had reached the top of the slope, Qalingu joined his companion and hopped aboard... The sled was advancing slowly because it was going over powder snow that squealed under the runners. Just then they came across fox tracks. Qalingu, who was behind the sled, noticed and shouted, "These tracks are very fresh!"

"*Ii!* There it is, up there! It's sitting on top of the hill!" said Ilaijja.

"Whereabouts? Is it an Arctic fox?"

"Yes! There it is, up there!"

"*Ai!*" said Qalingu. "I see it clearly! I'll try to get nearer *ai!*"

"Yes!" agreed Ilaijja.

"Get my ammo," continued Qalingu, speaking softly. "Take it out of the satchel in the stove case!"

He crawled towards the animal, concealing himself behind a big rock. He called "psst! psst!" to the fox, which came running to the source of the noise. This is how one usually attracts foxes, by imitating the sound of a lemming. Qalingu aimed his gun, *Tikkuu!*

"I could hear the sound of it hitting the fox!" said Qalingu.

The fox writhed spasmodically before dying. The hunter grabbed it with satisfaction.

"*Ii!* Thanks," he said before firmly pressing his foot onto the animal and suffocating it.

With night falling, they pitched camp by a lake. Ilaijja untied the baggage from the sled and unharnessed the dogs while Qalingu built an igloo for shelter overnight. At this site, however, the snow was not very thick.

"I won't be able to finish the dome from the inside because there's not enough snow," said Qalingu.

"*Ai!*" said Ilaijja.

From the outside, he was plugging the cracks that remained between the blocks of snow. He added chunks of snow, shaping the edges with the knife. Now that the igloo dome was complete, they put their things in order, lit the camp stove, and put snow on it to be melted. Once there was water, they made tea...

In this way they travelled for the whole week, at the end of which, as they settled in for the night in a makeshift igloo, hardly any provisions were left. Yet there still remained one more stop on the way home.

In the igloo, Qalingu said, "*Ii!* The wind is howling something awful. Sounds like a blizzard coming." Pointing to the igloo's vent hole, he added, "We need to plug that hole up there. It should be stopped up to prevent hoarfrost from forming inside."

Ilaijja plugged the vent hole and the whining of the wind died down.

They were short of kerosene and no longer using their stove, in order to save the precious fuel, but they had an oil lamp and used it to heat the igloo, for freshly built igloos are cold. Qalingu would keep the meat of the fox he had killed, to take back as a gift to his family. The wind was blowing very hard. It would undoubtedly eat away at their snow house. Night having come, they tried to doze off but were roused from their sleep by the wind blowing through a hole it had pierced through the wall. Qalingu was the first to awake in the dark dead of night and, seeing their igloo filling with snow, he called his companion.

"Wake up! The igloo has been completely eaten away by the wind! We're being invaded by the blizzard! Get up!"

His companion stayed still for fear of the cold and did not move at all.

"Get up!" said Qalingu, but Ilaijja turned a deaf ear, not wanting to budge, and burying himself deeply under his covers. Qalingu insisted.

Ilaijja answered, "I don't want to move. I'm staying still for fear of the cold!"

Qalingu became more insistent. "Get up. You're in danger of freezing to death!"

Ilaijja tried to get up, but as he did so he said, "I'm afraid! I'm probably going to die! I've lost all hope." His teeth were chattering. He was covered with snow.

Qalingu went to plug the holes on the outside of the igloo with chunks of snow. Ilaijja in turn got dressed, walked outside, and found himself facing a wind so strong and so cold that he could hardly breathe... He was really like a child. The two of them went to work building a snow windbreak outside their igloo to protect it better. The wind, however, was blowing so hard that the blizzard continued to eat away at their snow house. Early morning was not far off, so they gave up on going back to sleep.

When Qalingu crawled in, he said, "When it starts to be light out, we'll get on our way. Here the wind just won't stop eating away at our igloo... We should instead make a new igloo in a place sheltered from the wind!"

They prepared to leave while the night was still pitch-black. Qalingu said, "Put the harnesses on the dogs. Let's get ready to leave."

Ilaijja put the harnesses on the dogs, but they refused to budge. They would not move for fear of the biting cold. To harness a dog, he slipped its head through the neck of its harness, then its front paws through the neck straps and, once the harness was on, shouted, "*Uit! Uit!*" He then slipped all seven tugline loops onto the *nuvviti* one after another.

When the two men had finished harnessing the dogs and tying down the load, they set the *kalirtisaikkut* and attached the main tugline to the sled. Qalingu walked ahead but, because of the raging blizzard, could see nothing and stopped, for fear of losing his companion, who was urging the dog team on, "*Uit! Uit!*" The dogs could not pull properly, for they feared the cold. Ilaijja advanced in this manner for a long while and should have caught up to Qalingu, who had gone ahead. But being just an adolescent and afraid of the blizzard, he began to think, "I'll probably get lost... I'll probably never again see my mother's home... But if I lose my companion, how will I avoid getting frozen? I'm starting to get afraid..."

They had completely lost sight of each other. The dog team came to a halt, as did the sled and its occupant. The dogs could go no further because of the raging blizzard. Meanwhile, Qalingu had clearly gone astray. He had lost his bearings and did not know where he was. He walked for a long time, using the wind as a compass. A strong *atuarniq* was blowing. He was afraid and his thoughts were on his companion.

"Had I not gone ahead, my young companion wouldn't be in danger of freezing... He can't do much by himself, so he's certainly going to freeze... If he gets lost, it'd be better if we both got lost... But if we both die, my little family, my little boy, Qumaq and her mother, will be looking everywhere in vain. They'll have false hopes and be ever more hungry, with no provider... The others will probably abandon them... I'm helpless because of this severe blizzard... I don't even have anything to drink to keep me warm, and although my companion has a stove with a bit of kerosene, I'm very anxious for him..."

During this time, Ilaijja, who had halted with the sled, was abruptly and unwillingly pulled away in the direction of the wind by the dogs, which had smelled something. He was pulled away quickly and might have been thrown off at any moment as the sled hurtled over the uneven ridges of snow. He managed to hold on by hanging to the leather strap that held the load in place. The dogs' sense of smell finally took the sled back to the abandoned igloo. His thoughts turned to Qalingu. "My companion will certainly freeze... I'll be unable to go home alone... I'll probably get lost on the way, poor little me who lacks intelligence and gets lost easily!"

Qalingu, now in the thick of the blizzard, was fast losing hope. His face was encrusted with snow and he could not make out the slightest thing. Nonetheless, he plodded on into the wind. His cheeks were freezing and his entire body was feeling the cold. With night falling, he decided to take shelter on the side of the hill away from the wind, while there was still some daylight. Without even a snow knife, he began digging a hole for himself in the snow, all the while afraid of being smothered by the blizzard.

Meanwhile, Ilaijja was waiting and doing nothing in their old igloo. He had been there all day and was starting to feel very hungry. For a long time, he chewed on a piece of beluga stomach, dipped in oil, and drank cold water, no longer having any fuel for heat. With another night coming, he tried to sleep but could not because the familiar howling of the wind was fading away.

At the camp where they had left their family, Sanaaq and her folks were worried. Ningiukuluk made Sanaaq even more anxious by saying, "Sanaaq *ai!* That's some blizzard. It's really no weather for being exposed to the elements far from home! I had a *qunujaq* some time ago. You'll have to take good care of your little boy because I dreamed of something broken!" This was an omen that someone close would die.

"You're probably right," answered Sanaaq, "but I still hope they're alive. We don't have any news of them yet... Those beliefs of yours just aren't true. I don't want to believe in them!"

Ningiukuluk became angry because her views were being dismissed. As she left, she exclaimed, "*Irq!* I'm leaving because no one believes me."

Sanaaq slipped her baby into her *amauti* and told her daughter, "Qumaq! You must not come with me now!"

Sanaaq followed Ningiukuluk. She crossed the threshold and walked down the front step. Qumaq could not keep herself from following her mother, crying all the while, "*A a a!*" She fell and hit her face after stumbling over a ridge of snow. Sanaaq said, "Ningiukuluk! I'd like to give you some explanations... We've been told not to believe at all in such things. They're not really things to believe in *ai!*"

Ningiukuluk simply agreed with her

Daylight had now come and the two sled travellers, Qalingu and Ilaijja, would at last find each other. Qalingu was walking towards their old igloo. As he walked he said, "*Aa!*" Still anxious, he caught sight of the dogs. "Thank goodness!" When he reached his companion, he said, "You came back here?"

"Yes! I was dragged here against my will by their sense of smell... That's how I managed to end up here!"

"The dogs are truly to be thanked! Let's go! Let's get on our way!"

"Yes!" said Ilaijja.

They got their dogs going, without even a going-away meal, because they had almost nothing left to eat. They both had empty stomachs.

At the camp, Sanaaq was carrying her son in her *amauti*. He was getting a bit big to be carried about in this manner. He was starting to crawl on his belly. She went out... Soon after, she began cutting and sewing some material to make boots with. She gazed at the horizon, far off in the distance, straight ahead of her, looking for travellers on a sled. She then said, "Those things over there, wouldn't they be people coming on a dogsled? They look like little dark spots..." She went back in and said, "Arnatuinnaq! Go look! Seems to be people coming on a dogsled... Look at them through the telescope."

"Yes!" said Arnatuinnaq. "Qumaq! Quick, get me the telescope up there in the *kilu!*"

Qumaq fetched it from the *kilu* and brought it to her. Arnatuinnaq went out and looked through the telescope.

"You're right," she said. "There are people with a sled, over there. Looks like they're having their daily meal!"

Qumaq and her little brother were overjoyed as Sanaaq in turn took a look.

The two travellers were indeed having their daily meal. They barely managed to get the stove lit and hardly had any provisions left. They drank a very weak tea and, between them, their only food was a small piece of meat. It clearly was not enough and Qalingu was glad to let his companion have it. He pretended that he did not want to eat, even a little bit, in order to leave him his share. He took care of his companion, out of love for him. The two of them got their dog team going again. The wind was blowing in their backs but, as they came closer to home, it dusted them with powder snow from the ground.

Arnatuinnaq prepared a meal for the travellers. She melted some snow for tea and chopped off a piece of frozen *ujjuk,* which she had received as her share of the game caught by another person. She cut it into small pieces, to make boiled meat. Then she went out again, for they were about to arrive. Everyone in the igloo stayed out for a long time as the boiled meat cooked over the oil lamp, whose flame was getting too high.

Sanaaq said to Arnatuinnaq, "Isn't there an oil lamp smoking in our home?"

"No, not at all!"

Sanaaq went in and shouted, "*Ii!* Our oil lamp is smoking! It's full of smoke... Quick, give the vent hole up there a few blows with the axe! Make it wider! Hurry!"

Arnatuinnaq went in after giving the vent hole several blows with the axe.

"*Autualu! Ii!*" she said, on seeing Sanaaq's nostrils and face black with soot, from inhaling the smoke. "Your face is all covered with soot and so are your nostrils!"

"No wonder," said Sanaaq. "It was full of smoke!"

Qumaq was told by her folks to stay outside, so as not to breathe the soot. The travellers had now arrived and were bringing their baggage inside and unharnessing the dogs...

20

SPRING HUNTING ON THE SINAA

With spring arriving, Qalingu and Ilaijja went hunting on the *sinaa.* Ilaijja harnessed the dogs and said, "*Autualu!*" on noticing that a dog was missing.

One of their dogs was nosing around in an abandoned igloo. Qalingu, meanwhile, was coating the undersides of the runners with wet snow, using a *nanuirvik*. When the undersides were completely frozen, he planed them smooth and iced them again. Once they were properly iced, he stood the sled upright and attached a *naqitarvik* and also a *kalirtisaikkut.* He lashed his *qajaq* to the top of the sled. After tying it down, he went inside to put on his dehaired sealskin boots, which were impermeable to seawater. From among his mittens, he took the ones made of black dehaired skin. Finally, he put on sealskin overpants.

They now took off downhill to the shore and the land-fast ice. Some of the dogs saw their tuglines slip under the runners. Others were almost hit by the sled. Some, finally, were simply dragged along. Qalingu shouted, "*Uai!* Pack of bums that let themselves be dragged and do nothing but eat! Shame on you!"

After making their way downhill, they continued across the ice sheets of the foreshore, the tuglines often catching on snags and spurs. Qalingu would go to release the lines. Once freed, the dogs would start trotting, some pulling hard, others less so. The bad pullers waddled as they walked. The good pullers had arched backs, their bodies tightly drawn by the effort. They were heading out to sea now, the two hunters continually darting from one side of the sled to the other, throwing a piece of wood at any dogs that failed to obey their orders. Before arriving at the *sinaa,* they crossed an area of fresh ice, parts of which were coated with frost crystals. Their progress slowed down considerably.

In the open water, they spotted a *puiji.* Qalingu saw the top half of the seal emerge and fired. He hit it and it squirmed wildly... Qalingu had killed it. After hauling it onto the ice, he decided to skin it. He cut the animal open lengthwise, skinned it down to the blubber, cleaned the blood-spattered skin with seawater, and divided the seal into many parts to be distributed later. The two of them ate the meat attached to the lumbar vertebrae and prepared the small intestines and liver by setting them out to freeze. They divided up the entire kill to provide all their camp mates with a share. When the liver was frozen solid, Qalingu laid it on top of the *qajaq*. They would now go home, so they untangled the tuglines. Ilaijja went about this quickly, for the ice was starting to crack and drift.

Back at the camp, their loved ones often climbed the *nasivvik* in order to look off into the distance. Taqriasuk had a telescope with him. He also had a pipe that he wished to smoke, but no matches for the already filled pipe. He proceeded to chew the pipe's contents energetically and almost choked. No wonder... Just then he spotted the hunters arriving and, although he had believed they would return empty-handed, he could see them bringing back a heavy catch.

Qumaq was beginning to grow up and had fun cutting out blocks of snow. She was trying to build a snow house. Snow covered her all over and frost coated her *manu*. From time to time, she would call out, "Oh! I'm having fun building a house with the snow knife!"

Aanikallak, a bit further away, was doing the same. While she and Qumaq amused themselves, each of them building an igloo, they suddenly heard a large plane and were very frightened by the noise it made... They scampered off to their homes. Qumaq tripped and fell several times, so overcome with fright was she. Her mother asked, "What's with you? *Ii! Aalummi!*" and she ran out to see. "Look at the big plane! *Qatannguuk!*"

The plane disappeared. The children were still very frightened.

21

MUSSEL FISHING UNDER THE ICE

Sanaaq, Arnatuinnaq, Qalingu, and Aqiarulaaq were going fishing for mussels under the *qulluniit.* Qumaq wanted to come along. Qalingu filed the cutting edge of his ice chisel and then honed it with a stone. Sanaaq prepared to go fishing by putting on her *alirtiit* and boots. Qumaq was aware that they were preparing to leave. She kept going in and out, following the others. She said, "Mother! I want to go mussel fishing with you!"

"You're not going down under the ice. We're the ones going down… You might bang into something… You're going to stay home with your maternal grandmother!"

"I want to go with you! And I won't go under the ice!"

"Go then!" answered her mother. "But eat before you leave so you won't get hungry there... I'm going to breastfeed your little brother!" Sanaaq also changed the baby's diaper.

Once Qalingu was ready, they set off, taking a bag, the ice chisel, and a bucket. Qumaq followed not far behind. With the sea retreating under the ice, they hurried to the point underneath which the ebbing waters met the shore. Qalingu began bashing away with the ice chisel to open up a tunnel down into a large *qulluniq*. With his hands he removed the shards of ice. He looked really tired. When the opening was wide enough, he knocked the last shards out and, with the water level no longer falling, everyone rushed to climb down under the ice.

"Let's go! Let's go down," said Arnatuinnaq very happily... And they went down.

"There are a lot of mussels," said Sanaaq. "Over there on the side of the big rock."

"There's another one!" shouted Arnatuinnaq, "*Ii!* But I can see big crabs! They're repulsive!"

"Oh no, not at all!" said Sanaaq. "They're not at all repulsive! I'll tear their legs off and eat some crab."

"I'll taste a piece," conceded Arnatuinnaq, "but now I'm disgusted by these *kinguit!* I want to go back up to the surface."

"Before you've filled the bucket?" asked Sanaaq, teasing her.

Arnatuinnaq tasted some of the crab and wanted to eat some more... She found it good—she who had been so disgusted. She even went looking for other crustaceans... Meanwhile, Qalingu had half-filled the bag with mussels. He had also gathered seaweed, *qiqruat, kuanniit,* and *aliqatsaujait.*

It was now time to climb out. Sanaaq was eating mussels while collecting them. When Qalingu reached daylight, before his companions had climbed back up, he looked over the mussels he had gathered. To his great disappointment, some were full of sand... He had picked them up too fast. Since some of the shells he had gathered were empty and his bag was very heavy to carry, he became suspicious and began taking a closer look. When everybody had reached the surface, Qalingu said, "My kinfolk! I've gathered only empty shells. I picked them up without even looking!"

Sanaaq and Arnatuinnaq burst out laughing.

"He wanted to do it so fast," said Sanaaq, "that he gathered only empty shells! It's because he was in the dark!"

They headed home. When Qumaq saw them, she shouted, "I want to eat mussels!"

"But the mussels I gathered are just empty shells," answered Qalingu. "They're full of sand... I'm ashamed. Eat some kelp instead."

And they went home. Qalingu pulled his load on a little sled. Sanaaq was very thirsty because of the salty taste of the mussels. When they arrived home, Arnatuinnaq took the mussels as a gift to Ningiukuluk, who said, "Thank you so much! There are really a lot of mussels!"

Qalingu ate some mussels with oil. He also opened some for Qumaq. He then went with Qumaq to barter mussels for tea at the store. Qumaq said, "Father! Some sweets too!"

After bartering with the *Qallunaat* for tea and candy, Qalingu told his family, "This is what I got in exchange!"

22

SPRING HUNT

The time of the *ullutusiit* was beginning and soon it would be spring. Qalingu announced that he would go hunting the next day for *uuttuq* and that some of the things he had just bartered for would be provisions for the trip. He made some wooden stakes for use as upright supports for his seal-hunting screen. Sanaaq also made him a hunting cap out of Arctic hare skin. She cut it out and sewed an inner band to it. At daybreak the hunters prepared to leave. The warming air was causing the snow to shrink and dwindle away. They took their hunting caps. Sanaaq stayed outside a long time with her baby in the *amauti*.

"We'll probably lose our snow house today," she said, "because the air is getting warmer... Arnatuinnaq! Make a sunshade out of some bedcovers. Also put anything wet out to dry... I'm going to stay indoors for a while."

Qalingu was hunting *uuttuq*. He prepared his hunting screen while his companion, Maatiusi, stayed with the dogs to keep them in place. Qalingu bent over double and advanced unnoticed to an *uuttuq*. It suspected nothing. He aimed carefully and fired. He made a hit and ran to the animal. When he got there, he smelled a strong odour and said, "It stinks like a male seal in rut! It's really a male seal in rut!"

The odour was very strong. Maatiusi heard the gunshot and set out at full speed by dog team. When he arrived, he said, "Thank goodness, you've caught a seal! Its blubber will provide our dogs with something to eat!"

"It's a male seal in rut! Skin it, Maatiusi!"

His companion opened it up lengthwise and the two of them tried to eat it. Even though it was not to their liking, they ate it, for want of other food. Maatiusi said jokingly, "What a nice-tasting seal! It really has a very strong taste."

Because they had eaten so much meat all day long, their belches stank of it. After they finished eating, they went back to watching the ice from atop a hill. While they were busy looking, their dogs, now hungry, began plundering the load of meat on the sled. Qalingu heard the noise they were making as they tussled with each other. He said, "Maatiusi! Sounds like they're after the load on our sled! Go quickly because they're stripping us of everything."

* * *

Spring had arrived. It was the season of the belugas. Maatiusi and Qalingu prepared to go hunting again on the *sinaa*. Qalingu said, "Maatiusi! Get ready! I'm going to take a look from the lookout... Put paw protectors on the dogs! Palungattak won't be coming with us."

He climbed the inuksuk and scanned the *sinaa* with a telescope. He spotted something in a patch of open water, between the ice floes.

"Look at that!" he said.

He hurried off because he had just seen some *qilalukkaanaq* carried on the backs of their mothers. He scrambled down the hill, sinking into the snow with every step. Meanwhile, Maatiusi had harnessed the dogs and put paw protectors on them, one after another. There were five dogs. He then had his going-away meal and quickly gulped down his tea in one long swig. Qalingu, who had just come down the hill, said, "Hurry up! I saw a large number of belugas in a patch of open water, between the ice floes, a whole pod of belugas!"

They got their dog team going and quickly headed to the *sinaa*. On arriving, they took up position behind an ice hummock, after taking care to avoid making any noise while walking. They were now in a good position to fire. When the belugas surfaced, all at once, they made a big noise with their blowholes. Qalingu raised his rifle, aimed, and fired. He hit a beluga and shouted, "*Ii! Autualu!* It's sinking straight down!"

Maatiusi in turn fired and struck dead on, fatally hitting a pregnant female that rose back to the surface. His face flushed red with emotion, for it was the first beluga he had killed. His whole body was shaking. Qalingu said, "*Suvakkualuk!* Just look at that!"

Qalingu nervously grasped the shaft of his harpoon, attaching the head and the harpoon line. He then threw it at the wounded animal... The harpoon head hit the animal hard but slipped on a bone... Qalingu thought his prey was going to sink. But it soon resurfaced and he immediately reattached the head to the harpoon and threw a second time. The harpoon struck home. He said, "Maatiusi *ai!* It's your first beluga!"

Maatiusi smiled slightly in response. A profound quivering ran through his entire body, probably out of gratitude or satisfaction. With the assistance of the dogs, they tried to haul the animal out of the water and onto the ice. Maatiusi stood in front of the dogs to urge them on. "*Hau! Hau!*" he called to them.

But suddenly the leather rope snapped, lashing Qalingu in the face. He screamed, "*Aatataa!* My face!" His cheek was bleeding profusely, and he saw many flashes of light.

Maatiusi was very afraid, and thought, "Had I not killed the beluga, he wouldn't have hurt himself..." He was full of remorse.

When Qalingu's pain began to subside, the two men started hauling the beluga again. With the ice chisel, they bashed away at the bumps in the ice that stood in the animal's way and managed to haul it up and onto the sled, then set out for home. The load being a heavy one, they advanced very slowly and had to walk beside the sled, pushing it continually. They could not keep it from rolling over whenever it crossed an ice ridge, and could set it right again only with great effort... They finally crossed the land-fast ice and were almost home when their folks saw them and said, "*Aa!* They've killed a beluga!"

"We're going to have *mattaq* to eat!" shouted Arnatuinnaq joyfully.

Qalingu called to Ningiukuluk, the midwife who had delivered Maatiusi, "Your *angusiaq* deserves our gratitude. Today he killed his first beluga... As for me, I lost mine and it sank! And when the *nuvviti* snapped in two, I was almost killed right then and there. I saw many flashes of light and was hurt in the face!"

Ningiukuluk was delighted by the feat of her *angusiaq* who had killed a beluga. Though old, she began to jump for joy and, suddenly feeling full of fervour, called out to everyone present, "But what do all these men do who stay home and do nothing? Haven't you just been delivered from starvation?"

They now cut the animal up into portions while putting the sinewy meat aside. Ningiukuluk, meanwhile, continued to extol her *angusiaq*. When the cutting was done, gifts would be distributed to one and all by throwing them out to the crowd. In the meantime, Ningiukuluk would apportion the four sinewy pieces of meat among the women, after cutting them with her ulu. Sanaaq exclaimed, "I'm going to remove the sinews from my share of the meat!"

Arnatuinnaq, Akutsiak, and Qumaq munched on raw cartilage—pieces of the beluga's larynx. They also ate the *qalluviaq* of the heart, and pieces from the rear flipper. Sanaaq removed the sinews by ripping them out with her ulu. She cleaned them off, using her teeth to remove the remaining meat, and set them out to dry. Aqiarulaaq did likewise. She then called out to the others, "Come and eat the beluga's tail!"

Everyone came to the feast. They were very cheerful, holding their ulu or knife for a piece of the meat. Qumaq had a piece of *mattaq* cut out by her mother. Arnatuinnaq too removed the sinews from her share of the meat, using a small piece of cloth, but she had trouble removing them. The sinews were fresh and still a bit alive.

"It's really very difficult," she said. "I can't quite yank this one out!" The cause of her anger was a little sinew with meat attached. "I'll try again *ai!*" She began again, trying with all her might... but to no avail. "That's alright! I don't want to try anymore. I'm afraid it would just make me angry!"

"You're really stupid, Arnatuinnaq!" said Sanaaq, insulting her younger sister. "What a display of intelligence!"

They now brought together all the little gifts to be thrown out to the crowd. Ningiukuluk, who had delivered Maatiusi, was full of enthusiasm.

"*Aa!* Look at all the stuff!" said Sanaaq. "There are even bars of soap. How nice! Toss some over here, to my side."

After catching what had been thrown to the crowd, everyone went home, their arms loaded with the meat that had been divided up and the gifts that had been distributed. Tobacco... Matches...

"Qumaq! Show me what you caught," said Arnatuinnaq.

"Here it is. All of that!"

"Look at all of what she collected in the give-away! She has sinews and matches!"

23

SCENES OF SUMMER LIFE

Sanaaq and her family saw a plane arrive once more in the sky, and it seemed to be low on fuel... It looked as if it would land there, as Sanaaq and her family looked on dumbfounded. Inside the plane were two occupants, who were also short of food. Qalingu went closer and said, "*Autualu!* His eyes are wide open with fear, the poor man!"

* * *

Summer was coming and large motionless clouds could be seen, apparently held back by strong winds from the cloudless part of the sky—a sure sign that a thunderstorm was forming. The two *Qallunaak* headed to the tents. As night fell, it began to thunder loudly.

"I'm going to tell Qumaq not to go to sleep," said Sanaaq. "A storm is brewing and I'm afraid she'll be badly shaken by the sound of thunder!"

Arnatuinnaq, who was very afraid, went to stay with her camp neighbours, where there were lots of people.

"I'm afraid and without protection!" she said, coming in. "I have no one who can really reassure me."

"Are you afraid of being struck by lightning?" asked Aqiarulaaq. "It's getting closer and closer. Just listen! The rain is pouring, with huge raindrops... The *nikkuit* that I put out to dry will probably be ruined, as well as the *iluliarusiit* and the *uliuliniit.* I'm worried about them, but I forget, there are also the slices of beluga tail... With this heavy rain, nothing is safe... Arnatuinnaq *ai!* Let's both eat some *nikku.*"

Arnatuinnaq ate some *nikku* from the beluga's shoulder blades and some ordinary *nikku.* She then said, "I don't want any more. I no longer feel like eating because I'm afraid. Stuffing my mouth no longer gives me any pleasure... I'll go back to eating when it stops thundering. *Irq!* Look at that big flash of lightning!"

Aqiarulaaq ate some *nikku* and dipped it in oil, but it was not enough for her and she cried out, "Aanikallak! Cut me a piece of blubber with skin. Some seal blubber, from the seal here on the ground."

"*Ii!*" said Aanikallak. "Filthy creatures! Those big maggots are so disgusting! They look dangerous... They're really wriggling about!"

"Listen *ai!*" mused Aqiarulaaq. "People say that maggots make you fatter! My kinfolk, I'm going to get jowls from eating them. What do you think?"

She was teasing, but Aanikallak answered tit for tat. "Maybe it's because my mother ate maggots that she's starting to get jowls... She even has a double chin and is a bit plump!" she said, laughing.

Arnatuinnaq had previously planned to make boots but instead had gone visiting. She could not sit still, though, worried as she was by everything she still had to do and by her fear of thunder.

"But what's happened to the thunder?" she said. "It seems to have stopped!"

So she decided to go home. She tried to finish her boots because she wanted to go fishing on the foreshore the next day. She chewed on the skin of the sole to soften it and did the same with the skin of the top half before assembling them. She first did the *mirsutaq*, then the *ilullitaq*, and finally the two folds gathered together from the back of the leg to the heel. The next day, at sunrise, she dressed and made ready to go fishing on the foreshore. She took a packsaddle to be carried by a dog on the way back. The tide having reached its lowest level, Arnatuinnaq and Aqiarulaaq walked down to the foreshore, chatting all the while.

"Look at all the clams!" said Arnatuinnaq. "Let's gather clams!"

She dug into the sand with a scraper to unearth the molluscs. Aqiarulaaq, who was very slow, had taken along only a small bucket for the clams she picked. Meanwhile, Arnatuinnaq, when hers was full, would empty it into the packsaddle. She gathered clams for a long while. Suddenly Arnatuinnaq shouted, "*Ii! Ai!* There's a big insect! Look at the centipede!"

"I'm going to look for *kanajuit* over here," said Aqiarulaaq, unperturbed. "Look at the big *suluppaujaq!* It looks dangerous... It's disgusting!... I don't want to look for sculpins anymore!"

"I've filled my bucket again," said Arnatuinnaq, "and the packsaddle is full. I'm now going to catch some little sculpins a bit higher up on the beach. The dog should be able to go home all by itself, for the tide is starting to come in."

"Oh, is it ever cold!" exclaimed Aqiarulaaq. "My boots are letting water in. And it's cold! The water's leaking inside in several places that have worn through. Never mind! Let's fish a little more!"

Arnatuinnaq forgot all about the dog, despite the rising tide. She was lifting many stones.

"*Aa!* That one over there! Is it a *kanajuq* or a *nipisaq? Ii!* Not at all! It's a dirty *ningiurqaluk!* It's disgusting!"

Just then, Arnatuinnaq noticed—too late—that the rising tide had surrounded her dog and her packsaddle full of clams. She ran to the animal and called to it, all the while thinking apprehensively, "If it swims, it may not get away because the packsaddle is too heavy for it..."

She called to it, "*Hau! Hau!*" The dog began to swim to shore with the packsaddle on its back.

Aqiarulaaq, too, approached and said, "Look at that dog! It was caught off-guard by the tide..."

"It was surrounded by the water while standing on a small mound... But it's coming!"

Arnatuinnaq was feeling more confident now, after being so afraid. She was reassuring herself about the swimming dog. Once it had made its way across, she pulled it to shore by its leash, without looking at the bag's contents. The tide was now high. She looked in the packsaddle and saw that it was completely empty.

"*Ii!* The clams I gathered are all gone... Not a single one remains. The stitching on the packsaddle's bottom came loose!"

"Too bad! But the tide is high... Do you have your bucket of sculpins?"

"No, I left it back there! It too has probably been swept away by the tide!"

She hastened to go and look. The tide had carried it off while her attention was on the dog. Her bucket was floating on the water and the sculpins she had caught were clearly lost... She even tried to wade into the water in her boots, but she could not grab it and came back with nothing... She felt overcome by sorrow, thinking about all she had gathered on the foreshore... No wonder. She was going home having lost everything.

* * *

Sanaaq was braiding some sinews into a thread to be used for sewing skins onto Qalingu's *qajaq*. It was midday and, since awaking that morning, she and her family had not left their tent.

"Give my little boy something to eat! Cut off a piece of *mattaq* for him, Qumaq!"

Qumaq cut into a piece of *mattaq* with an ulu.

"Take it, little brother!" she said.

"Yes!"

"*Ii!* What's he doing?" exclaimed Sanaaq. "*Autualu!* He's swallowing and choking, the poor thing! How do we get rid of whatever's choking him?"

Qalingu was filling a barrel. Later, he would make a laced bag to put meat in. He removed the rind of the blubber and cut it into pieces. As the pieces piled up, he put them onto a plate and carried them to a spot near the barrel. He threw away the rinds he had removed and kept the blubber pieces, the meat pieces, and the guts—some of which he had thrown away. Sanaaq was cutting thin slices of meat. Qalingu told her, "The barrel isn't completely full... A little more blubber should be put in... It'd be nice if we caught another beluga!"

"It sure would," replied Sanaaq, "but we should find a way to dry the slices of *mattaq* I've cut up."

"When I'm done, I'll make a meat-drying rack out of a crossbar... Watch out! My son's going to slip and fall on a piece of blubber!"

The little one did, in fact, slip on the blubber... He was smeared all over with grease and had hit himself on the face. "*Aatataa!* I'm hurt! Mommy! *Aappuu!*" he wailed.

"*Ii! Autualu!*" exclaimed Sanaaq. "Look, he's really skinned himself! He's given himself a bump on the forehead... *aalummi!* Let me see, let me make you *aappuu!*"

Qumaq, realizing that her little brother had hurt himself, came running and tried to console him. She said, "Little brother! Let's play together! Let's have fun, over there, throwing rocks... Let's also play with the little boat... Where's your little boat?"

"Look! I've given myself a big lump! I've got a real bump on my forehead!"

"Let's go! Let's go down there! Akutsiaq! Come with us!"

"Yes!"

They both started playing with the little boat and were quite happy. Akutsiak shouted, "Hey! I'm going to fall into the water!"

She indeed fell in and began to cough and splutter. "*Hai! Hai!*"

Qumaq burst into a fit of laughter and grabbed her by the hand. Akutsiak was furious over being made fun of. She said, "Don't laugh at me, dirty Qumaq! Didn't I fall into the water because you told me to come?"

She was soaking wet, for she had fallen the full length of her body into the water. She began to wring her clothes and hang them to dry elsewhere so that her mother would not know. Predictably, though, Ningiukuluk started to call, "Daughter! Come and set this sealskin on a drying rack!"

Akutsiak hesitated because her clothes were not dry yet, but went home nonetheless and was given a talking-to by Ningiukuluk. "Why did you pretend you couldn't hear me? Is your dress all wet?"

Her daughter nodded and set the skin on the drying rack, using a *kaijjiaq*.

* * *

Qalingu was making an *ungirlaaq* out of *mattaq,* using half of a beluga skin and lacing it with a leather strap. Once the bag had been laced, he filled it with meat, after placing it inside a stone cache, whose interior he had carefully dried. After filling and closing the bag, he covered the cache again with stones and wedged it shut. When he was done, he went home and said, "*Ai!* There are lots of belugas out there. Looks like they're staying at the same place, on this side of the little point. I'll keep my gun ready!"

Sanaaq took the thin slices she had cut and laid them on the drying rack, saying, "The dogs don't look hungry... They're lying around and don't even feel like stealing the food!"

Her little boy joined her after playing with Qumaq. The legs of his boots had slid up the entire length of his legs. Everyone now went into the tent.

24

THE LEGEND OF LUMAAJUQ

In the tent, Arnatuinnaq heard a strange noise from outside.

"What is it?" she said. "Could it be someone shouting?" She went out to see. "*A!* What's that big thing in the distance? What could that possibly be, that black thing among the belugas? Come and see!"

Her whole family, Qalingu, Sanaaq, and her daughter Qumaq, went out to see. Qalingu in turn said, "What is that big thing? I can't make it out. Look, Sanaaq! Can you make out what that is?"

"Yes! *Ii!* It's all black and it's making noise! *Qatannguuk! Qatannguuk!* Take a look! What's that black thing among the belugas that's making sounds?"

"What? Whereabouts?" said Aqiarulaaq. "Let me look! *Ii! Autualuk!* There are lots of yellowish belugas and among them is something else that's not a beluga. Let's try and find out what it could be!"

Aqiarulaaq went to consult Ningiukuluk and Taqriasuk. Ningiukuluk said, "I know what it is from what I've heard people say. Among those belugas is a *lumaartalik*. Whenever such a beluga surfaces to breathe, it drags behind itself a being who sings '*Lu lu lumaaq!* Up there, up there, I want to go to the top of the hill, *lu lumaaq!* I want to go there because it's clean, *lu lu lumaaq!* Up there, up there, on top of the hill, I want to use my scraper, *lu lumaaq*...' After expressing itself in this manner, it dives again... The beluga is attached to a Lumaajuq. It's a very old beluga!"

Now that the animal had been identified, Qalingu lost interest and did not even go near the belugas. Sanaaq and Aqiarulaaq did likewise. Sanaaq said, "Look, my kinfolk, at all the migrating belugas, with a Lumaajuq among them!"

"*Ilai qatannguuk!*" said Aqiarulaaq. "The belugas are yellowish in colour, probably because they're very old and no good to eat!"

"Yes! Ningiukuluk and Taqriasuk must know about this, for they are old and wise. I'll ask Ningiukuluk. Ningiukuluk! Have you heard about these beings?"

"Yes! A *lumaartalik* is inedible. You may even die if you eat one. It can bring about death because it's a very old beluga. You must not even shoot at it!"

Taqriasuk recounted the legend of their origin:

"A very long time ago, a blind boy killed a polar bear with an arrow. But he was tricked by his mother, who led him to believe that he had accidentally killed their dog, Uugaq. They indeed had a dog by that name. The mother had a daughter a little younger than the boy. The mother went with her daughter to cook the bear meat a bit further away, while the blind boy stayed home, although he was the one who had killed the bear. They were gone the whole day. While the blind boy was at home, he heard birds flying north in their migration and he called out to them, 'Give me back my sight!' The mother and daughter had boiled the bear meat, and the daughter pretended to eat some, but in fact she tucked some pieces for her brother into her jacket by sliding them down her neck. She then headed home and gave him the meat, telling him it was from their dog Uugaq, for she was afraid of their mother, who was claiming that he had killed their dog Uugaq. Thanks to his sister, the blind son did not die of hunger, though knowing full well that he had killed a polar bear. When he again heard the cry of the migrating birds flying overhead, he once more called out, 'Give me back my sight!' Then and there some loons visited him. They led him to a small lake, to give him his sight back. The loons plunged the blind boy underwater after telling him to move his body the moment he began to choke, to let them know. Just when he was about to drown, they brought him back to the surface to breathe. He could now make out a lemming's burrow off in the distance, atop a small hill... The loons plunged him a second time underwater, until he again began to choke, this being indicated by a movement of his body. They brought him back to the surface. Because his sight had improved, they let him go home by himself. On the way back, he came to the level land where the polar bear's skin was staked to the ground. He ripped it to pieces so that it could no longer be used. His mother realized that he was not blind anymore and went to meet him... When summer arrived and they were all alone in their camp, the mother asked her son how the people at the neighbouring camp hunted belugas. The son answered that a hunter would catch them with the help of his mother, whom he would attach to the end of his harpoon line... The son's mother, who envied the other camp's hunting success, insisted that she be attached to the end of her son's harpoon line when they went beluga hunting. He had successfully convinced her, falsely, that she would be needed to help him capture his prey. Despite her ill will towards her son, she told him, 'That one! That one! That little grey calf! Harpoon it!' But he harpooned the largest of the belugas, an all-white beluga. Because she was attached to the harpoon line by her waist, she was dragged over the shoreline rocks and out to sea as if she were a float..."

That was Taqriasuk's tale. Sanaaq exclaimed, "*Aa!* So that's it! The woman who became Lumaajuq is this dark-coloured form that appears at the surface behind a beluga!"

"I understand the story you've just told," said Aqiarulaaq, "and it's very nice to hear, just like Lumaajuq's song!"

"Thank you!" said Qalingu. "We now know that she's the one among the belugas!"

"I'm grateful to you," added Arnatuinaaq. "It's the first time I've heard about Lumaajuq and seen her! I'm glad to have heard Taqriasuk's tale, which was passed down to him by our ancestors. I'm glad he's still alive, despite his advanced age. He's a very good grandfather, who knows much about all subjects!"

"That's not what I think!" said Qalingu. "I'm not very glad. I wanted to capture another beluga, and it seems that these ones are not edible and could poison us!"

"It's a lucky thing," said Aqiarulaaq, "that the belugas didn't arrive at night. Qalingu would've hunted them in the dark and he might have killed one, without being able to see properly. Had he done so, we'd all be dead now from having eaten one of them!"

"There are many Lumaajuit to be found among belugas," said Sanaaq. "The one we just saw and heard has gone under water, but many other ones like it may still come here!"

"When I saw it," said Arnatuinaaq, "I first thought it was something I had never seen before and then, because it was daylight, its dark colour reminded me a lot of an *avataq,* although it was in fact the old woman who had become Lumaajuq!"

"I heard that legend because I'm old," said Taqriasuk. "She's said to be easy to recognize because she's pulled by a beluga... She was an Inuk, a very long time ago, and she'll probably stay in that form until the end of the world... The line attached to her is bigger than the ones used by the Inuit, because over time it's been covered with *mattaq!*"

Qumaq watched and silently listened to everything while thinking, "I saw a Lumaajuq with my folks. One day soon I'll try to draw or carve a likeness of it..."

All day long the belugas surfaced and frolicked at the same place, but Qalingu refrained from hunting them, for fear of dying. After all that Taqriasuk had recounted... The whole day, his thoughts turned over and over in his mind.

"Because of what Taqriasuk said, I haven't killed a single beluga, although many were in view. All because Ningiukuluk and Taqriasuk, as elders, knew better about everything... Had we not listened to them, we'd probably all be dead by now... There have been belugas here the whole day and we could have easily killed some... I'm glad we've got elders among us. If none were around, we wouldn't have been told and, along with all our camp mates, we'd have eaten some and probably be dead..."

Qalingu went to share his thoughts with Taqriasuk.

"Taqriasuk, thanks for your knowledge about what's dangerous... Through you, I've learned that the meat of some belugas is fatal!"

"A long time ago, my grandfather taught me the dangers of life... To this very day, I've never forgotten what he taught me. But now that I myself am an old man, I must tell it to others... Because I'm getting too old, I'll soon be unable to help you by telling you what I know, for I'll not be around much longer. You must act wisely towards what's dangerous and not dangerous on earth... It's not just the belugas with Lumaajuq that may threaten your life. Ordinary belugas can also be a source of danger... In summer, when they are not skinned immediately and are exposed to the sun, their meat, if boiled, will smell strong and may be fatal. You must pay very close attention, even if it has no special taste or smell!"

"Thanks for all this knowledge," replied Qalingu. "Keep on teaching the youngest among us about dangerous things! They must learn. I fully understand that an Inuk must know everything about food. Even though you're old, your words are useful and will outlive you... Your teachings as an elder will continue to be passed on. Thank you, Taqriasuk!"

"It isn't just the belugas with Luumajuq and those whose meat is rotten that are deadly or dangerous. There are also the very skinny ones, whose meat should not be consumed. Their meat too can cause death, even though, in appearance, it seems good to eat! The fact that these belugas are very skinny is a sign that they're dangerous. When I kill such a beluga, even if I'm starving or if it's the first time in my life I've killed one, I absolutely will not eat it!"

"I now understand why the meat of certain mammals isn't edible. I'm glad you're still alive because I didn't know these rules. My father and my mother are dead and I no longer have anyone to give me advice on what I must and must not do. All I know is how to hunt, but without really knowing what's dangerous... Tell me more of what you know to make me wiser... As you're very old, if that tires you, I could also ask Ningiukuluk to teach me!"

"I'm not tired... It's the only way I have to help you... The belugas aren't the only ones to pose a mortal danger. Some other mammals are even more dangerous, others less so... I'm old now and I've already been made ill by some mammals. Among them are very skinny ringed seals, whose meat, like the beluga's, must absolutely never be consumed when the animal is too skinny. If its skin is of good quality, you may use it after throwing the meat away, even though the meat isn't rotten, because the skinniness may result from an illness. I don't mean seals that normally are skinnier in spring. I don't mean them but those that have almost no blubber, the ones that have a strong yellow colour... Those seals are the ones whose meat poses a mortal danger. There are also the ringed seals that, without being skinny and without having been wounded by bullets, have some sort of illness... Eating their meat is very dangerous. There are also the seals that have had serious injuries, either new or old ones, due to ice, that have bones or ribs broken by the ice... Those ones you can eat without danger, as well as those that have funny-looking pelts!"

"Taqriasuk! Thank you for explaining all these things. It's reassuring to have elders."

"It's known that animals with only skin on their bones have parasites. As do very skinny birds. It isn't just the Lumaajuit that are dangerous. Some other mammals, such as foxes, can be too."

"Thank you! I won't forget any of what you've told me and which I didn't know before. I need to be taught. Those who aren't elders are less knowledgeable than those who are. Without elders the Inuit are nothing, for there is much knowledge that the elders alone possess!"

"My knowledge comes not from me but from my ancestors. It seems to be mine but, in fact, it comes to me from people who preceded me. I pass it on to all of you, to all of your descendants and all of your kinfolk!"

25

THE FIRST CATHOLIC MISSIONARIES

A big boat appeared in the distance. Qumaq saw it first and said, "There's a big boat!"

Sanaaq called out to her cousin, "Yes! *Qatannguuk!* Look at it! Have a good look!"

Qalingu ran to warn the *Qallunaat* at the trading post, telling them, "A big boat is arriving *ai!*"

The *Qallunaat* went to unload the big boat, accompanied by Qalingu. Both *Qallunaat* and Inuit did the unloading. While they were on board, Qalingu noticed an *iksigarjuaq*. He looked like a very kind man. He seemed to find Qalingu friendly and spoke to him.

"*Ai!* What's your name?"

"My name is Qalingu."

He then noticed an *ajuqirtuiji* who also looked like a very kind man and who invited Qalingu to follow him to his cabin. He did, and there the minister offered him a book, without saying what it was... Qalingu took it back with him, thinking it to be nothing important, that is, he was told nothing about the book and was taught nothing, so he clearly had no idea what it was. Nonetheless, the *ajuqirtuiji* did tell him what he thought of the *iksigarjuaq*.

"You must not listen at all to people like him, for they are big liars! They will come and move into your camp!"

Because of this warning, Qalingu remained very reserved when the Catholic missionaries came and moved into the camp. He helped them only grudgingly, for fear of being tricked. Qumaq, her mother, and their family stayed on the dry land. The *iksigarjuaq* disembarked and went to Qumaq and her family. He shook many hands and smiled broadly at Qumaq and her little brother. But Qumaq was reserved.

"*Ia-a!*" she said shyly, her little brother too.

Qalingu left the big boat and went ashore. He took back a large bag of gifts for his family. Qumaq came to meet him. Her little brother tried to come too, but he still had trouble walking. Qumaq was growing up to be a big girl. Qalingu gave his son and Qumaq some oranges and then went home, carrying his son on his shoulders and taking Qumaq by the hand.

Sanaaq said to her husband, "Look at that! You were given presents for your family?!"

"Yes!" said Qalingu.

He hurriedly returned to the *Qallunaat*, who gave him many gifts. He was even short of containers to put them in. They treated him well, for it was their first meeting. In exchange for a sealskin and a few small objects, he was offered cloth for a pair of pants. Coming back to his family, he said, "We won't let Qumaq go to the *iksigarjuaq* because he's a liar. That's what the *ajuqirtuiji* told me!"

"What do you mean?" said Sanaaq, very astonished. "Why? Just listen to that! We now have to be afraid of being tricked!"

The next day, Qumaq very much wanted to go and visit the *iksigarjuaq*, but Sanaaq tried to stop her. Qumaq was on the verge of crying. No one could change her mind, and finally she was allowed to go, accompanied by Arnatuinnaq. Qumaq was very happy. When they arrived, the man picked her up in his arms. With Arnatuinnaq, she played billiards. Qumaq was even given a short catechism lesson and no longer wanted to leave. She and Arnatuinnaq nonetheless headed home. On arriving, Arnatuinnaq said to Sanaaq, "He's very kind and really puts you at ease!"

"But why did the *ajuqirtuiji* call him a liar?" said Sanaaq and Qalingu. "Is he one himself?"

"He probably didn't tell the truth," answered Arnatuinnaq. "The *iksigaarjuaq* carried Qumaq in his arms and even began to teach her what's good and what's bad. That's how she was treated! The other man probably didn't tell the truth!"

Arnatuinnaq wished to follow the Catholic faith, but had not yet said so. "I want to join their faith," she often thought to herself.

In truth, she still had to talk it over with her family... She was afraid, though, of being prevented from doing so by Sanaaq, her older sister, and by Qalingu. She was scared that her family would give her a hard time. The thought made her very ill at ease.

"Never mind *ai!* Since I'm afraid of no longer being well treated, it's not possible for me now..."

Meanwhile Qumaq was thinking, "It'd be better if I followed the *iksigarjuaq,* even if I have to face the opposition of my kinfolk. It doesn't matter... Can't be helped... As for my body, it will die, and then where will I go? What does my body matter!"

She was eager. Aanikallak shared the same ideas, but she felt helpless because her mother forbade her from following the *iksigarjuaq*. Qumaq, whose mother was still making some effort to hold her back, stuck to her choice. Aanikallak too persevered, despite strong opposition.

Arnatuinnaq, Qumaq, and Aanikallak all wished to convert. Qumaq was very keen. Arnatuinnaq was afraid and self-conscious. She made obstacles out of anything for herself. As soon as someone talked to her, she immediately began to have doubts, just as Maatiusi did. Qumaq was very happy and said, "I'm going to follow this faith because I think about it continually!"

She strove to push herself whenever she felt like lazing around. She developed a habit of working fervently and, though she had other occupations, began to pray more. Anything became a motive for her to think about her family. She had found a way to be happy now.

26

A CHILDREN'S QUARREL

Qumaq was growing up. Today, she was going to do the laundry with Akutsiaq. She gathered everything to be washed and put it into a bag, saying, "Mother! We're going to wash, I and Akutsiak... Give me some soap!"

Akutsiaq and Aanikallak, who were still little girls, accompanied her and took along some little things to be washed. Qumaq had a heavy load and chatted on the way.

"Tomorrow *ai!* We'll go fishing on the foreshore, at the far end of the cove!"

"We'll go *ai!*" said Akutsiaq.

"I won't go," said Aanikallak. "I have bad boots that let in water and are in very bad shape!"

"It's because you're lazy!" said Qumaq. "You don't take care of them!"

"Oh! I'm going to tell my mother!"

"Don't!" answered Qumaq, who wanted to be forgiven and was looking for a way out. "Don't do that! Here, I'll give you this bar of soap... Tomorrow, we'll have fun making a little tent *ai!* Aanikallak! Here *ai!* Take the soap... It's real soap!"

"That Aanikallak is really a tattletale," said Akutsiaq. "She even tells things that aren't true!"

Once they had arrived, they began to wash in the river. Qumaq was fast and had already gone through a lot of laundry when her two much slower companions were still at the beginning of theirs. Aanikallak washed very poorly and left some parts dirty. She was ridiculed a second time by Akutsiaq.

"*Autualu!* Look, Qumaq! That's been really badly washed. It's still dirty here and there!"

Aanikallak, predictably, again began to sulk. She glared at her companions and started to cry. She called out, "I'm going to tell my mother you've been very mean to me!"

"*Ii!*" shouted Qumaq suddenly. "That old jacket over there is being carried off by the current!"

Akutsiaq jumped to her feet and began running. She ran after what was being carried away by the river, saying, "*Irq!* I've got to grab it fast, when that stone stops it!"

She managed to grab what the current had snatched away before it got to the waterfall. She then washed the laundry that Qumaq had brought. Once they had finished, they wrung the laundry and laid it to dry on the ground. Qumaq stretched out a large *atigi* for it to drip-dry. Unable to wring it with her hands, she let it drain on a rock. They stayed a long while.

Meanwhile Aanikallak had gone to tell her mother.

"Mother! Qumaq and Akutsiaq are always being mean to me!"

When her mother heard that, she said, "*Suvakkualuk!* My daughter has been badly treated. I'm going to find those two rascals who think so highly of themselves!" She believed her daughter, who had not told the truth. She indeed went ahead and scolded them. "Why have the two of you been picking on my adopted daughter? You wicked tormentors!"

"She didn't tell the truth!" answered Akutsiaq. "We simply told her that she hadn't been washing properly! We just treated her as being clumsy... We don't have any bad feelings against her!"

"You're really hurtful! She's not to be humiliated, for she's mine and mine alone!" said Aqiarulaaq, who then went home, the little girls doing likewise.

27

A COMMUNITY FEAST OF BOILED MEAT

Ningiukuluk was cooking outside. She was preparing *aqiluqi* and was bothered by the smoke. When the pieces of meat were done just right, she pulled them out with a fork. She did not follow the example of Makutsialutjuaq who, according to legend, burned her hands when pulling the pieces out with her fingers. Onto a plate she put the various pieces. There were pieces with bones: *siqruit, kuutsinaat, akuit, taliit, qimminguat, kiasiit, sakiat, tunirjuit, tulimaat, kujapigait, kuutsiniit, niaquit, alliruit, qungisiit, ittunguat, pamialluit, akitsirait,* and *ulunnguat.* She also cooked the guts: *kanivaut, tinguit, aqiaruit, qitsalikaat, qinirsikallait, matsait, qinirsiit, inaluat, uummatit, qalluviat, pavviit, umirquit, qaritait, puvait, iggiat,* and *turqujaat...* These were the pieces that she boiled.

She called for everyone to come. "*Uujun-ukua!*"

Sanaaq and all of her camp mates gathered for a community feast. Qumaq got a rear flipper and Akutsiaq a front flipper. Qumaq was keen on saving the little bones from her share of the meat, Akutsiaq likewise.

"I'm collecting my little bones!" said Qumaq. "We're each going to do that, *ai!* Akutsiaq! We'll play a game of pulling bones out of a mitten, by using a sinew with a noose at the end!"

After eating her rear flipper, Qumaq saved the following little bones: a *qimminguat, arnanguat,* an *iglitikallak,* a *paannguaq,* a *natsinguaq,* a *qajuuttalutuq,* a *sirpalutuq,* an *illiti,* an *utsuluttuq,* and an *angutinnguaq.* Akutsiaq, Qumaq's partner, saved the following little bones: a *qimminguat,* an *aquviartulutuq,* a *sappa,* a *qulliq,* a *kaivvasuk,* an *illaulusuk,* an *utsulutuq,* and a *kuutsitualik.* They would now play the bone game.

"Akutsiaq!" said Qumaq. "Use the sinew noose to pull some little bones out of a mitten *ai!*"

Qumaq began pulling some bones out with the noose. "*Aa!* I caught one!"

They each took turns.

"*Irq! Autualu!* I've just been pulling for nothing! Look, Qumaq! *I i i!*" She laughed. "I haven't caught anything at all! You're so lucky. You've caught a lot, Qumaq!"

With their little bones, they each made the outline of a snow house and a meat cache. Qumaq tried to break into Akutsiaq's meat cache while Akutsiaq's pawn was asleep. She was careful not to make any noise, but Akutsiaq, who was being very attentive, said, "Listen! What's it doing, that one there?"

"Over there! There goes a mouse!" answered Qumaq through her pawn. "It's gone in to hide... I'm going to look for it!"

Qumaq's pawn lied to conceal its intention to steal what was in the cache and because it had been taken by surprise. The two pawns were now going to fight each other. They were tossed into the air and the one that fell convex-side down was the loser... That was the bone game.

28

SPRING HUNTING, FISHING, AND GATHERING

Spring had come. Qumaq and Akutsiaq went to gather some *airait.*

"Akutsiaq!" said Qumaq. "We're going to gather some *airait* on the plateau!"

"Sure! Wait *ai!* I'll first look for something to dig the ground with and a bag to put them in."

"Sure, go ahead! Hurry before night falls!"

Akutsiaq went home for what she needed. On her way she walked through a patch of soft snow and got her boots wet. As she came in, she said, "Mother! Qumaq and I are going for a walk. We're going to gather some *airait.* Give me something to put them in and a digging tool!"

"To dig with," answered her mother, "take the old file. And to carry them, take the little bag."

Akutsiaq rushed to catch up to Qumaq, who had already set off.

"Qumaq!" she shouted to her. "Wait for me!"

They harvested many *airait* on the little flat mounds where the snow had melted.

"Here's an *airaq!*" said Qumaq. "I'm going to dig it out... It's really a fine *airaq!*"

She unearthed it by digging all around it and then yanking it out. She then cut the stem off with a stone, on a rock, and put it into her bag. She and Akutsiaq kept digging the ground up for more *airait.* They chatted.

"We've got enough!" said Qumaq. "Are we going home *ai?*"

"Yes!" said her companion. "Look, Qumaq! Some people with a sled are approaching... They've been hunting on the *sinaa...* Let's go! Let's hurry over to them!"

They ran down the slope. The snow, however, had turned quite soft and when Qumaq sank into it she was flung forward with all of the *airait* she had gathered raining over the snow. She began to cry with grief, for having lost all of her *airait.* Her companion picked them up.

"Qumaq!" she said. "Don't cry, little one! Here they are. Put them into your bag. Look, over there, the people on the sled. They're almost here... Don't cry anymore! They've been hunting on the *sinaa.*"

The two girls arrived home.

"Here are some *airait!*" said Qumaq, tossing them at her mother on the *ungati.*

The girls ran off to meet the new arrivals. The sled passed Akutsiaq but caught Qumaq by her feet in the tuglines and dragged her along in the snow. Qalingu and his companion, who were bringing back an *ujjuk,* both used their feet to brake.

"*Au!*" yelled Qalingu.

Qumaq was dragged over the bumps and hollows of the ice. When they finally came to a stop, she freed herself and walked to the sled... Akutsiaq joined her. The men got moving again, arriving at home shortly after and unharnessing the dogs.

"You're going to have *kujapik* meat to eat!" announced Qalingu. "I've killed an *ujjuk!*"

They finished unharnessing the dogs and rolled up the tuglines. Once free, the dogs lapped up little mouthfuls of snow, having become thirsty from the blood they had drunk.

Qalingu and his companion carried in the pieces of meat. Maatiusi received a shoulder as his share. This was the portion that usually went to the hunting companion of the person who killed the animal. Though not required, it was customary for him to get a shoulder. If he did not want it, he could choose another piece more to his liking. As for the others, the ones given ordinary shares, they could receive a thigh or short ribs, or spare ribs with their vertebrae. To Qalingu went the other shoulder with the head attached. Sanaaq was preparing to take a share to someone.

"A knife!" Qalingu asked her. "I'll first cut some handholds into it!"

Between the two of them they carried a *kiataq* and an *aksunaaksat*. Only for the purpose of making leather straps would the chest skin be removed from an *ujjuk*. Maatiusi received an *aksunaaksaq*. The hunting companion who is entitled to this piece is called an *aksunajjatuq*. The others, the ones who did not take part in the hunt, have no right to these pieces although they may, as a favour, be given some. Similarly, they have no right to a share of the small intestine, unless offered a share.

Sanaaq laid the *kujapiit* on a *mangittaq* and called out to her camp mates, "Here are some *kujapiit!*"

"Yes!" they answered.

Aqiarulaaq, her ulu in hand, hurried over to this small feast for the women. Sanaaq sharpened her ulu and, once the cutting edge was honed, began to eat. Aqiarulaaq cut off a thoracic vertebra by slicing through a joint and ate its meat, adding some pieces from the heart. After scraping the meat off a vertebra, she threw the bone away and it was immediately fought over by the dogs. Meanwhile, the men were eating meat from the *kuutsiniit*. Once they had finished, they rinsed their hands in a bowl and dried them off... They were done.

That evening, Sanaaq and Aqiarulaaq prepared to go line fishing.

"Sanaaq!" said Aqiarulaaq. "Let's go fishing for *kanajuit!*"

Before leaving, they baited their hooks with pieces of blubber—some leftover chewed rubber—and took along a leather strap as a *nuvviti.* They set off. Sanaaq had to step over several cracks in the ice.

"The water is very murky here! Looks like the pack ice is breaking up... It will be harder and harder to walk over after the high spring tides!"

They began to fish by jerking their lines.

"Feel that," said Aqiarulaaq. "It feels like a sculpin. Doesn't seem to be hungry!"

"Listen! I can feel one! Yes! *A a a!*" Sanaaq drew it in. "I've caught a sculpin *ai!*"

"I envy you! I probably won't catch any. They're all getting away... I must be scaring them off with my hook!"

Sanaaq caught many sculpins and strung them onto her *nuvviti.*

"I feel like heading home," said Aqiarulaaq. "I probably won't catch any... It'd probably be better if we went to the foreshore, over there *ai!* Where the ice has broken up."

"Wait a bit, I'm catching quite a few," said Sanaaq, as she pulled in another one. "Listen to it! A sculpin!" She drew it in. "*Ii!* It's a dirty *ningiurqaluk*. I'll throw it away!"

"*Irq!* Don't throw it away! Give it to me!"

"*Ii!* Leave it! Are you in the habit of eating *ningiurqaluk?*"

"I'm not, but since I haven't caught any..."

"*Ai!* Then take some *qanirqutuit* and some ordinary sculpins!"

They went home and, once there, began cleaning the fish.

"I didn't catch any," said Aqiarulaaq. "They all got away. I brought nothing back!"

They cleaned the fish and put them into a cooking pot. Qumaq and Akutsiak went to draw some seawater. They dropped their pail down through an ice crack and, when they were done, returned home.

29

HUNTERS ADRIFT ON THE ICE

After another hunt for bearded seals, *kujapiit* were once again placed on a *mangittaq*. The invited women came together to feast on heart, *qalluviaq,* and *qiaq*. Akutsiaq removed the peritoneum from the *ujjuk*'s small intestines using a sinew. When she was done, they ate it.

"Is it ever good!" exclaimed Sanaaq.

After eating, they rinsed and dried their hands.

Meanwhile, Qalingu was carrying stones to the hilltop to build an inuksuk. When he was finished, he wiped his telescope with an Arctic hare's foot and looked through it at the surrounding landscape. Something caught his eye.

"It's probably an *ujjuk,*" he thought. "Down there, near the ice crack... I can't make it out very well because of the columns of warm air... I'll get a better look from further below... The two of us will go down to the ice floes!"

He drew closer as he descended and, looking again through the telescope, he could clearly make out the form of an *utjuk*. He went to his hunting companion and said, "There's an *uuttuq* out there! It's an *utjuk!* I'll try to get nearer... Stay here and watch! If I am carried away on the drifting ice, you'll come and look for me in a *qajaq!*"

He made ready to leave with his harpoon and white hunting cap. He set off, carrying the harpoon line and the harpoon head on his back. He crossed the land-fast ice and headed to the ice floes that had come in with the rising tide. When he had almost reached the *utjuk,* he stopped momentarily to rest and watch from atop an ice cake, using a hummock in the ice to judge his distance. There was no mistaking it. He was next to the *uuttuq*. He drew nearer, but it was asleep and completely unaware of him. He caught its attention by making some noise... The *utjuk* raised its head... and Qalingu fired his rifle... He hit it and started running straight to the animal. He was glad that it was not in a hazardous spot.

Taqriasuk, his camp mate, had followed everything from the look-out. He began to descend on foot.

"Maatiusi! Qalingu has killed an *utjuk!* Take the dogs to him. He's not far off!"

Maatiusi harnessed the dogs. "*Ha! Ha! Hau! Hau!*" But they were in a poor mood for pulling, their paw pads being in bad shape. He finished harnessing them and set off, holding the lead dog's tugline and letting the others follow. Eventually he came to the edge of the ice crack. He halted for a while, scared to go across. The ice had shifted considerably. He finally stepped over the crack, taking care to follow Qalingu's footprints. His dogs followed the footprints until they came within sight of the prey and picked up its scent, whereupon they bounded ahead at full speed—the very same dogs that were previously so loath to get going.

On arriving, Maatiusi said, "I took my time because for a long while I thought I wouldn't be able to cross the big ice crack, which seems to have widened!..."

"*Ai!*" said Qalingu. "Not surprising. Let's go! We'll let the dogs pull it...Hurry, there's a dark cloud, a sign that an *uanniq* is coming *Uit! Uit!*"

They set off in the direction of dry land. Qalingu wielded his ice chisel to smash away hummocks in the ice that hindered the passage of the *utjuk*. They advanced toward the coast, above which loomed a large and increasingly visible blue-black cloud.

"Maatiusi *ai!*" said Qalingu. "Don't be afraid! We won't be carried off with the ice."

"But we will! I'm afraid! We're drifting with it!"

"We aren't! There's just a little stretch of open water... When the tide comes in later today, it will push the drift ice to shore and we'll cross straight onto the land-fast ice."

They were separated from the land-fast ice by a narrow stretch of water. They weren't afraid, for the sea was very calm. As they whiled away the time, waiting for the rising tide to bring them to shore, they saw a large number of *puiji*. The open water shrank to nothing and they were finally able to cross over. Their dogs were panting, their tongues hanging out.

On arriving home, Qalingu said, "For some time it was no longer possible for us to cross over to the land-fast ice!"

"But over there," replied Sanaaq, "to the south, there isn't any open water... You could have come back that way."

"Time to sharpen my skinning knife! I'll skin the animal and make straps out of its skin... Its guts have probably begun to putrefy and its flesh has become all soft."

They started skinning and everyone received a portion of the meat. Qalingu and his hunting companion had killed many *utjuit* that spring, thereby procuring large amounts of *kiatat* and *aksunaaksat*.

The dogs fought over the scraps on the skinning site.

"Maatiusi!" said Qalingu. "Empty the small intestines and the stomach too. They might contain deadly parasites... Empty them into an ice crack. I'll make a float out of them for my harpoon!"

"*Ii!* They're disgusting," shouted Maatiusi, emptying the contents. "All these dirty *amaukkaluit!*"

"There's really nothing to be disgusted about," said Qalingu. "Hurry up!"

When he was done, he rinsed his hands several times in a little pool of water.

30

INUIT CHEWING GUM

The temperature turned colder that evening and the mushy snow froze again. They went to sleep at nightfall and awoke the next morning. Sanaaq lit her oil lamp and, while still in bed, prepared the morning breakfast by making tea. When done lighting her lamp, she fell back into a deep sleep... only to wake up again.

"*Ii!* Our lamp is smoking! Wake up! The bottom of the teapot is covered with a thick layer of soot! The poker has almost completely burned up!"

It was morning, so everyone woke up. Arnatuinnaq went outside the roofed snow house and called out, "Sounds like a ptarmigan up there. It's chattering *a a a!*"

Qalingu rushed to give chase. "Get me my cartridges!" he shouted. He went after them and took aim at the ptarmigans several times, killing four.

On his return, Sanaaq and Arnatuinnaq skinned the birds for eating. Sanaaq ripped open the breast of one. She removed the heart and offered it raw to her little boy, who tore into it with his teeth. They then ate the different pieces: the keel of the breast, the back, the drumsticks, the appendix and, finally, the gizzard—after removing its internal membrane...

"Mother!" exclaimed Qumaq. "Give me the head to eat! Give me also the wings with their skin, and I'll eat the marrow. I want to make chewing gum out of the marrow and little feathers."

Qumaq prepared the *qaunnaq*. She plucked little feathers from a ptarmigan skin and began chewing on them. She then added oil residues from the lamp and some boiled blood. She was now chewing her gum.

"Give me some, little sister!" asked her little brother several times.

She gave him some, but he soon swallowed whatever he was chewing.

"Give me more!" he said.

"*Ii!*" said Qumaq. "You've been swallowing so much that almost none is left!" Despite the little one's crying, she refused to waver. "I won't give you any more because it's almost all gone!"

Sanaaq, once again, tried to console him by diverting his attention. "Let's go for a walk *ai!* I'll carry you on my back. We'll go up the hill and from there we'll be able to look at everything around us and we'll make some tea outdoors!"

Qumaq, her mother, and her family went for a walk while Aqiarulaaq prepared boiled meat outside, using driftwood as fuel.

"The pieces I've been boiling have become very tender. I only wanted them half-done... They've been in too long!"

Qalingu and his companions had stayed home. They played cards for a long time and enjoyed themselves considerably. They did not even notice that a fine powdery snow was falling outside, nor that Sanaaq and those with her had failed to come back yet. Suddenly the dogs began to bark loudly... Maatiusi went out to see what was going on and saw the dogs fleeing in all directions. He immediately came back in, saying, "A polar bear has just wandered in here!"

His card partner jumped to his feet...

"Get my rifle!" he said.

"Where's the bear?"

"It's over there!"

They fired several shots, but it got away.

"It's a shame," said Qalingu, "that we let that big male slip away because of our clumsiness! What a shame!"

Akutsiaq was trembling with fear, shivering and crying. Aqiarulaaq ran away from where she had been preparing her boiled meat, and the dogs pounced on the opportunity by wolfing down the pieces of meat... It was unfortunate because she no longer had any fuel left. She went back out to see what was happening. She said, "The pieces I was boiling are gone! They've been devoured by the dogs... We won't be having any boiled meat. Not the tiniest morsel remains! My pot has rolled over down there. The dogs have eaten everything, so I won't be cooking any more. Dirty dogs! They're still all excited!"

31

LEARNING HOW TO SEW AND THE COLLAPSE OF THE IGLOO

It was daytime and Sanaaq was making boots. Qumaq moistened the portion to be sewn by chewing on it. Sanaaq asked, "Isn't it moist enough for me to make a *sulluniq?*"

"No, it's not soggy enough yet. I'm going to moisten it more."

Sanaaq made some sewing thread out of sinew. Her son often grabbed her leftover sinews (the child was a real pest!) and stuffed them into his mouth. Sanaaq sewed the *sulluniq*. After attaching the *qalliniq,* she softened and stretched the *atungaksaq,* which she had moistened. She then cut the piece out, notched it to mark where she would sew, and made some tacking stitches. She was making *qaliruat.* When she was finished, she said, "I've done the *silalliq!*"

To make the *ilulliq,* she now removed the leather's *mami* with the ulu.

"Mother!" exclaimed Qumaq. "I want to eat the *mami!*"

"Here, take some!"

"Yes!"

"Qumaq *ai!* Make a little chain out of the seal's small intestine. We're going to make *nikku*. Remove it from the seal."

Qumaq opened the animal lengthwise with a knife, dirtying her hands as she emptied the contents of the small intestine.

"*Ii!*" she said. "The stuff inside is disgusting! I don't want to continue... Look, it's full of *qumait!*"

"*Ai!* Never mind, leave it! It's a little *siiqrulik!*"

Everyone was now home and Sanaaq went about sewing soles onto the boots she was making. Her son, now awake, was a real nuisance. From a *mangittaq* taken from an old *qajaq* skin, she prepared to cut the soles out. Her pattern was the bottom of a boot. With her ulu, she cut out a piece for the heel and a piece for the soles of the feet. When the cutting was done, she softened the leather with her *kiliutaq* and began sewing, using braided sinews smeared with blubber.

"My son's so tired that he's whimpering all the time," she said. "I'm going to put him to bed right away. And to top it off, our igloo's getting dangerous and threatening to cave in!"

She put her child to bed and stretched out alongside him. Once he had fallen asleep, she hurried to sew the soles onto the boots.

Sanaaq's snow house was really on the verge of collapse. She was worried and woke her son up. "Son! Wake up!"

"*Aa!*" he moaned, for he was still groggy.

Sanaaq spoke to Arnatuinnaq. "Pack our belongings. The dome of the igloo is probably going to fall on our heads!"

"Yes! I'll get packing. *Ii!* It sure is caving in on us... and I haven't finished. Ouch! I've been hurt! I've been hurt in my back! *Aatataa!*"

"I'll give you a rubdown with snow," said Qalingu. "Bare your back!"

"*Iikikii!* Is it ever cold!"

"Arnatuinnaq! Do you have anything broken?" asked Sanaaq.

"No, I don't think so. But I ache all over!"

Qumaq was constantly going in and out. Her mother warned her. "Stop going in and out like that!"

"Yes," she agreed, while continuing her coming and going.

"I told you to stop that! You'll get hurt!"

"But I'm collecting my toys!"

"*Uai!*" said Qalingu. "Those dirty mutts have broken into the entranceway. Hand me a club!" He began clubbing one dog after another.

"We've been robbed! They've taken off with all the meat we had left. We'll pitch our tent *ai!* Over there, where the snow has melted."

They brought some stones to anchor the guy ropes and others to hold down the base of the tent, then raised the tent. Arnatuinnaq and her companions brought stones while Sanaaq arranged the interior.

"Qumaq! Bring me a stone to hammer with. I want to move that big stone that's in the way." Sanaaq hammered away at it. "It won't budge! Let it stay put then."

Qalingu angled the door into place.

"Qumaq!" he said. "Hold the doorframe upright for a moment. I'm going to install the door... Arnatuinnaq! Bring me some nails and a wooden bar."

"Where are they?"

"In the tin can!"

"There aren't any."

"Let me see! I'll look for them."

"Could these be the ones?" asked Sanaaq.

"Yes! Those are the ones!"

That evening, when they had finished, they undressed for bed. Sanaaq undressed her son and said, "*Ii!* His feet are wet because he's been splashing around... He probably won't be able to wear his boots tomorrow if the weather doesn't dry them out... Son, your feet are soaking wet!"

They then went to sleep.

32

FISHING FOR IQALUK

It had rained overnight. Early in the morning, Qalingu awoke and said, "*Autualu!* We're completely flooded! Wake up! The ground's covered with water!"

They all woke up and hurriedly dressed. With his knife, Qalingu hacked out a channel to drain the water away from the tent. As before, his son was already splashing in the water and, as before, was soon soaking wet.

"*Irq! Autualu!* My son fell flat on his stomach in the water. His clothes need to be wrung dry."

"But what will he wear when it stops raining?" asked Sanaaq. "I was wanting to go fishing for *iqaluk*... Arnatuinnaq *ai!* We'll quickly sew him some new clothes. The lake ice should now have lots of holes."

"It does!"

When the rain stopped, Qalingu left to hunt for *uuttuq,* taking along his hunting screen. Pools dotted the sheets of land-fast ice and, further out, meltwater covered the pack ice too. He sighted an *uuttuq*. He crawled to get nearer and killed it. Plugging the wound with a cartridge case, he walked back, dragging his catch behind him. There was a long trail of blood because the seal was bleeding profusely. His family spotted him.

"He's killed a seal!" shouted Arnatuinnaq. "He's dragging it behind him. We'll get some tea ready... Let's make an arrival meal!"

When he arrived, he said, "I've killed a seal *ai!* Its back has lost some of its fur. All that dragging has left a mark because the ice has sharp edges... It's not a good idea to drag seals over the ice."

"Arnatuinnaq!" said Sanaaq. "Remove its small intestine and make some *nikku!*"

"Don't!" said Qalingu, cutting in. "We'll make a meat bag out of its skin. The skin has no market value, Sanaaq."

Sanaaq said, "I feel like going *iqaluk* fishing today. I'll talk to my *qatanngut* about it!"

She went to her cousin's place and entered.

"*Qatannguuk ai!*" said Aqiarulaaq. "Have a seat!"

"No, I've only come to talk to you."

"About what?"

"I want to go fishing for *iqaluk* today!"

"Let's go now *ai!* Will there just be the two of us?"

"No, Arnatuinnaq will come too. We'll walk, but I've got to go and prepare myself *ai!*"

"Sure! I'm coming right away."

Sanaaq prepared a load of everything she would be carrying on her back. Aqiarulaaq prepared her load too. "Since my load is too heavy," she said, "I'll carry my teapot in my hands. Let's go! Let's start walking."

"But I'm not ready yet," said Sanaaq.

"You're really slow getting yourself ready *ai!*" replied her cousin.

They set out on their way and walked for a long while. They then took a rest and cooked outside. Arnatuinnaq, the third one in the group, gathered fuel for a fire. She yanked up heather and small shrubs of black crowberries.

"*Qatannguuk!*" shouted Aqiarulaaq. "Go look for something to put the teapot on. I'm going to build a fireplace!"

They built a support out of stones. Arnatuinnaq went for water, filling the teapot by dunking it. She came back and started cooking. They lit brushwood and stoked the fire continually, in the lee of the wind. The smoke made blowing on the fire bothersome.

"My eyes are all swollen because of the smoke! The cooking's not coming along right. The water's hissing, though."

They had their meal. Sanaaq's son ate eagerly, completely smearing his face.

"*Nuakuluk!*" chided Arnatuinnaq. "Looks like you've bitten somebody to death!"

When she had finished eating and the water was boiling, she added some cold water to the teapot. They then started walking to their fishing ground, which soon came into view. Arnatuinnaq said, "The sole I sewed on has come unstitched and slipped to one side. I'm going to remove it."

Once they had arrived, they went onto the lake with their fishhooks and bait.

"Is the ice breaking up?" asked Sanaaq.

"No!" said Aqiarulaaq.

The lake had many holes. To fish in them, they jerked their lines with their hands. They were now angling for fish at the ice holes, each angler at her own.

"Listen!" said Sanaaq. "Sounds like a trout!"

They could see straight to the bottom. Aqiarulaaq leaned over for a closer look and immediately saw something.

"An *iqaluk!* Look at it! But it doesn't seem to be hungry."

"*Ii!*" said Sanaaq. "I've caught an *iqaluk ai!*"

Arnatuinnaq had not had any bites yet. It was now Aqiarulaaq's turn to catch an *iqaluk*. When she pulled it in, she tried to remove the hook but the *iqaluk* was wriggling vigorously.

Sanaaq pulled in a second one from the same hole and said, "This is really fun! I've caught another one!"

"Mother!" said her son. "I want to eat the eye! Come on, let me eat the eye!"

Sanaaq removed the eyes. "*Ii!* One of them has burst," she said.

Arnatuinnaq had not caught any *iqaluk* yet. She went over to Sanaaq, saying, "I'm so envious of those who catch lots of *iqaluit!* I haven't caught anything yet, but I'm going to fish here. Move back, let me take your place!"

"Go ahead, take it!"

Arnatuinnaq was angling. Still not getting any nibbles, she said again, "I want to go home. I won't catch any *iqaluk!*"

"Wait a little!" said Aqiarulaaq. "Let's go over there and leave the *iqaluit* we've caught here!"

Leaving their catches behind, they walked further out and began fishing again. Right away Arnatuinnaq caught a very big *iqaluk*.

"Look, both of you, at the big *iqaluk* I've caught!"

Her two companions, however, were catching nothing, so they got up to return to their first fishing hole.

"What's that over there?" said Sanaaq.

"Whereabouts?" asked Arnatuinnaq.

"Those things, over there, like spots?"

"*A-ii!*" said Arnatuinnaq. "Something's moving about there... What could it possibly be?"

"What could it be, *qatannguuk?*" echoed Sanaaq. "Looks like where we left our trout... Those wouldn't be dogs, would they? Have the trout we caught been eaten? Arnatuinnaq, hurry up and run! Our trout have probably been eaten!"

As they came close, the things flew off.

"They're gulls!" said Arnatuinnaq. "They're flying off, filthy creatures! Look at that filthy creature still holding a trout in its beak!"

"Did they take everything?"

Once her companions caught up to her, Arnatuinnaq said, "The trout the two of you caught were all devoured by the gulls. Everything is gone!"

"What a shame!" said Aqiarulaaq. "Gang of gluttons! Big throats! Big throats that gulp down a whole trout without even chewing. *Suvakkualuk!*"

"Let's try fishing a little bit longer, *qatannguuk!*" said Sanaaq.

Although they did some more angling, no more fish were caught.

"Let's go home *ai!*" said Sanaaq.

They headed home.

"A pity the trout we caught were all devoured by the gulls," said Aqiarulaaq. "Just because we went out there, to the other place."

"But we were lucky to have gone there," replied Arnatuinnaq. "Had we not I wouldn't have caught any trout!"

Before going home, they again cooked outside.

"Let me have the few tea leaves that are left," said Arnatuinnaq.

"Chew them thoroughly," said Sanaaq. "Otherwise there won't be enough to make the tea as dark as it should be... Our provisions of tea are all used up."

She chewed and put them into the teapot, thus darkening the water a bit. They finished and set out for home. Arnatuinnaq carried on her back the trout she had caught. It felt heavy, being very big.

One of their folks at home, Qalingu, went to take a look from the hill. He came back and said, "The women who went fishing are appearing in the distance! One of them seems to be carrying a heavy load on her back... Looks like big *iqaluit!*"

"*Ai!*" asked Taqriasuk. "Are they coming here?"

"They're coming this way!"

When the fisherwomen were almost there, Qumaq and Akutsiaq rushed to meet them.

"Mother!" said Qumaq. "Did you catch any *iqaluit?*"

"No, mine were devoured by gulls!"

Qalingu cut the *iqaluk* into pieces. "Let's invite the others to come and eat!" he said.

Qumaq went to tell the others about the invitation. "I was asked to tell you to come and eat some *iqaluk!*"

And everyone came together for a community feast.

33

QALINGU MAKES A PUURTAQ AND QUMAQ HER FIRST BOOTS

The next day, Qalingu was sitting on a rock and getting ready to strip the skin off a seal with a knife. He now had ample stores of meat, having killed many seals. When he finished removing the skin, he said, "Arnatuinnaq! Come and pull!"

She began pulling the seal carcass out of its skin. He then inflated the skin, now turned inside out, by blowing into it, in order to scrape the blubber off. When the scraping was done, he took the skin to Sanaaq for her to sew a patch over the anus to cover it.

"I'll need a small piece of sealskin with the fur removed," said Sanaaq.

She sewed a patch over the anus and, when she had finished, Qalingu filled the bag, stuffing it with pieces of meat and blubber. Then he wiped it with vegetation and carried it to a stone cache. With a leather strap, he tied slipknots around the rear flippers, that is, around its knees, and also around a front flipper. It would be carried on each side by Arnatuinnaq, the young Maatiusi, and Sanaaq. Maatiusi cried out, "Wait a bit! You've got to stop a moment because my hand is being squeezed by the leather strap!"

They halted and advanced a little further, but, just as they had almost put the meat bag into place, it began to rip...

"It's been torn by a sharp stone," explained Qalingu. "But it's only a little tear."

He closed up the stone cache and erected an inuksuk over it. Once he had finished, he went home.

Night was now falling. Arnatuinnaq called out, "An *uuttuq* down there!"

"I'll go *ai!*" said Maatiusi. "I'll use the seal-hunting screen... I've got to hurry!"

"Are you really up to it?" asked Sanaaq.

* * *

Sanaaq was scraping the inside of a sealskin. It had fur and was that of an adult seal, not a young one. As she started to remove the flesh, she said, "The skin has become really thin. It's a seal that's been moulting... Look, Arnatuinnaq! Its *mami* is all black. The fur is falling off all by itself!"

"Let me eat some of its *mami!*" said Arnatuinnaq. "It's really good *mami!*"

When Sanaaq had finished, she washed the skin because it was shedding. It could not be scraped with a *kiliutaq.* She laid it out to dry on a rock, with the furry side on top. She then went inside, saying, "Someone should go outside and keep an eye on the skin I laid out to dry. It could lose its fur because of the heat. It's really sunny!"

"The dogs ate a piece of our skin!" exclaimed Arnatuinnaq.

"A big piece?" asked Sanaaq.

"No, one of its rear flippers."

"Never mind! I'll mend it and hang it on a drying rack."

She went about her mending. Once the operation was done, she asked, "But where are the leather straps to hang it with?"

"On the edge of the *kilu,*" answered Arnatuinnaq.

After making eyelets all along the edge of the skin, she hung it on the drying rack.

Qumaq had grown up a little and was now trying for the first time to make boots by herself. She cut out what was needed to make the *qalliniq* and also to make the *atungaq*. She then began to sew. She stitched very badly, making holes in the skin and sewing asymmetrically, without really noticing how poor her work was. When she was done, her mother, Sanaaq, took a look and said, "Qumaq *ai!* It's the first time you've made boots. We'll offer them to your *sanaji!*"

Ningiukuluk, her maternal grandmother, had also delivered her. As a *qillaqut,* they would offer a plate, some tobacco, a sealskin, and the boots that the little girl had just sewn.

"Your *arnaliaq* has made her first boots!" said Sanaaq as she brought the gifts.

"What? These things are for me?" said Ningiukuluk. "That girl, my *arnaliaq,* I made her skilful! And now I'm being given boots... They are truly beautiful boots!"

Ningiukuluk found the boots to be very beautiful because they were the work of her *arnaliaq,* even though they were not at all well made... She even tried them on as a way of honouring her *arnaliaq,* and because she had received them as a *qillaqut* gift.

34

GATHERING EGGS

Qalingu and Irsutuq were leaving in their two *qajaak*. They were going to gather eggs. As part of their preparations, they took a box to put the eggs in and a bag. Qalingu lashed his *qajaq* to his sled for the trip across the *qainnguq* to open water. Because he and his companion would be travelling by *qajaq*, they took something to sit on while paddling.

"We'll be back tomorrow," said Qalingu.

They set off in their two *qajaak* and headed to Pikiuliq Island. Because they landed while the tide was still coming in, each had to carry his *qajaq* to dry land. Qalingu began walking about on dry land and, as he made his way, eider ducks and gulls took off from the ground. A bird that had been laying flew from its nest as he passed by. Qalingu saw the eggs in the nest and called out, "I've found some eggs!"

He put the eggs he had gathered in the box he had brought and the down from the nest in his bag. He decided to leave one, out of compassion for the eider duck, which was continually flying about in close proximity, full of anxiety for its eggs. Some of the eggs contained a chick embryo, others a germ, and still others no visible germ. Irsutuq too found some eggs, but only a few. He went to his companion and said, "I really don't have a knack for this. I've only gathered a few eggs!"

"It's because you see poorly, on account of your advanced age."

"No, I don't see poorly!"

Some gulls swooped down from above. They feared for their eggs and their chicks. The two men stopped and began checking over the eggs they had gathered by dunking them in the water of a small lake.

"We'll check the eggs we've gathered," said Qalingu, "to see whether they've got any embryos... The ones with embryos float. The other twenty don't have embryos. I'll use them for bartering!"

After checking the eggs, they made their daily meal by boiling eider meat and eggs... They had also collected down. After loading their *qajaak,* they paddled off.

"There are some places, over there towards land, where the water is darkened by the wind," said Qalingu. "You can hear it howling... We'll soon be caught in the wind!"

"Just our luck! That's not reassuring. Is it getting closer?"

"Yes!" answered Qalingu.

Despite their efforts to hurry by paddling as fast as possible, the wind began to blow in strong gusts. They barely avoided capsizing several times because of the dark waves it threw up.

"I'm losing hope!" said Irsutuq. "We don't seem to be making headway into this wind... It will probably blow us out to sea... I'd like to take shelter from the wind behind the island!"

"Let's go then, *ai!*"

Their kinfolk—Sanaaq, Arnatuinnaq, Qumaq, Akutsiak, Taqriasuk, and Aqiarulaaq—were watching from a hilltop.

"I'm very worried about them," said Aqiarulaaq, "because we can't see them... They said yesterday they'd come back today."

Taqriasuk looked through the telescope and said, "I still can't see them and yet there's no one left on Pikiuliq Island!"

"*Ai!*" exclaimed Sanaaq. "I wonder where they could possibly be... Perhaps in the areas where the wind's blowing very hard?"

Arnatuinnaq saw something.

"That's probably them! The two of them appear at times in the storm, but they often vanish from sight because of the breaking waves offshore. Try looking at them through your telescope!"

"Yes, I can see them! They're caught in the storm... They'll probably seek shelter from the wind behind the ice floes."

"I'm scared!" said Qumaq.

The wind was subsiding now and the women walked down to the shore while their husbands continued to watch on the hill. On their way, they picked up some brush for fuel.

"We could gather some fuel for making boiled meat," suggested Aqiarulaaq.

Arnatuinnaq and Sanaaq pulled up large quantities of heather and black crowberry bushes.

"There's enough to cook with *ai!*" said Aqiarulaaq. "Each of us will take an armload."

Once they had arrived home, Arnatuinnaq went for water in which to boil Aqiarulaaq's meat. After filling the outside cooking pot, she said, "I'm done! It's ready!"

Aqiarulaaq had just come in when she cried out suddenly, "Listen! Dogs growling at each other. Sounds like they're eating the meat I put in to boil... Arnatuinnaq! Go quickly and see!"

"They sure are eating it! All the meat is gone!"

"What a shame!" said Aqiarulaaq. "Those were my only pieces of meat... I won't be able to cook now... The worst thief among the dogs is going to have a paw tied to its neck!"

Arnatuinnaq tied one of the dog's paws to its neck... It began to whimper, "*Maa maa...*"

"Serves you right!" said Arnatuinnaq.

Their lookout arrived at that very moment, saying, "The weather is clearing up. They're both coming!"

"All the meat I cut has been eaten by the dogs! What a crying shame!" said Aqiarulaaq.

"Which one did it?" asked Taqriasuk.

"Once again it was that miserable Taqulik!"

"Too bad, but this time it's going to die, that dyed-in-the wool thief!"

"I could try and look for something to make boiled meat with at Ningiukuluk's place, because we've got nothing left…"

Taqriasuk agreed. So Aqiarulaaq went looking for a gift. She entered the tent and said, "Ningiukuluk! I've come begging for meat. All the pieces I'd been boiling have been eaten!"

Ningiukuluk, who disliked giving, replied, "I won't give you any because you're a fool and because you're often robbed of your food. I don't want to be short of food through the fault of others. You're really stupid! Just go away!"

Yet she had plenty of meat. Aqiarulaaq went to Sanaaq's place and told her, "*Qatannguuk!* I've just been rudely sent away by Ningiukuluk after trying to get some meat... I didn't get any, not even a little morsel. I was given a flat no!"

"*Ai!*" said Sanaaq.

The two *qajaak* were about to arrive.

"The *qajaak* are arriving, out front!" announced Arnatuinnaq. "They're heavily loaded. Let's go to where they'll be landing!"

They all went. Ningiukuluk also wanted to go, despite feeling very embarrassed. She went anyway and when she arrived, she looked about furtively, saying, "Look at all the eggs they've got! How nice it would be to eat eggs! Aqiarulaaq *ai!* You'll come and get some meat at our place!"

"I won't go again. I already asked for some today!" answered Aqiarulaaq.

They went back and forth on the shore carrying the many things that the travellers had brought back. They got ready to boil the eggs and eider ducks. They skinned the ducks, removing the skin with the feathers.

Ningiukuluk was no longer the centre of attention. With no more gifts being brought to her, she felt envious and dearly wished to receive more... Her daughter Akutsiaq, feeling the same way, visited her neighbours for something to eat. She expected those who prepared the boiled meat to offer her some. She waited a long time in the expectation of being offered food. When her hosts began to eat boiled meat, she joined them and, finding it very good, ate eagerly, soon finishing off the eggs and the pieces of duck she was given. She even scraped the fat off the duck skins with her teeth.

"Pass me the soup pot!" she said after eating.

It was passed to her. Although its contents were very hot, it did not give off any steam. She gulped down a mouthful, unaware that it was boiling hot, and scalded herself badly. "*Aatataa!* My throat has been scalded!"

"But why are you eating so greedily?" asked Aqiarulaaq.

"I'm not! I don't eat greedily!" shot back Akutsiaq.

35

SPRING HUNT ON THE EDGE OF THE ICE

It was spring. Qalingu and Taqriasuk were travelling by sled to the *sinaa.* Qalingu saw something right away and yelled, "Belugas!"

"Whereabouts?"

"Over there out to sea! They are coming this way and will probably swim under the ice of the cove."

The belugas did come and they all surfaced together. When the firing started, however, they immediately dove under and remained there for a long while. Not being wounded, they never reappeared.

"All the same, I got a shot at them," said Qalingu. "*Ai!* What a pity! I scared your game animals away. I was afraid I wouldn't get another chance to shoot."

"Couldn't be helped. But there's no need to let me shoot first. I'm getting old and my vision is failing... I can't even make out the front sight on my gun anymore..."

"*Ai!* How many winters have you been through?"

"*Ai!* I've been through eighty-nine winters!"

"*Suvakkualuk!* You really are very old, yet you're not at all frail!"

"Sometimes, though, I wish I had a walking stick..."

"If you want, I'll buy a piece of wood and make you one."

"It would really please me if you did!"

The two of them were now hunting on the *sinaa*. They saw some *puiji* and Taqriasuk fired on them. No sooner had he fired than he hit one, and Qalingu set out to recover the body and tow it back with his *qajaq*. On the way back, while landing, he saw another *puiji*. He fired and missed. Taqriasuk in turn fired at the animal that his companion had missed, hitting it with his first shot.

Qalingu set off in his *qajaq* for another tow. Again and again he went back and forth, towing seals killed by his hunting partner. Back on the ice once more, he said, "I was thinking... You said you couldn't even make out the front sight on your gun anymore, yet you're still a very good marksman!"

"Sometimes my vision gets better!"

"Are you telling the truth?"

"Do you think I'm not telling the truth?"

The two of them headed to dry land. Their kinfolk were watching from a hilltop. As she climbed the hill with Aqiarulaaq, Sanaaq suddenly shouted, "Look at them! They've come quite close... They're heavily loaded... What could they have possibly killed?"

"I'd say that Qalingu has killed an *ujjuk*. I'm sure it's not my old man who killed it!"

With the hunters arriving, the women walked down to the campsite. The hunters had to climb up the shore, having arrived at low tide, and they halted several times because of their heavy load. During these stops the panting dogs pulled on their tuglines.

"*Uit!*" said Qalingu. "The runners on our sled are no longer upright... It'll really be something if we manage to climb all the way!"

"That's true!" said Taqriasuk. "Let's get at it, let's try to get all the way up!"

By the time their sled finally reached dry land, its runners had become completely skewed and were no longer upright.

"Leave it here *ai!*" suggested Qalingu. "I'll go get my little sled!"

He went to fetch it and arrived at his tent, saying, "I've come for a sled. The runners on ours have gone askew!"

"Drink some tea first *ai!*" said Sanaaq. "The bannock has just been baked."

"I'll just have a drink. My hunting companion must be tired of waiting."

He then returned to his companion, pulling his little sled behind him.

"I took a while," he said on arriving. "I was thirsty and wanted to have some tea."

"I was starting to get really cold after you left!"

They transferred their load to the new sled, which proved to be more suitable. When they arrived at the tents, Aqiarulaaq said to her old man, "I really didn't think you'd catch so many seals. I thought only Qalingu would get any. But now I've completely changed my mind about you!"

"My vision got better," said Taqriasuk, "so today I hit bang on while Qalingu shot very poorly!"

36

A CHILD'S CARELESSNESS

Qumaq was growing up and for the first time went for a walk alone. She wandered back and forth, walking very fast and gathering *uqaujait, sursat, killapat, kakagutit,* and all kinds of other plants. Unaccustomed to being alone, she was afraid and easily startled. She soon headed home, collecting willow leaves on the way. She mused, "I feel like gathering plants, but there are many *igutsait.* So I'll go home... And so what if my cup isn't full... That'll be enough, for I'm very scared of big bumblebees." She saw another bumblebee and began to run away. "It's tiny and it still scares me," she thought. "Yet it's just a little insect..."

She pretended to be unafraid and tried to feel confident, while heading straight home and giving up on any further gathering. Her brother saw her and came to meet her.

"My little sister's coming! I must go and meet her. Little sister, let me see the plants you've gathered," he said, approaching Qumaq.

"But there are very few!" said Qumaq.

"I don't think there are too few! I'll spit oil on them, to moisten them... Those ones look like bumblebee food or willow catkins."

"No, there are none of those here. I didn't gather any bumblebee food, because I was afraid."

When her brother got home, he went inside and said, "Look, Mother! Arctic willow leaves collected by my sister. Look at all of that! Mother!"

To Sanaaq it did not look like much. "Is that all you gathered? Did you have trouble finding them?"

"No!" said Qumaq. "On the contrary, there were a lot!"

Sanaaq's son cut off a piece of blubber from an *ujjuk* in the *aki* and tried to spit oil from it onto the little willow leaves...

"Son! Your *manu* is getting stained," said Sanaaq. "Don't spit any more oil! There's enough already. They're well oiled."

Oil trickled down his forearm as he ate the leaves. "Take some *ai!*" he said when he was done and getting ready to leave again. "Father, make me a little boat!"

"Out of what?" asked Qalingu.

"Out of this piece of wood."

"Let's go to it!" said his father, and he set to work making a little boat.

"Use that for the mast. Father! Hurry! I want to go and play with the little boat!"

Qalingu began to hurry.

"Is it done, Father? Give it to me quick!" insisted the child.

As he was about to leave, his father said, "Take care not to fall into the water!"

He played with the little boat, chattering non-stop. "There it goes... It's going over there... Wait a moment, we'll first go a bit out to sea... It's got a heavy load!"

He repeatedly waded into the water, and several times the water came up over the top of his boots. He had been told many times to be careful, yet he went ahead and climbed onto a rock with a very slippery surface. The soles of his soaked boots had meanwhile shifted to one side. Suddenly he slipped and fell into the water... He stayed there a long time, for he was all alone. He wailed and whimpered but could not shout that he had fallen into the water… His parents had no idea what was happening.

"Listen! Does that sound like someone crying?" said Sanaaq, suddenly worried.

Qumaq went out to see.

"It's crying alright... He's probably fallen into the water!"

"Out of my way! I'm coming!" shouted Sanaaq as she rushed outside. "*Autualuk!* My son has fallen in!" She hurried over and rushed to pull him out. "*Aalummi!* Did you slip, little one? Come! From now on, you'll no longer play all by yourself with the little boat! My son fell into the water! He got out just in the nick of time... We didn't know what was happening for quite a while!"

She carried the boy, who was weeping and dripping with water, so much so that she got all wet too. She took him home, pulled his boots off, removed his clothes, and put other ones on.

"Keep your boots off for a while. Your boots are soaking wet and need to be dried."

She left him bootless on purpose, for fear he would fall again into the water. He said, "Mother! I want to put my boots on."

"Later! Wait for them to dry. You're being really unreasonable! Remember, you just fell into the water!"

He would not let up, so his mother lay down beside him on the sleeping platform until he fell asleep.

Qumaq went to wash the clothes that her little brother was wearing when he fell into the water. Akutsiak came with her.

"Let's wash here," suggested Qumaq.

"Yes, let's! But I'll be clumsy like before... I'll never manage to get the dirt out and I'll be slow."

"No wonder. You're always taking a break from your work!" said Qumaq.

On hearing this, Akutsiaq went home to tell her mother how she had been offended. She simply left her wash behind, because she felt so humiliated.

"Mother! I'm home because Qumaq has been very mean to me!"

She voiced her discontent by telling lies. She felt badly treated although what she had been told was merely the truth.

"*Suvakkualuk!*" exclaimed Ningiukuluk. "Let me handle this. I'll find her... Qumaq! Why did you tell my daughter off again?"

"She's not telling the truth! I simply said she was always taking a break from her work. I only said that!"

"*Ai!*" said Ningiukuluk.

Qumaq no longer liked Akutsiaq. Hardly surprising. Akutsiaq tattled on others, complained all the time, and would not tell the truth. Qumaq too went home. And there she said, "Akutsiaq left behind the things she was washing. They'll probably be torn to bits by a dog because she left them in the pool!"

"But why did she leave them behind?" asked Sanaaq.

"Because she went home!"

"Did you make her angry?"

Qumaq made no reply. She did not wish to repeat what the other girl had said. It was not worth it. So she changed the subject.

"Let me eat too! I want some meat from the *kujapigaq* and also some dried small intestine that's been pounded!"

37

A HOUSEHOLD QUARREL

Qumaq's little brother woke up and began walking about barefoot. He asked again and again for someone to put his boots on, but everyone turned a deaf ear. Qumaq said, "*Irq!* He's going to hurt his feet, the little one! I'll put his boots on."

"Go ahead," said Sanaaq, "but take good care of him! Don't let him wander off anywhere. He could fall into the water again!"

"I'll take good care! I feel bad about not looking after him properly... If he had drowned, I would've deserved being scolded by you."

"His breathing is still not back to normal. It's probably because of the water he swallowed... I dread the moment when his father comes back... I feel like running far away, for fear of having to face his anger."

"Why?"

"Out of fear... It's true! I'll run away because I'm terrified of facing him!"

Her son began to vomit water continually… as Qalingu walked into the tent. Seized by fright, Sanaaq told him, "My son fell into the water today… I'm frightened because he's still not fully recovered… He slipped while playing with the little boat and was in the water for a long time… Qumaq and I realized too late…"

"Why are you so scared?" said Qalingu. "Is it because you let him fall into the water or is it because you're afraid of my anger? The *umiarjuaq* is about to arrive. His only chance of pulling through will probably be for him to leave… I'll go and see the *Qallunaat* at the trading post *ai!* I'll go and talk to them, for his condition will probably get worse!"

"But couldn't he get better without having to leave?" protested Sanaaq timidly.

Qalingu got ready to visit the *Qallunaat* at the trading post.

"Let me soften your boots quickly!" offered Sanaaq, starting in earnest.

She did not dare oppose Qalingu. He went straight to the employees at the trading post and to the *iksigarjuaq*. Sanaaq was unhappy. She feared seeing her child leave. She thought over and over, "If he goes, he may end up crying a lot, especially if he's among people he's never seen… If it takes time for him to recover, he'll be gone for long… I can't accept his having to leave… He'll probably get better if he just stays here… I don't want to be separated from my son because I love him very much!"

Qalingu spoke to the trading post staff. "My young boy fell into the water while playing with a little boat. I've come for his sake because his condition is getting worse. He's throwing up water all the time!"

"If he fell into the water," answered the chief factor, "he should leave on the big boat. He'll have a chance of recovering!"

"He will go!" concluded Qalingu. And he immediately went back to his family.

"The chief thinks he should go," he said as he arrived. "Here are some *niaquujait* for him, for the trip!"

He gave them to Sanaaq, who responded heatedly. "He won't leave! I'll run away and take him with me. He can get better quite well just by staying here! If he goes, he will suffer all kinds of troubles... No way is he going. He isn't even old enough to think for himself! I don't want to be separated from him!"

Sanaaq tried to have the last word. She fought to make her view prevail. Qalingu, for his part, refused to waver, concerned as he was to see his son get better.

"Accept it," he said, "or else his condition will get worse!"

"He certainly won't leave! I absolutely cannot accept it! I insist! I'm going to run away with him... I'll get up very early and, while you're all asleep, I'll leave and take him with me!"

"He's going to go! Accept it!"

"He won't go. He's my son and I love him! If anything, you're the one who'll leave... He will not go!"

Both of them stuck to their guns, so much so that Sanaaq had used up almost all of her strength and resistance... Everyone now went to bed... and to sleep.

38

SANAAQ'S FLIGHT

Sanaaq woke up very early the next morning. She rubbed her eyes and began to prepare to escape with her son. She dressed carefully in order not to wake the others. She did everything very slowly, so as not to interrupt their slumber. She dressed without making a noise, and they all remained sound asleep... She took hold of her sleeping son and placed him in the back pouch of her coat. He certainly was able to walk, but, out of affection for him, she was unwilling to make him walk so soon after awaking.

No sooner had Sanaaq placed the child in her back pouch than he began to cry. Qalingu stirred. But he was too sleepy and dozed off again right away. Sanaaq rushed out to keep her child from crying. Once outside, he stopped crying and she was on her way. Some dogs started following her, but she threw stones at them, thus deterring them from coming any further. But they continued to watch the direction she was going in, for they were accustomed to following their mistress. A little later her son awoke and began to cry once more, for he was hungry and not feeling well. She explained to him her intention not to take him far.

Back in the tent, meanwhile, Qalingu and Arnatuinnaq had woken up. Qalingu said to his sister-in-law, "Your older sister has run away. She's gone!"

"*Ii autualuk!*" said Arnatuinnaq. "I wonder where she could have gone! Let's both go looking for her, Qalingu! *Aikuluk!*"

"I have trouble believing she did that just to keep her son from leaving... It's as if she didn't want him to get better... Let's go, Arnatuinnaq! Let's look for her with Maatiusi's help!"

Qalingu went to his camp mates and said, "My wife took our son and ran away without my knowing... Maatiusi! Join Arnatuinnaq and me in searching for them. Qumaq will be minded by my sister Aqiarulaaq."

"I will!" said Maatiusi.

All three went looking for the runaway. The dogs sensed they were looking for someone and bounded ahead, in the direction taken by Sanaaq.

"The dogs seem to be on Sanaaq's trail!" remarked Qalingu. "All we need do is to follow them and start searching!"

They searched all day without spotting Sanaaq.

Meanwhile, Sanaaq was beginning to think of going home, for her son was crying from hunger.

"I love my dear son so much," she thought, "and I'm making him suffer... At home, there's lots to eat while here there's nothing... If I love my son, how can I make him suffer from hunger and prevent him from going away and getting proper care? I must go home. I've acted with no regard for common sense. If they want to take him away, I should accept it, even though it makes me unhappy... I know it's for his own good... I must accept it, if I truly love him!"

And Sanaaq headed home. Her folks were still looking for her.

"I really feel like going home. I'm very tired!" said Arnatuinnaq.

"No!" replied Qalingu. "I won't go home until I've found them! My wife and my son must be weak and hungry... I'm afraid they'll be attacked by a polar bear... I'll continue to look for them until I find them... The two of you can go home if you so wish!"

"I will," said Arnatuinnaq. "I'll go home because I'm tired and hungry. Let's both go home."

"I agree," answered Maatiusi.

They both went home while Qalingu kept searching.

Sanaaq, however, was already back home with her child and both were eating to their hearts' content. Aqiarulaaq came and, on seeing her, said, "*Qatannguuk!* What's been going on with you? We thought you were lost!"

"Where are my kinfolk?" said Sanaaq.

"Qalingu and his young sister-in-law have gone searching for you, with Maatiusi, while I minded Qumaq!"

"He's searching for us? But he's the one who was responsible for my running away by wanting to send my son to a far-off place! If my son leaves, so will I!"

Now Arnatuinnaq and Maatiusi arrived on the scene.

"*Angajuk!*" exclaimed Arnatuinnaq. "I was looking for you! Have you been back for a while? I wanted to go home because I was tired and hungry... Qalingu decided to keep searching until he found you, even though he has no food... He had no idea you might have gone home... He's worried sick about the two of you!"

"I was weak," answered Sanaaq, "and very hungry. So was my son. I had to go home. I felt sorry for my child... Now, his condition's improving. Arnatuinnaq! Take care of him while I go looking for Qalingu!"

39

CONJUGAL VIOLENCE

Sanaaq left to go looking for Qalingu. Both were now in search of each other. As he looked, Qalingu began to think, "My wife may be dead… Maybe a wild animal has killed her... Anyway, she must be dying of hunger..."

Meanwhile Sanaaq was telling herself, "My husband must be tired... Had I not run away, he wouldn't be in such a condition... I'll go home only when I've found him!"

Qalingu was accompanied by his dogs, whereas Sanaaq was alone. Qalingu's dogs had smelled something and had located Sanaaq, but without her son. Qalingu too spotted her and was now thinking, "My son is surely dead! I'll make Sanaaq pay for causing my son's death!"

When he caught up to Sanaaq, he questioned her. "Where's my son? Is he dead?"

Sanaaq kept silent. Because she said nothing, he asked again, "Where is he? Is he dead?"

He began to hit Sanaaq. He beat her with his fists while heaping insults on her. "*Ivvilualuk!* You're completely out of your mind! You've been furious ever since you found out that my son had to go away!"

"My son's at home!" shot back Sanaaq. "I left to go looking for you because I love you, and now that you've found me you accuse me of all kinds of evil things! My son is fine. Arnatuinnaq is taking care of him. If I wasn't fit for you, why did you marry me? I love you and that's why I went looking for you, and here you are beating and hurting me!"

The two of them headed home. Qalingu felt very bad about beating his wife. Sanaaq had to stop and rest several times because of her severe pain. Although Qalingu regretted what had happened, he was still angry and simply continued on his way. He left his wife behind so that he could go home and see his son again. When he arrived, Aqiarulaaq came to visit and asked him, "Did you see my *qatanngut* who went looking for you?"

"I saw her in a totally mindless state. She could no longer walk because I had hurt her by hitting her!"

"You're the one who's mindless! She went looking for you, out of love for you!"

Qalingu stood silently before his sister. Aqiarulaaq added, "I'm going to tell everyone how my cousin got beaten up, when it was out of affection for her husband that she'd gone looking for you!"

Sanaaq arrived just then. Qalingu felt bad and angry and his folks were very unhappy.

Sanaaq continued to suffer and was unable to work. When the *Qallunaat* were informed of her condition, they told her she would have to go away with her son by plane. She prepared to leave. At the time of departure, she was asked about the cause of her pains. She answered, "Qalingu beat me when I went to meet him. I had abducted my son because he was going to be taken away, but because we were starving we returned home. Meanwhile Qalingu had gone looking for us with others. I left my son at home and went looking for Qalingu because I love him. When we caught up to each other, he accused me of causing his son's death and he beat me and swore at me... I have no desire for vengeance against him and if I must leave, I will, for it's no fun at all to suffer as I am now..."

"It will be necessary for you to go away," she was told. "Your son seems alright now and no longer needs to leave, but you must go!"

The plane had arrived. Sanaaq prepared to leave and made arrangements for her children, who were heartbroken to see her go. They were left in the care of Arnatuinnaq, who would look after them like a second mother, with Aqiarulaaq's assistance if need be. Thinking about his wife, Qalingu felt unhappy. He suffered from having behaved badly. He felt very uneasy towards his kinfolk, the *Qallunaat,* and his son. When he saw just how sad his folks were, he felt responsible.

40

A SORROWFUL QALINGU

When the police officers learned that Sanaaq had to leave because of injuries due to spousal abuse, they came to give Qalingu a warning. He greeted them, red in the face and speechless.

"We'll let it go this time, but if it happens again, you'll go to jail for five years!"

Qalingu fell into a worsening state and became increasingly ill tempered, although he tried to lift his spirits. After the warning from the police, his sister Aqiarulaaq felt no sympathy for him anymore.

Sanaaq was gone for a long time. An operation was needed to mend her bones. When Qalingu learned she had to be operated on, he became even unhappier. His folks resented him for causing Sanaaq to leave. Aqiarulaaq, feeling very depressed, wrote her cousin a letter and sent it by the next plane.

As Sanaaq's convalescence drew to an end, preparations were made to send her home. The news delighted Qumaq and her little brother when they were told, but Qalingu was shaken. He feared a confrontation with his wife.

When Sanaaq arrived, her kinfolk, accompanied by the whole community, came out to welcome her and shake her hand. Aqiarulaaq broke into tears and said, "*Qatannguuk!* I missed you so much! I've been unhappy since you left and I haven't stopped hating my brother."

Qalingu too spoke to Sanaaq. "After what I did to you, I'm now afraid to be your husband. I no longer feel worthy of having you as my wife and I'll make myself your servant because I fear you!"

"But you're a true Inuk," answered Sanaaq. "You're able to do anything and you're in the prime of life! I'm the one who's been weakened and who's no longer able to do much. Now, if you want me to remain single, if you no longer want me as your wife, it's up to you."

"I don't want you to be single. I want to help you and listen to you always, for I'm ashamed of what I did to you!"

Although he had tried to improve since the incident, Qalingu felt very unhappy and was still haunted by what he had done. For this reason, he wished all the more to listen to his wife's advice.

Sanaaq, now disabled, was again in pain. She had trouble with anything that required effort. So she let Arnatuinnaq take her place in doing the chores.

Qalingu no longer hunted because his wife was very weak and because he tended to tire quickly, having long been inactive. His son was now in good health. The child was glad not to have gone away and to have his mother back.

Qumaq too was glad, even though her mother was still so weak. She made a top out of an old sewing spool. With an ulu, she cut out a piece of wood to make a peg for the top and a piece of cardboard to make it spin. She handed it to her brother, saying, "Here's a toy for you!"

41

SANAAQ'S RETURN TO HOSPITAL

Sanaaq's condition was deteriorating, so her camp mates came to pay a visit.

"*Qatannguuk!*" said Aqiarulaaq. "You'll have to go away again. It's important for you to recover completely."

"It sure is. I can't sleep at night. I can't eat and I'm again having pains, more acute than before."

Qalingu went to tell the *Qallunaat*.

"My wife is ill again. Maybe she didn't get enough treatment... If she has to be taken away again, I'll be unhappy, but she's suffering a lot and I don't want her to die!"

"If she's very ill," he was told, "we won't be able to treat her here. She'll have to be taken away again, perhaps as soon as tomorrow."

Qalingu, saddened that nothing could be done locally, added, "I really am the one to blame. A while ago, I hit her when she was behaving badly. I hit her without meaning to hurt her and it's my fault if she's not doing well now. If she must leave, I'd like to go with her!"

"You can't go with her. You're not ill. Only Sanaaq has to go. She should get better this time, and you'll not be held accountable as long as you don't repeat the same offence."

Qalingu went home and said, "*Aippaa!* You'll have to be taken away again, but this time you're going to be cured completely!"

"Alright, if that's what has to happen, even though it doesn't please me at all!"

When a plane arrived, she was taken away to the hospital where she would be treated.

"As soon as you're cured," she was told, "you'll go home. Don't bother yourself about having to be taken away!"

She nonetheless longed for her family. Whenever Inuit, either men or women, are sent to hospital for treatment, they are always very anxious to return home. They fervently wish to return to their loved ones. They miss the country food and suffer from staying in an overheated place. Sanaaq, after being in pain for a long time, now noticed a daily improvement in her health. She and the other Inuit were happy, for they were being well taken care of. Yet they dearly wanted to go home. They preferred their country, where there was no overheating. Sanaaq was thankful to the nurses and the hospital, her pains having gone. But she could not forget her son. She thought continually about him, from the moment she got up to the moment she went to bed.

After a long while, Sanaaq regained much of her strength, so much so that she often went for walks outside. She was back in shape and would soon be going home. Out of affection for her, the other Inuit at the hospital came to see her off on the day of her departure.

Her folks were likewise very happy to have her back. Everyone was on hand to greet her when the plane arrived. She herself was happy to be finally back with her family, but she was also tired from the trip and, since it was late, her whole family decided to go to bed. Sanaaq tried to sleep but could not. All kinds of thoughts came to mind.

"If my son had died, how would I have reacted? Maybe that would've broken me... Had he been the one to go away, I would've been shattered..."

She eventually fell asleep, late at night. She had an *uqumangirniq*. Her body became paralyzed and she dreamed that someone very bad was trying to enter her home. Still asleep and dreaming, she heard footsteps in the entranceway. She opened her eyes in her sleep and then tried to shut them, but could not. She feared seeing a big *tuurngaq*, but her body was frozen. Unable to close her eyes, she thought, "I'll shut my eyes as soon as I see something!"

Another thought crossed her mind, with her eyes now closed: "Maybe if I tried to move during the *uqumangirniq*, I'd actually move and I'd break free of it..."

She made an abrupt movement in her sleep, while dreaming that the big *tuurngaq* who had been trying to enter had succeeded and was now grabbing hold of her. Increasingly afraid, she tried to kick her feet and move her body. And so, bit by bit, she managed to move and come out of her deep sleep.

"I really had an *uqumangirniq*," she told herself, "and if I just roll over onto my other side I won't have another one!"

But before she could roll over, she fell asleep again and had a new nightmare. Fear took hold of her and she let out a scream. She tried to talk but could made no sound... Qalingu, who was sleeping beside her, finally awoke and saw her trying to talk while the rest of her body remained still. He grabbed her by the hand and tried to wake her.

"What's wrong with you, Sanaaq?"

"Oh, thank you! I've been having nightmares all night long... I wanted to roll over onto my other side but was just too drowsy... I dreamed that a *tuurngaq* was trying to grab me... I had the impression he was really there... If I had managed to roll over, I think I would've snapped out of it!"

The next morning, everyone woke up, but Sanaaq was still groggy from lack of sleep. She spent the whole day not wanting to do anything.

42

RITUAL FEAST FOR THE FIRST KILL

Qumaq was growing up. She was now a young woman. Her brother too had grown up and was almost old enough to think for himself. His father had bought him a *qukiutiaruk,* and he was going to fire it for the first time. He took aim at a stone and completely missed it five times... His mother watched closely, fearing the recoil might throw him back. Sanaaq told Qalingu, "My son shouldn't fire too many times. He might hit someone by accident!"

"It's better if he's trained to shoot now," answered Qalingu. "Otherwise, when he reaches adulthood he might be thrown off-balance even more and lack judgment. By then, it'll be harder for him to learn."

"*Ai!*" said Sanaaq.

Her son took his new rifle and went hunting for *aqiggit* with his sister Qumaq. When they reached a small plain, Qumaq was the first to see a ptarmigan.

"Look, little brother. An *aqiggiq*. Are you going to shoot? Look over there!"

He fired.

"Yes, I got it, little sister! I broke its wing!"

Both brother and sister ran after the injured bird. With its broken wing, the ptarmigan could no longer fly... They ran for a long time, holding back their shouts of glee, so as not to lose sight of it... The little brother finally caught hold of the bird.

"I caught an *aqiggiq!* I got my first *aqiggiq!* Come, let's go home, little sister!"

"Yes! Let me carry your rifle. It must be very heavy!"

"Go ahead!"

They came home and walked in. Their mother was inside. When her son opened the door, she said, "This *aqiggiq,* are you the one who killed it?"

"Yes!" answered her son.

"He killed the *aqiggiq* after hurting it in the wing," recounted Arnatuinnaq.

"*Suvakkualuk!*" said Sanaaq. "We'll quarter it, all of us together. First take it to his *arnaquti!*"

Sanaaq went to Ningiukuluk's place. She entered and said, "Your *angusiaq* has just killed his first *aqiggiq!*"

"I'm so delighted to hear that! We'll all quarter it together... I'll hold the head of the first *aqiggiq* of my *angusiaq!*"

Ningiukuluk left with Sanaaq. She took hold of the *aqiggiq* and began calling. "*Ilakka!* come right now for an *aliktuuti!*"

"Listen! We're going to have a quartering!" said her camp mates as they went outside.

Irsutualuk, Arnatuinnaq, and Qalingu all came. Ningiukuluk took hold of the head, Sanaaq a foot, Qalingu a wing, Irsutualuk the other wing, and Arnatuinnaq the other foot.

"What fun this is!" said Ningiukuluk.

"Let's go! Pull! This is so much fun," said Irsutualuk.

"I hope nobody will snatch the part I'm holding onto!" joked Ningiukuluk.

The boy who had killed his first *aqiggiq* began laughing heartily. The two playmates, Qumaq and Akutsiaq, both watching closely, also burst into laughter.

"Look, Qumaq, someone's snatched what my mother was holding onto," said Akutsiaq.

"*Ii,* look at her! She's laughing anyway!"

The quarterers stopped their work. Ningiukuluk began eating her share of the *aqiggiq*. Qalingu ended up with part of the breast, Irsutualuk with a piece of flesh, and Arnatuinnaq with a foot... Everyone was dunking their pieces in seal oil. All the eating had dirtied their hands, which they rinsed with wet snow. After cleaning themselves, they wiped their mouths. Ningiukuluk was offered a pair of scissors as a *qillaquti* gift. She was also given chewing tobacco and a bar of soap that Sanaaq brought to her home.

"Thank you!" said Ningiukuluk. "All the gifts I have here are for tying umbilical cords... This soap will be only for me... Akutsiaq, my daughter, will never use it, not even for doing the laundry... As for the scissors, I'll take great care of them... They'll never be used for metal cutting!"

Taqriasuk came back to the camp, after a long time keeping a lookout on the hilltop. He thought, "What have they been up to here? I can see a lot of footprints in the snow! All day long I've been keeping a lookout. I'm hungry and I'm going home. The whole day I haven't seen the smallest game animal... Yet I looked in all directions through my telescope!"

"*Ii,*" said Ningiukuluk. "Here comes our old man! And we didn't wait for him before quartering. We were in too much of a hurry! ...I put something aside for you to eat, have some! It's thanks to my *angusiaq* that we've got food to eat."

Taqriasuk began eating some of the *aqiggiq*.

"I'm really happy to be eating!" he said.

Aqiarulaaq had been gone the whole day to gather fuel for the fire and was not back yet. Meanwhile, Aanikallak had stayed home. She was old enough to make herself useful. Once Taqriasuk had finished eating, he went home.

"Hasn't my old woman come back yet?" he asked.

"No!" said Aanikallak.

Qalingu went to visit Taqriasuk. When he entered, he said, "*Ai!*"

"Qalingu, *ai!* Today, I searched high and low on all sides with my telescope, but I saw absolutely nothing, not even a seal on the ice. I'm really happy that your son killed his first *aqiggiq* today."

"When I bought him his rifle, he couldn't hit a target... He managed to catch an *aqiggiq* today by breaking its wing. I'm not surprised he didn't kill it with a single shot."

Taqriasuk was tired because he was very old. He went to bed. His old woman, Aqiarulaaq, came just then. She brought the fuel she had gone to gather: *kuutsiit, sigalat, mamaittuqutit, issutiit,* and *paurngaqutit.* The fuel would be used for cooking outside at a place where the snow had melted. She went to bed, because it was evening, after having a bit of tea. They were still living in an igloo, although the dome was threatening to cave in on them.

Morning arrived and Qalingu awoke. The weather was very bad and it was snowing heavily. They had hardly any food left, however, so he decided to go hunting with Maatiusi, despite the weather... As they travelled by sled, the weather improved and it stopped snowing.

Qalingu spotted an *uuttuq* and decided to go after it while his companion kept an eye on the sled and dog team. He slipped a white hareskin cap over his head, took a few cartridges and, circling around the seal to the north, crawled towards his prey. He killed it. It was a female with its baby. The seal he had just killed was lying on the bed of its snow shelter. The baby seal did not even dive into the water when its mother died. It simply stayed by her. When Qalingu reached his prey, he also shot the baby seal. His hunting companion caught up to him at that moment. Now that they had a seal, they decided to go home, where they had run out of seal oil and were reduced to cooking outside with fuel gathered from the tundra.

Aqiarulaaq went out and spotted the approaching sled with its travellers. She called out to Sanaaq, "*Qatannguuk!* A dog team is coming. Why's it acting that way? Let's go, the two of us. Look cousin, they're loaded. Seems like they've killed a seal. Let's go and meet them!"

To cheer on the arriving dog team, Aqiarulaaq shouted, "*Aa, aa!*" and Sanaaq began pulling on the sled's main tugline. The travellers were happy.

43

QALINGU LEAVES TO WORK AMONG THE QALLUNAAT

The same day, in late afternoon, a plane appeared.

"Listen to that drone. Sounds like a plane!" said Qalingu. "Over there! It's arriving… There are two men aboard!"

It was a single-engine airplane. The Inuit were very nervous and the children were crying. Everyone went to greet them. When the door to the airplane opened, little Qalliutuq was very afraid.

The two *Qallunaak* spoke the Inuit language. Their chief asked Qalingu, "Who are you?"

"I'm Qalingu!"

"Do you want to come and work among the *Qallunaat?*"

"No! I've never been away from here. I don't know the language of the *Qallunaat.*"

"If you accept, you'll be treated very well. You'll start off receiving two hundred dollars a month and your family will get a house. The plane will be back in a week."

"OK," said Qalingu, who decided to help his family. "I'd like to give it a try." Speaking to Sanaaq, he added, "I'll be away working for two months. You'll be given assistance."

She agreed.

Qalingu made his preparations. He was afraid he would not be allowed to come back. Airplane travel scared him, this being his first time... and the plane was very fast. His family—Qumaq, Sanaaq, and Qalliutuq—broke into tears at the thought that he might never come back... When the airplane disappeared in the clouds, they went home very sad because Qalingu was gone.

While the family looked after the home, the *iksigarjuaq* would drop by with food—all kinds of things in tin cans. Sanaaq was invited to his place and she went with a bag. She found the tins to be quite nice-looking.

"Look, Arnatuinnaq!" she said, coming back. "Look at the presents we've been given: canned food!"

"I'd like to see if it's any good. May I have a taste? It's pretty good, the stuff in this can. And these *usuujait,* what are they? They're too salty, throw them away. Yes, they've got a very bad taste!"

They were not accustomed to *Qallunaat* food, so they did not like it. But they did appreciate the oranges. Just then, Qalliutuq began to vomit.

"The boy's throwing up!" said Sanaaq. "Hand me the pot! Toss those cans out! We can't keep the bad ones."

The next day, at dawn, the airplane came back. The weather was very nice and everybody went out to the plane, even old Taqriasuk. The *Qallunaaq* was an Inuit agent. He said hello, shook hands, and smiled. But no one understood a word of what he said. The airplane stayed for the night. Taqriasuk carried the visitors' baggage into the Catholic missionary's house and Maatiusi too carried some in. When they were done, they were offered a dollar. Thinking it was something important, they showed it to the missionary.

"Look!" said Taqriasuk. "Look at what we just got, I and Maatiusi! A simple piece of paper. What is it?"

"It's money," said the missionary. "If you take it to the merchant, you'll be able to buy anything with it."

"*Ai!*" said Taqriasuk.

Night was falling. The Inuit agent, using the missionary as an interpreter, asked, "What's your name?"

"I'm Taqriasuk!"

"How old are you?"

"I have no idea!"

"You're probably very old because you look quite elderly. You'll regularly get money without having to work, because you're old. You can spend your time doing nothing. You'll buy what you want every month. You'll get money for your children too, for anyone who isn't sixteen yet. When they pass that age, the money stops. But for the old there won't be any age limit."

After this conversation, Taqriasuk went home and said, "I was told I'll get money."

"*Ai!*" said Aqiarulaaq. "That's great!"

As for Sanaaq's family, they would get a house next summer, a real house, she was told. That evening the Inuit agent paid a visit.

"*Ai!*" she said.

"Hello," he replied, while lavishing much affection on her child. He then said to her, "Next summer a house will be built for you. In addition, starting tomorrow, you'll get money for your children."

Sanaaq was astounded to be promised so much when she had never been helped before. After the *Qallunaaq* went back to his place, Aqiarulaaq came to visit Sanaaq.

"Hi, *qatannguuk!* Tomorrow we're going shopping! This has completely taken us by surprise, cousin! We were told that my old man would regularly get money at the end of every month."

"Looks like our children too will be getting money!" said Sanaaq.

Qalingu, meanwhile, was working among the *Qallunaat*. He was made to do just about anything. At times he yearned to go home, because he missed his little boy and his wife. He had never been gone so long from home. Often, the thought even came to his mind that he would never be allowed to go back... At bedtime, he frequently could not fall asleep, for the thought haunted and bothered him.

Back home, those who had stayed behind were also feeling his absence. They had never been apart for so long and Sanaaq often found her little boy crying because he missed his father so much. The next day they went to the store. The Inuit agent was already there with the company clerks. Ningiukuluk also came in. She was very old and went about her purchases without knowing how much anything cost, for she had never paid attention to the prices of different items. She bought felt, flour, chewing tobacco, baking powder, and printed fabrics to make a dress for Akutsiak and a sweater for her younger sister, Tajarak. Sanaaq and Aqiarulaaq were also making their purchases. They bought a lot of things and wrapped the ones that would be hard to carry away. While Ningiukuluk was still in the store, Sanaaq and Aqiarulaaq went to look for a small sled.

"*Qatannguuk!* We'll haul away our purchases together. Give me a leather strap to pull with. Too bad we won't have any more straps to tie down the load. I'll hold it down while you pull!"

When they came back with the sled, they spoke to Ningiukuluk.

"We've just got back," said Sanaaq. "It took us some time to get ready!"

"I'm not at all tired of waiting," replied Ningiukuluk.

"We tried to be fast," added Aqiarulaaq. "We were afraid you'd get cold!"

"I'm not cold. Just a little cold in my feet. My feet are giving me a headache!"

"You should get going," said Sanaaq. "Walk all the way home!"

"I'm going. I'm tired of standing in one place!"

Qalingu was busy working but had trouble concentrating on his work, worried as he was about his family and thinking a great deal about them. "I don't know what my family is doing or how my little boy is… They may be short of food and hungry… They must be missing me and thinking I'll never come back... My wife's probably trying all the time to console my little boy, who's crying and unhappy… As for Qumaq and Arnatuinnaq, they'll both be working non-stop, even during snowstorms… So when will I go home? Maybe next month?"

He was becoming increasingly despondent. He had been away for a long time and for two months now had not stopped working. Then came spring and the *Qallunaat* told him, "Qalingu! You're going home next week."

On hearing this, he was overcome with joy. He smiled all the time now and prepared for his departure. His pockets were full of *kiinaujait* because he had been working for a long while.

44

A SUCCESSFUL DAY FISHING FOR ARCTIC CHAR

With spring coming and many water holes appearing on the lakes, thoughts in the Qalingu household turned to fishing. Aqiarulaaq went to visit Sanaaq.

"Cousin! I feel like going fishing with Maatiusi and Arnatuinnaq. Qumaq will also be coming!"

"We'll go tomorrow *ai!* Great idea! We'll leave tomorrow. I'll prepare something to eat for the trip and make some bannock because it's far from here... We'll camp overnight and go by dogsled over the ice!"

Arnatuinnaq, Maatiusi, Qumaq, Aanikallak, and Akutsiaq went to see the Catholic missionary and the store employees.

"Tomorrow we're going fishing," said Arnatuinnaq to the missionary.

"I'll go with you! It'll be a great pleasure for me," he replied.

They all went to see the chief factor at the trading post and Maatiusi told him, "Tomorrow we're going fishing. I'd like some biscuits for the trip."

"I'll go with you, and I'll take enough provisions."

They left and returned to Sanaaq's home.

"All of the *Qallunaat* will be going with us," said Maatiusi.

Aqiarulaaq and Sanaaq were delighted. The next day, everyone prepared to go. They took along their fishhooks and provisions. Ningiukuluk and Taqriasuk remained behind at the camp because of their advanced age. The others travelled by dogsled over the wet snow. Maatiusi drove the dog team. When they reached their destination, they made tea for their *ullugummitaaq*. Arnatuinnaq went to draw water from a river.

"Isn't this fun!" she exclaimed.

Meanwhile, Aqiarulaaq was building a fireplace. The chief factor remained seated in order to attach his fishhook properly. Maatiusi was baiting his with a piece of blubber.

"*Qatannguuk!*" said Sanaaq. "It's coming to a boil. Time for our tea! Let the children have theirs first."

When everyone had had their tea, they walked onto the lake ice.

"Isn't this fun!" said Sanaaq. "Son, pay attention so you don't fall through the ice. Qumaq! You too!"

The chief factor started fishing.

"There's an *iqaluk* at the end of my line, Maatiusi!"

"Mine too. Look at the one I've caught!"

But the one the chief factor caught was much bigger.

"I just missed an *iqaluk!*" said Sanaaq.

"I've got one too!" shouted Aqiarulaaq. "This is great!"

"The *iqaluit* won't stop biting at my bait," said the missionary. "Here we go! I just caught a very big *iqaluk*, a *nutilliq!*"

"I haven't seen the tiniest little *iqaluk!*" said Arnatuinnaq. "Qumaq! Come and fish with my line for a moment while I go smoke a cigarette."

"Look!" said Qumaq. "A big *iqaluk!* Yes! I just caught a very big *iqaluk!*"

"I sure envy Qumaq for landing such a catch!" sighed Arnatuinnaq.

After Qumaq caught her *iqaluk,* she gutted it with a knife. Her mother and all the other anglers were very happy that Qumaq had got one. The missionary too had caught some Arctic char.

"I'm very happy to have caught so many fish," he said, stuffing them into a bag.

The chief factor, for his part, had caught two.

While the two *qatannguuk* were fishing, Aqiarulaaq suddenly shouted, "Over there, *qatannguuk,* are some *iqaluit* swimming in small schools. They're heading to shore, in your direction. One of them is very big!"

"Yes!" said Sanaaq. "Right there! Very many *iqaluit.* Look at them. They're fighting over my bait... I've got one *iqaluk,* and another one, and still another!"

The chief factor walked over to Sanaaq because she was landing a lot of fish, and he started fishing beside her.

"I've got an *iqaluk!*" he said. "I've got one! Another one! Another one... None are left! I've taken them all!"

That night, they would be sleeping under the stars, without a tent. With Aqiarulaaq, Sanaaq looked for a suitable campsite. Her son trailed behind, while Qumaq gathered *qijuttaq* and Arnatuinnaq went to do the cooking. The chief factor stayed near the fireplace, as did the missionary. Arnatuinnaq was looking for a flat stone. When she came across one, she picked it up but found it too heavy to carry. Maatiusi helped her.

The chief factor said, "Maatiusi, give it to me. Let me carry it!"

"*Ii!*" said Maatiusi. "I dropped it and it broke!"

He went looking for another one.

"Isn't this one suitable?" asked the chief factor.

"No," answered Arnatuinnaq. "It's too thick!"

"Here's one," said Maatiusi. "It should do the job, shouldn't it, Arnatuinnaq?"

"I'll bring it over," said the chief factor, "because Maatiusi dropped the other one."

And he carried it to the fireplace. Arnatuinnaq built a large fireplace beside the spot where she had prepared the tea. She lit the fuel under the flat stone, whose upper surface became burning hot. Onto this she put blubber, which crackled and gave off steam, and then one of the fish that she had cut into slices. In very little time, the fish slices were cooked on the flat stone. Everyone had some, including the chief factor and the missionary. Both of them enjoyed what had been cooked on the stone. After their first taste they asked for more. When everyone had finished, tea was served. As there were only four cups, people took turns drinking the tea.

After finishing their meal, they looked for a place where they could sleep in the open, there being no tent. Some of them created a makeshift tent out of bedspreads, by tying the edges together with a leather strap. They were Sanaaq, Arnatuinnaq, Qumaq, Aqiarulaaq, and Sanaaq's son. The others—the missionary, the chief factor, and Maatiusi—had no tent. They went to sleep in the lee of an L-shaped rock. They did, however, have a few bedspreads and some brush for bedding.

During the night, a strong wind picked up and those who slept outside were cold. They got up very early. Maatiusi lit the fire in the fireplace and made some tea. Being next to the fire, he was no longer cold. While the women of the group continued to sleep, the early risers began fishing once more on the lake. On approaching a crack in the ice, they saw large numbers of Arctic char and said, "Look at all the fish! Today we're going home!"

Meanwhile, Sanaaq's companions were just awaking.

"Arnatuinnaq, wake up!" said Sanaaq.

"Yes!"

"Mommy, are we going home?" asked little Irsutuq. "It's not warm in the tent!"

"We'll go home after we've fished a little bit more, I and my *qatanngut!*" said Sanaaq.

When breakfast was over, they both went fishing.

"*Ai qatannguuk!*" said Aqiarulaaq. "Take care not to go through the ice. This past night it didn't stop melting!"

Arnatuinnaq was cooking while Qumaq and Irsutuq stayed in their tent. The men of the group were back. They had caught many *iqaluit*. Maatiusi had landed a big one—an *isiuralittaaq*. They began preparing to go home.

The chief factor found Arnatuinnaq very attractive. While she cooked, he even tried to kiss her, right in front of Qumaq, who thought, "*Ii,* that one, that bad *Qallunaaq* who was our companion, he's behaving badly. It's really offensive!" Arnatuinnaq, however, did not mind, and the two of them would be having sexual relations throughout the spring, unbeknownst to Arnatuinnaq's kinfolk.

Maatiusi was preparing to leave with Irsutuq while Qumaq chatted with the missionary.

"I again affirm my desire to follow your religion once we've returned home. I'll go to prayer every day. My stepfather, Qalingu, when he comes back, will be happy for me and I'll be happy all my life!"

The missionary replied to Qumaq, "If you always try to do good, Qumaq, and if you persevere in doing good, you will find happiness!"

With the return of Sanaaq and Aqiarulaaq, everyone prepared to leave. After having another cup of tea, they resumed their journey and soon arrived home, at Ningiukuluk's place.

"So you're back?" said Ningiukuluk. "Now we'll be able to eat fish! Thanks!"

She received fish from the kinfolk of Sanaaq and Aqiarulaaq. So did Taqriasuk. They had stayed home because they were very old.

With spring well underway, people began to long for Qalingu's return, because the airplane was supposed to be arriving.

"But when will my father arrive?" asked Irsutuq.

"I was told he would arrive tomorrow," answered his mother.

"That's great! Tomorrow I'll stick around so that I can go and welcome him back. Little sister, they say my father will be arriving tomorrow!"

"*Ai!* That's great!" said Qumaq. "We'll save some fish for tomorrow, Mom!"

Arnatuinnaq told Sanaaq, "I'll go look for fuel, so that we'll have enough tomorrow to keep us warm. That's delightful news! We won't be alone at home anymore."

Sanaaq went to Ningiukuluk's home. She walked in and said, "*Ai!* Ningiukuluk!"

"*Aa!* Sit down, Sanaaq, and have some tea!"

"Thank you, Ningiukuluk!"

When night fell, Sanaaq left and Ningiukuluk went to bed.

"*Uuh,* am I ever tired! It's tiring to be old. I feel exhausted each evening!"

She fell asleep. In the morning she awoke to a nice sunny day.

"My stepfather's going to arrive," said Qumaq. "What a happy occasion!"

When the airplane appeared, all of the Inuit came to welcome its passengers. Qalingu climbed down from the plane. On seeing his father, Irsutuq felt overwhelmed.

"Father! You've arrived!" They headed to the village, with the baggage. "Dad, may I carry these things? Where were you?"

Qalingu had brought gifts for everyone in the whole family. The chief factor came to visit. Taqriasuk also went. They recounted everything that had happened in his absence.

"Over there," said Qalingu, "at our work site, three of us were Inuit. One of us, a young man, missed his mother and father a great deal and we sometimes thought we'd never be allowed to go home, despite our wish to go home. We were told the Inuit would always have work... By going away to work, I made a lot of money. I'll buy a canoe and an outboard motor!"

"At the end of every month," said Taqriasuk, "I've been getting money. I've bought felt and braid cloth—to tell the truth, just about anything... I'm very grateful!"

Qalingu was eager to go hunting now, for he was very happy to be back in his country. Maatiusi was happy to see his hunting companion return.

45

THE FIRST MEDICAL EXAMINATION

The airplane came again, with a nurse aboard. She brought her devices for diagnosing illnesses. The plane would stay two nights and the nurse would attend to the health problems of the Inuit. It was the first time that the Inuit met an *aanniasiurti*. The nurse used the missionary as an interpreter. That evening, the Inuit were invited to come. They heard for the first time that they would be examined. That same day, in the evening, they underwent blood tests. Maatiusi was the first to have a sample of his blood taken.

"*Aatataa!* That hurts!"

It was then the children's turn.

"No, I don't want to!" said Irsutuq, "because Maatiusi has just been hurt!"

Qumaq and Aanikallak ran off for fear of being hurt. Although they slipped away, they were still made to take a blood test. Qumaq's blood was too weak. As was Aanikallak's. They were told so.

"Sanaaq! Qumaq's blood is too weak and the same is true for Aanikallak's. They'll both have to go to hospital!"

That did not at all please Sanaaq and Aqiarulaaq. The two of them cried and cried. Their lungs were going to be X-rayed. The next day, they were ordered to strip to the waist. They felt very ashamed, because they had never undressed in this manner.

"Do it!" they were told.

After they had been tested, their lungs were found to be healthy. Taqriasuk, however, was advised to take it easy because he was very old. The same recommendation was given to Qumaq and Aanikallak because they would soon be leaving on the airplane to be among the *Qallunaat*. The nurse also questioned Arnatuinnaq.

"Are you often unwell?"

"No!"

Their weights were measured: Arnatuinnaq, 122 pounds; Qumaq, 77; her little brother, 26; Sanaaq, 118; Qalingu, 141; Taqriasuk, 136; Aqiarulaaq, 112; Aanikallak, 76; Maatiusi, 101; Tajarak, 40; Irsutualuq, 215, and Angutikallak, 143. The last two were too fat. Angutikallak was told that he was overweight.

"Angutikallak! You will not eat seal blubber too often. You're too fat for someone as young as you!"

"Yes, yes! I'll surely do as you say!"

"And you, Arnatuinnaq! You're pregnant. Your baby will be born next month."

On hearing this, she felt thoroughly ashamed, for she had no husband. Sanaaq, her family, and everyone in the camp were learning the news for the first time. They thought, "Could it be Maatiusi's child or maybe Angutikallak's?"

Once she had gone home, Arnatuinnaq told her older sister, Sanaaq, "It's the chief factor's child!"

Some of their camp mates were very astonished and displeased at what Arnatuinnaq had said. When the time came to leave, Qumaq and Aanikallak were weeping warm tears, as were their families. The Inuit realized for the first time that some unpleasant things were being done to them. Qumaq did not cry too much, however, because she had begun to listen to the teachings of the Church, and her thoughts were often on the Catholic faith.

"In truth, I won't always be happy!"

There were many things they had not yet understood by the time of their departure. From then on, however, Aanikallak and Qumaq were constantly learning and understanding more and more.

46

BIRTH, NAMING, AND CONVERSION

And so, among those close to her, Arnatuinnaq gave birth to a little girl. Sanaaq was the midwife. Ningiukuluk, who wished to acquire a *sauniq,* made a request: "I wish to have a *sauniq* so that I may walk all the time and accompany those who go travelling anywhere!"

Ningiukuluk was overjoyed, having acquired a *sauniq.* And the baby with no father was now called Ningiukuluk.

After Arnatuinnaq had given birth, the chief factor wanted to marry her straightaway, out of affection for his little daughter. The problem was that he could be transferred anytime to a place among the *Qallunaat.* Arnatuinnaq was an Inuk and did not understand the *Qallunaat* language. A *Qallunaaq,* however, had fathered her baby. Arnatuinnaq wanted her first child to be baptized by the Catholic missionary.

"Tomorrow she'll be baptized!" she said.

Sanaaq and Qalingu both loved the baby. And Ningiukuluk, who had acquired a *sauniq*, gave away some of the felt she had bought for a pair of stockings, which Sanaaq made. The child's father gave her a shawl to cloak her body, flannel for her shirts, and material for her clothes. To the mother, he gave felt and material for an *amauti* so that she could carry the child on her back. Sanaaq made it, stitching it together after cutting it out, using her own *amauti* as a pattern. She very much wanted to carry the little baby in her own coat pouch. Arnatuinnaq, for her part, passionately loved her first child. And Irsutuq, Sanaaq's little boy, was always kissing her. He had grown and often accompanied Qalingu on hunting trips.

Maatiusi was not at all happy. His betrothed, Arnatuinnaq, had a baby that was not his. He wavered, however, between a desire to marry her and the opposite...

With the coming of summer, the *ajuqirtuiji* and his assistants arrived and attended to the Inuit. He questioned Qalingu and Sanaaq.

"But this baby, who is her father?"

"Her father is a *Qallunaaq!*" answered Qalingu.

"Her baptism has no value," said the minister, "for she is the fruit of sin. Her mother and you are truly lacking in common sense!"

"You are right," replied Qalingu. "If we're not acceptable to you, it doesn't matter. We can't always act perfectly. We must be humble, but this little baby will be baptized by the Catholic missionary!"

"How is that possible when neither you nor the baby's mother are Catholics? I'm the one who will baptize her!"

"No! I love this baby too much. You've just said she's not worthy of baptism, so we want her to be baptized by the Catholic missionary, whom we'll now follow. You may have worthy disciples, who'll always do good. But we aren't worthy of you, so we'll be confessing at the Catholic mission."

"I'm the one who'll baptize the child because you follow the Anglicans!"

Arnatuinnaq left and went to the Catholic mission, where she said, "This one, I want her to be baptized by you!"

The Catholic missionary agreed. "I'll baptize her in a few moments!"

And everyone, including Qalingu and Sanaaq, came in, because the baby was going to be baptized.

"I am going to baptize your child. She will be the first one among you to be baptized! Though she is only a little baby, she will now be washed of all uncleanliness. She shall be named Ningiukuluk Maria!"

As the first to be baptized, this baby became a source of great joy for the whole family.

Qumaq had gone far away. The airplane brought her news from her family. This is what was written to her:

"To Qumaq, from her mother, *Ai!* Qumaq. Right now we're doing fine. We have a newborn child, a little girl-cousin for you. She's been baptized and is called Maria! *Ai!* Qumaq! Be patient, because you'll be coming back! I send you my greetings, you and Aanikallak too! My cousin Aqiarulaaq is doing fine. Always be thoroughly obedient, the two of you. You'll come back when you've recovered. Qumaq! *Ai!* You're sent greetings from your little brother and from Arnatuinnaq, as well as from your stepfather!"

Qumaq received her mother's letter with the news about her folks while in hospital. The news of the baby gave her a start. She thought, "Had I been more diligent, I'd already be baptized... How I envy her! My little cousin is already baptized... When I go home, I'll carry her on my back often. But I don't know when I'm going home!"

Qumaq told Aanikallak, "Aanikallak! We got a letter! We've been asked to obey at all times. Our folks are fine, so they say. How delightful it is that we got a letter, Aanikallak! Read it and then give it back to me."

"*Aa!* Thanks!" said Aanikallak. "But I want to go home!"

"How true! Let's both cry, Aanikallak!"

“Let’s!”

They both began to cry and people thought that they were angry with each other, when they were just homesick. Some people also thought that they were in pain. Their families back home very much longed for their return. Sanaaq could not help but think about Qumaq often.

“Qumaq may arrive anytime! I must not get discouraged. She’s going to come back soon… When she’s back, she’ll probably have grown and her clothing will be too small for her, that’s for sure!”

47

A BROKEN HEART AND POSSESSION

Maatiusi was out walking alone in late summer. He was feeling down. All kinds of thoughts were turning over and over in his mind, even bad ones. He had been warned, in keeping with Inuit customs, that it was not good to dwell too much on something, but he ignored these warnings and let his despondency run free. He became used to mulling over his thoughts, in which Arnatuinnaq was first and foremost. He found her very desirable, thought much about her and, suddenly, while walking, caught sight of someone who looked like her. He believed it was Arnatuinnaq. Maatiusi saw a woman with the edge of her hood folded back and he really thought it was Arnatuinnaq. Being alone, he took her as a companion and talked and made love with her. He felt euphoric...

Members of his family began to be wary. No one understood why Maatiusi was often away at night and yet did not seem to be out hunting. Qalingu now usually went hunting alone, with only his little boy for company.

And Arnatuinnaq always stayed home. In fact, Maatiusi was possessed by a *nuliarsaq*. He no longer seemed to find any pleasure in going home. And his *nuliarsaq,* who was a very pretty girl, had great powers. She could make herself invisible. With her, he was happy, being himself a handsome Inuk. It was like having a real wife. He did not even notice her missing navel...

Maatiusi was unaware that he had changed, but those close to him, his camp mates, could see he was not doing well at all, even though they did not know why. His way of life was not the same as before. He seldom talked anymore, had become closed-minded, and avoided the company of other Inuit while still eating and working with them. He sometimes went hunting but no longer took care of his clothes. He dressed shabbily. Sometimes, his behaviour puzzled his camp mates. They would hear him talking aloud while alone and even making eyes at someone. At times, it looked as if someone was calling him. At other times, he would suddenly take off without warning. At still other times, it looked as if he was fainting... All this was the effect of his *nuliarsaq,* who was making love to him... People noticed too that his skin was damp. Those who lived with him found that Maatiusi often had a very foul odour...

Qalingu asked Maatiusi, "Are you sick?"

"No, I'm not sick!"

"What's wrong with you? You're living a life that's not like the one you lived before!"

"Not at all. I haven't changed!"

Clearly, he was not going to say anything. Qalingu no longer enjoyed him as a hunting companion and began to think, "Maatiusi must be possessed by a *nuliarsaq* because sometimes he converses with nobody and he smells very bad."

For her part, Aqiarulaaq was thinking, "All the Inuit feel that Maatiusi is in a bad way. It's probably because he doesn't want to say anything while having bad thoughts due to personal problems. If he doesn't talk, his condition will get even worse. We're his life companions and we should talk to him."

She decided to approach him.

"Maatiusi, what's with you? Maybe you have a relationship with a *nuliarsaq*. Could that be it?"

"No, not at all!"

Because he did not want to talk, the questioning led nowhere, and his condition only got worse.

Aqiarulaaq went to speak to Sanaaq. "*Qatannguuk!* Maatiusi clearly isn't saying a thing. Please, would you like to try and question him some time?"

"Maybe if I were alone with him," answered Sanaaq, "I could get him to talk. Couldn't I, cousin?"

So Sanaaq questioned him.

"Maatiusi, I'm going to talk to you because your condition is getting worse. You no longer appear to be the same person. You've got a *nuliarsaq!* You sometimes give off a *nuliarsaq* odour. If you stay that way, you'll go to *kappianartuvik!*"

Maatiusi was overcome with sorrow on hearing this from Sanaaq, but his *nuliarsaq* forbade him to talk and continually reminded him of this. Yet he very much wanted to talk to Sanaaq. Because his *nuliarsaq* feared he would, she tried to frighten him with a large knife and lashed him with a whip.

"I'll kill you!" she repeated again and again. "As soon as you talk, I'll kill you. I'll no longer have you as a husband!"

So, he did not say anything, fearing that he would be killed if he did so. Although he almost confessed to Sanaaq, he stopped himself, believing his *nuliarsaq*. She had worked hard to make him fear greatly the consequences of a confession. He had several reasons for saying nothing: the fear of punishment and also his deep fondness for his *nuliarsaq*.

"He hasn't talked yet, *qatannguuk!*" reported Sanaaq to her cousin. "He seems to fear the consequences of confessing. He's probably under someone's influence!"

His *nuliarsaq* was very grateful to him for not talking. She visited him more and more and Maatiusi became even more possessed. His sense of reason was almost gone and, whenever he left for the night, people were afraid he would lose his way. His camp mates were increasingly worried.

Arnatuinnaq's baby was growing and Qumaq and Aanikallak were back.

"It's really nice to have them back, our two absent girls!" said Aqiarulaaq.

Qumaq loved the baby as soon as she saw her.

"Little cousin *Ai!* You're so tiny. I'm going to take good care of you!"

And she recounted to her mother everything that had happened since her departure.

"*Anaanak!* I saw big houses for the first time. They were very beautiful. And cars, many of them too. And lights that often lit themselves. And stores, statues, plenty of things… Ships too. There are very many *Qallunaat*. Even at night, they don't stop. And there are animals that produce milk, and many other things. Over there we learned a lot at school. We were treated well all the time. We never went out. Sometimes it wasn't nice. It was very tiring. All the time we were made to sleep during the day so that we would get cured. Finally, because we were both cured, I and Aanikallak, we came back by plane. What happiness! The nurses loved us a lot!"

"Thank you so much, Qumaq, for being cured! The chief factor will be leaving very soon, even though he's liked so much by Arnatuinnaq and by all of the Inuit. He'll be leaving next week. Ever since she found out, Arnatuinnaq has been distraught because her lover will be going. Another person will surely take his place, but that one, the chief factor who'll be leaving, is the one she loves the most."

Maatiusi was often home and made only short visits with no real thought of working. He was very absent-minded, talked rarely, and disliked being with the Inuit.

48

CONFESSION AND CURE

Sanaaq loved her *nuakuluk,* who was at the stage of beginning to chew. She gave her fish to eat. And Qalingu often went fishing.

On the day that the chief factor departed on a big boat, his replacement arrived. Everyone was sad. Arnatuinnaq cried. The chief factor left a few little things behind for everyone, but his baby and Arnatuinnaq received more than the others. Arnatuinnaq was sad and thought again and again, "My handsome lover is going away. There'll never be a man as kind as him, and I no longer even enjoy staying home. I always feel like crying! He'll probably never come back!"

The new chief factor was often engaged in trade and the Inuit felt intimidated by him. He too found Arnatuinnaq to his liking and tried to seduce her, but Arnatuinnaq detested the man. She could not love her friend's replacement. She thought constantly about the first one.

Sanaaq spoke to her. "Arnatuinnaq, don't get thinking too much about this new *Qallunaaq*. He could leave!"

But she was not thinking at all about the new *Qallunaaq*. Then one evening, while on a visit to Aqiarulaaq's place, all alone and still grieving, she spotted a man on her path who looked like the chief factor who had left.

"*Ii! Ii!*" shrieked Arnatuinnaq, overwhelmed by fright.

Feeling faint, she ran into Aqiarulaaq's home and began talking to Taqriasuk and Aqiarulaaq.

"I was terrified when I saw someone who wasn't a human being, our former chief factor. I was almost possessed by an *uirsaq*... And he even tried to seize me, just now, when I was already here!"

"*Ii!*" said Aqiarulaaq. "What an experience! It's because you're still hurting, because you're lamenting too much, that you've almost been possessed by an *uirsaq!*"

Arnatuinnaq no longer wanted to go home alone, for fear of meeting such a being again. So Aqiarulaaq accompanied her to her home, to Sanaaq's place. She said, "Because she saw someone who wasn't human, Arnatuinnaq too almost got possessed by an *uirsaq, qatannguuk!*"

"It's a good thing, Arnatuinaaq, that you immediately confessed!" said Sanaaq. "You'll probably never see it again. It must be quite ashamed that you confessed right away. If you hadn't, it would've appeared to you again and again, even briefly. It's said that that's how non-human beings appear, by taking on the appearance of the person one loves!"

Arnatuinnaq spoke again. "I never thought I'd see a creature like that, on account of my being too attached to my friend, the former chief factor. It still hurts when I think that no one else will be as kind and nice as he was...!"

"It's fortunate you spoke right away," added Sanaaq.

Arnatuinnaq felt well. She forbade herself to think about him because she feared encountering another non-human being. She behaved honourably, for she wanted to be baptized like her child, and often went to pray. With Qumaq, little Irsutuq, and Aanikallak, she became a member of the Catholic Church.

Meanwhile, Maatiusi had still not confessed to having a *nuliarsaq,* despite having previously been engaged to Arnatuinnaq. It was as if he no longer cared for the real Arnatuinnaq. And so Arnatuinnaq was afraid of Maatiusi and his *nuliarsaq.* Maatiusi, however, knew he would never want to have the invisible woman as a wife, so he began to think, "There are two Arnatuinnaq. How can that be?"

Qalingu, Maatiusi, and Angutsiaq went fishing at the *saputi* for *iqaluit* that were swimming upstream. They felt happy as they fished. But Maatiusi could not be really happy. His two companions were caught up in the fishing—now and again running, often falling into the water, and standing back up each time... But Maatiusi was not really with them... He was fatherless, motherless, and without family. He lived at Aqiarulaaq's home, having taken the place of the man's deceased son Jiimialuk. Everyone took good care of him. While preparing the midday meal, Maatiusi thought, "*Uuu!* Am I ever tired! In the past, I was always really happy to be an Inuk, but now I'm tired of having a *nuliarsaq*. I hope Qalingu will come because I'm going to tell him everything... So what if I get killed by my *nuliarsaq,* who tells me again and again she'll kill me the moment I talk... Maybe it's not true and she just wants to keep me from talking."

Qalingu arrived just then. When he got his meal, he said, "Maatiusi *ai!* I fell several times into the water... Is it cooked? There's a good smell of tea and boiled fish!"

Maatiusi did not say a word. He did not even try to look at Qalingu. He wanted to talk but because he hesitated too long he could not.

Qalingu asked, "Maatiusi, are you feeling down? I'm really happy to be fishing!"

"Yes! All summer I've found nothing to make me happy!"

"But now you could be happy! All the Inuit and the *Qallunaat* too know you've got a *nuliarsaq*. If you confess, you won't be in that situation anymore. Who does your *nuliarsaq* look like?"

"Like Arnatuinnaq!"

"But Arnatuinnaq is still among us!"

"I thought I'd have Arnatuinnaq as my wife. Then, while walking far away, when I was sad because of her, I saw it for the first time... The edge of its hood was turned back and… it forbade me to talk. If I did, it said it would cut my head off with a knife... Yet I still felt attached to it. That's why I took so long to talk!"

"Maatiusi! From now on you'll be truly happy and you'll never see it again. It said it'd kill you just to keep you from talking..."

As soon as he had talked, Maatiusi truly felt much better. He had rid himself of his *nuliarsaq* thanks to his travelling companion and for this he was really happy. From then on he would no longer have such torments. As for the others, who had still been fishing, they decided to head home with the start of a heavy downpour...

END

GLOSSARY

Abbreviations: dual (dl.), plural (pl.), vocative (voc.)

Aa! Aaah! interjection to express pain

Aakut-tuasi old children's rhyme

Aalalaalaala humming of a tune

Aalummi! exclamation to express tenderness toward children

Aanaqatak person's name

Aanikallak person's name, literally "little Annie"

aanniasiurti physician or nurse; from *aanniaq* pain, painful illness

Aappuu! child talk; interjection to express wish to be consoled

Aaq! interjection to express disgust

Aatataa! onomatopoeia: interjection to express pain (Ow-ow-ow!)

Ai! interjection to address someone, to question, to express resignation, or to ask for agreement

Aiguuq! interjection used by spouses to address each other

Aikuluk reciprocal kinship term, used by in-laws, of the opposite sex and the same generation, e.g., the wife of a man's brother or the sister of a man's wife

Aippa, voc. **Aippaa!** kinship term used by spouses to address or refer to each other: Husband! Wife!

airait, pl. of **airaq** edible root of field locoweed *Oxytropis hyperborea*

airaq see **airait**

airqavaq, pl. **airqavat,** dl. **airqavaak** long-sleeved winter glove, used when building an igloo

ajuqirtuiji, pl. **ajuqirtuijiit** Anglican minister, literally "the one who teaches"

Ajurnamat! "Can't be helped!" "Nothing can be done!" Condolences after bereavement

aki part of the home (tent or igloo) left and right of the entrance, used as a kitchen or larder

akitsirait, pl. of **akitsiraq** seal spare ribs with their vertebrae

aksunaajjatuq hunting companion who gets an **aksunaaksak** as his share

aksunaaksaq, pl. **aksunaaksat** cylinder of skin cut from around the trunk of a bearded seal to make leather straps

akuit, pl. of **akuq** seal femur

Akutsiaq person's name, literally "pretty rear end of a woman's garment"

aliktuuti ritual quartering of first bird killed by a child

aliqatsaujaq, pl. **aliqatsaujait** algae (*Laminaria*)

alirti, pl. **alirtiit** sock made of fur, now made of felt, worn inside boots

Alliriirtuni recent term for "Monday," the day when customary prohibitions do not apply

alliruit, pl. of **alliruq** lower jaw of mammals

Am! Am! onomatopoeia: sound of lapping

amaukkaluit, pl. of **amaukkaluk** worm in the intestines of humans and bearded seals; especially common in the small intestine, according to Mitiarjuk

amauti women's garment with a back pouch for a baby

amiksait, pl. of **amiksaq** skin to cover a boat

ammuumajuq, pl. **ammuumajuit** mollusc: truncated soft-shell clam (*Mya truncata*)

anaana, voc. **Anaanak!** mother, mommy

anaanatsiaq grandmother or a person like a grandmother, i.e., a female relative of the same generation

angajuk, vocative of **angajuq** kinship term: a man's older brother, a woman's older sister

angusiaq term used by a midwife for a boy that she (or he) has helped deliver, literally "the male [s/he has] made"

Angutsiaq person's name, literally a "handsome man"

Angutikallak or **Angutikallaaluk** person's name, literally "little man" or "big little man"

angutinnguaq little bone, figurine of a man; also person's name

Apaapa!, see **apaapait** baby talk for food

Aqiarulaaq person's name, literally "little stomach"

aqiggiit see **aqiggiq**

aqiaruit, pl. of **aqiaruq** stomach

aqiggiq, pl. **aqiggiit** willow ptarmigan (*Lagopus lagopus*)

aqiluqi boiled meat, very tender

aquviartulutuq little bone, figurine of a person crouched on his/her heels

arnaliaq term used by a midwife for a daughter that she has helped deliver, literally "the female [that she has] made"

arnanguat, pl. of **arnanguaq** little seal bone, figurine of a woman

arnaquti a boy's term for the midwife who helped deliver him

Arnatuinnaq person's name, literally "real woman"

Ataa! see **aatataa!**

ataataksaq stepfather

atigi indoor jacket

atuarniq north wind

atungaksaq piece of leather for sole of a boot

atungaq sole of a boot

Au! command to sled dogs: "Stop!", "Don't move!"

Auk! command to sled dogs: "Turn right!"

Autualu! Autualuk! exclamation to express annoyance or distress

avataq float made from a ringed seal turned inside out and filled with air

avvik wooden board on which a skin is cut

Hau! command to sled dogs: "Come to me!"

Hra! command to sled dogs: "Turn left!"

Ia ia ia! onomatopoeia: laughter

Iaa iaa a a a! onomatopoeia: crying of a child

Ia-a! baby talk, interjection to express fear of an unknown object or being

iggiat, pl. of **iggiaq** pharynx

igliti baseboard of a sleeping platform

iglitikallak, pl. **iglitikallait** little seal-bone figurine that represents the baseboard of a sleeping platform

igutsait, pl. of **igutsaq** Arctic bumblebee

ii floating hook made of a small piece of wood with a spike in it. It is baited with a piece of seal blubber, which seagulls love, and is tied to a line anchored to the shore. Used to catch seagulls. See **iijuq:** "it swallows"

Ii! Iii! interjection to express fright, fear of failure, disappointment, or disgust

Iii! onomatopoeia: laughter

Iikikii! exclamation to express feeling of damp cold (dry cold is called **ikkii**)

Iirq! or **Irq!** interjection to express irritation with an unpleasant situation

iksigarjuaq, pl. **iksigarjuat** name given to a Catholic missionary

ila possessive: **ilakka** (my kinfolk). Kinfolk

Ilai! interjection: "Of course!", "That's right!"

Ilaijja person's name, Elijah

ilakka see **ila**

illaulusuk little bone, figurine of a fetus

illiti baseboard of the sleeping platform or little bone that represents it

illitikallak, pl. **illitikallait** little bone, figurine of baseboard of the sleeping platform

iluliarusiq, pl. **iluliarusiit** meat, fillet from the inside of a beluga

ilulliq inner stitching of double seam on the leg of a boot

ilullitaq inner stitching of waterproof double seam, for a boot

inaluat, pl. of **inaluaq** small intestine of ringed seals, of humans, and of small animals

Inuit see **Inuk**

Inuk, pl. **Inuit** an Eskimo, literally a human being

inuksuk stone cairn, often used as a landmark for long-distance observation

ipiraq harpoon line, which connects a detachable harpoon point to the shaft and the float

iqaluit see **iqaluk**

iqaluk, pl. **iqaluit** generic term for salmonids, in particular Arctic char. More broadly, can mean fish in general

iqaluppik, pl. **iqaluppiit** Arctic salmon or Arctic char

Irr...! onomatopoeia: call of a willow ptarmigan

Irsutualuk a person's name, literally "the big one who carries on his shoulders"

Irsutuguluk a person's name, literally "little Irsutuq"

Irtuu! interjection to express recollection of something to do

isiuralittaaq lake trout

issutiit heather

Itigaittualuk dog's name, literally "the big one that is missing a foot"

itingit see **itiq**

itiq anus; possessive: **itingit**—his/her/its anuses

ittunguat, pl. of **ittunguaq** vertebrae (*Axis*), literally "that resembles an old man"

Ittusaq person's name, literally "the one who is getting old"

Ivvilualuk! a kind of angry curse, roughly meaning "damn you!"

Jiimialuk person's name, literally "Big Jimmy"

kaitjiaq thin leather strap, cut in a spiral from sealskin

kaivvasuk little bone, figurine of an adolescent

Kajualuk dog's name, literally "the big red one"

kakagutit, pl. of **kakaguti** edible flower of the Arctic saxifrage

kakillanaquti plant, saxifrage

kalirtisaikkut short line running across the front of a sled, to prevent the main tugline from sliding under the runners

kallaquti small berry bush, bearberry (*Arctostaphylos alpina*)

kanajuit see **kanajuq**

kanajuq, pl. **kanajuit** marine fish, a kind of sculpin

kanivautit, pl. of **kanivauti** diaphragm of mammals

kappianartuvik hereafter for those who have broken the rules. Hell of Christianity (literally "the big scary place")

kaugaliaq, pl. **kaugaliat** cone-shaped mollusc, a kind of limpet or barnacle

kiasiit, pl. of **kiasik** mammal shoulder blade, with the meat

kiataq, pl. **kiatat** dorsal portion of skin on the upper trunk, here a bearded seal

kiatat see **kiataq**

kiinaujait see **kiinaujaq**

kiinaujaq, pl. **kiinaujait** coin, literally "which resembles a face"

kiliutaq scraper made from a caribou shoulder blade, used by women

killapat pl. of **killaapaq** ripe catkin of an Arctic willow. From **killak**—"teeth on a saw, rasp, or file"

kilu far end of a home's interior, at the end of the sleeping platform

kinguq, pl. **kinguit** scuds (*Gammarus*), a kind of amphipod

kuanniq, pl. **kuanniit** algae *Alaria*

kujapigait, pl. of **kujapigaq** thoracic vertebrae of ringed seals and small mammals, and humans. More broadly, the flesh surrounding these vertebrae

kujapigaq see **kujapigait**

kujapiit see **kujapik**

kujapik, pl. **kujapiit** thoracic vertebrae of bearded seals and large marine mammals

kunik stem of the verb **kuninniq**: smell, sniff, or kiss in the Inuit or Oriental fashion

kuu kuu kuu onomatopoeia: clams falling onto a plate

kuutsinaat, pl. of **kuutsinaaq** hip bones of seals

kuutsiniit, pl. of **kuutsiniq** lumbar vertebrae of mammals

kuutsiit, pl. of **kuutsiq** homonym of next word. Berry bush resembling a bearberry

Kuutsiq dog's name, literally "hipbone"

kuutsitualik little bone, figurine of a hipless person

Lumaajuit see **Lumaajuq**

Lumaajuq, pl. **Lumaajuit** "the one who says 'Lumaaq'!", old woman of the above legend

lumaartalik beluga attached by a leather line to an old woman called Lumaajuq ("the one who says 'Lumaaq'!"), according to an Inuit legend

Maa maa maa! onomatopoeia: dogs whimpering in pain

Maatiusi person's name, Matthew

Makutsialutjuaq person's name, old woman of a legend

mamaittuqutit, pl. of **mamaittuquti** plant, Labrador tea

mami fatty tissue under the skin

mangittaq skin blanket spread on the ground for laying food on. Often a piece from skins that once covered a *qajaq*

manu neck of the hood of a garment, piece under the chin

matsait, pl. of **matsak** spleen

mattaq edible skin of the beluga

mirsutaq outer stitching of a boot's waterproof double seam

misiraq rancid oil of marine mammals in which one steeps meat

Mmm! onomatopoeia: cooing of affection when one kisses a child, to make it happy

Muu muu muu! Miuu! onomatopoeia: dogs howling

nanualuk a big polar bear. From "Nanuq"—polar bear (*Thalarctos maritimes*)

nanuirvik pad of bear fur used to dampen runners with water

naqitarvik leather strap, with fastening straps, that runs along the outside of a sled's runners

nasivvik point of land that serves as a lookout, often with a stone cairn

natsinguaq little bone, figurine of a seal

natsiq, dl. **natsiik** ringed seal

niaquit, pl. of **niaquq** head of seals, humans, and small mammals

niaquujait, pl. of **niaquujaq** bun made by the Whites, literally "which resembles a skull"

nikku, pl. **nikkuit** dried meat

nikut-tuasi see **aakut-tuasi**

Ningiukuluk person's name, literally "little old woman"

ningiurqaluk saltwater fish, a kind of sculpin not eaten by the Inuit

nipisaq sea snail (*Liparis*), literally "which is sticky"

nuakuluk kinship term used by a woman for her sister's child

Nuilaq dog's name, literally "fur trimming of a hood"; because the dog's fur makes a good hood trimming

nuliarsaq invisible female lover, succubus

nutilliq fish, brook trout

nuvviti main sled tugline, which is slipped through the loops of the lines running from each dog harness. Also: sinew braiding, on which fish are strung by their gills.

paannguaq little bone, figurine of an entrance

Palungattak dog's name, literally "which has short drooping ears"

pamialluit, pl. of **pamialluk** seal's tail

paugusiq, pl. **paugusiit** wooden pole stuck into the snow wall of the igloo and supported by a vertical post. It serves as a support for the drying rack. From it hangs the cooking pot, over the oil lamp

paurngaqutit, pl. of **paurngaquti** black crowberry

pavviit, pl. of **pavvik** anklebone

Pikiuliq place name; given to places where various migratory bird species nest in early summer, and where the Inuit go to gather eggs; often islands

puiji , pl. **puijiit** marine animal whose head appears at the water's surface

puijiit see **puiji**

puttajiaq seriously wounded or dead marine mammal, whose body is floating on the water's surface

puurtaq bag of meat made from a sealskin turned inside out or from a beluga stomach

puvait, pl. of **puvak** lung

Qaa! onomatopoeia: snoring

qainnguq ice ledge along the shoreline at high tide mark

qajaak see **qajaq**

qajaq, pl. **qajait,** dl. **qajaak** kayak

qajuuttalutuq little bone, figurine of a drinking mug

Qalingu person's name

qaliruat, pl. **qaliruaq** boot made of sealskin that has had its fur removed

qalliniq part of a boot, covering the top of the foot and sewn to the sole

Qalliutuq person's name, literally "the one who is winning a fight"

Qallunaaq, pl. **Qallunaat,** dl. **Qallunaak** White man, literally "big eyebrows"

qalluviaq see **qalluviat**

qalluviat, pl. of **qalluviaq** arch of the aorta in the heart of marine mammals

qanirqutuut pl. of **qanirqutuuq** a kind of large-mouthed sculpin, literally "big mouth"

qaritait, pl. of **qaritaq** brain

qatannguт, dl. **qatannguuk,** voc. **qatannguuk** a woman's "female cousin"; more broadly, a female friend

qauliut wooden instrument for softening boot leather

qaunnaq Inuit chewing gum

qiaq caul, peritoneum

qiiii onomatopoeia: crackling sound of an oil lamp burning

qijuttaq firewood, brush wood, dwarf willow, or driftwood

qilalukkaanaq, pl. **qilalukkaanat** beluga calf

qillaqut, or **qillaquti** gift to a midwife as thanks for tying the umbilical cord

qimminguat, pl. of **qimminguaq** humerus of seals, also first knucklebones of the front and rear seal flippers. Little bone, figurine of a dog

qinirsiit, pl. of **qinirsiq** pancreas

qinirsikallait, pl. of **qinirsikallak** lymph nodes

qiqruaq, pl. **qiqruat** kelp

Qirniq dog's name, literally "black fur"

qitirsiraq, pl. **qitirsirait** finger-guard made from skin, literally an index-finger-guard, though also put on the ring finger and forefinger

qitsalikaat, pl. of **qitsalikaak** mesentery

qukiutiaruk .22 long rifle, literally "little rifle"

qulliq oil lamp made from steatite; also little bone: figurine of an oil lamp

qulluniq, pl. **qulluniit** ice cave created by the ebb tide, on the foreshore

qumait see Qumaq

Qumaq, pl. **qumait** person's name, literally "white-coloured intestinal worm" found in seals, humans, and fishes

qungisiit, pl. of **qungisiq** cervical vertebrae

qunujaq ominous prophetic dream

qurvik Inuit chamber pot. Can be used as a spittoon or a garbage pail. Formerly made of leather

quvianartuvik literally "the big thing that makes people happy." Modern meaning: "heaven"

sakiat, pl. of **sakiaq** short ribs of a mammal; also wife's brother or husband's sister

Sanaaq person's name

sanaji midwife

sappa little bone, figurine of wooden baggage compartment on a sled. Also called **iksivinnguaq**

saputi stone dam that is used to trap Arctic char when they swim upstream, in order to harpoon them more easily

Sarvaq! onomatopoeia: an object falling into the water. May also mean rapids

sauniq person's namesake, literally "bone"

sigalaq, pl. **sigalat** plant with a hard red berry, or ship biscuit

sigalat see **sigalaq**

siiqrulik very skinny seal whose knees can be seen through its skin

silalliq outer stitching of double seam on the leg of a boot

sinaa edge of an ice floe; literally "its edge"

Sinarnaaluk dog's name, literally "the big grey one"

siqruit, pl. of **siqruq** rear seal flipper

sirmiq, dl. **sirmiik**, pl. **sirmiit** coating of smooth frozen peat moss on a sled's runners

sirpalutuq little bone (meaning unknown)

Siu siu siu si si siu humming of a tune

sulluniit leg of a boot

sulluniq double stitching, folded over, of the leg of a waterproof skin boot

suluppaujaq eelpout, a small fish; literally "which resembles a feather"

sursat, pl. of **sursaq** thick fleshy root of the Alpine bistort

Suvakkualuk! interjection to express opposition, anger, or unpleasant surprise

Tajarak person's name

Tak tak! onomatopoeia: something hitting, knocking, or falling

Taka taka taka onomatopoeia: singing of a child

taliit, pl. of **taliq** rear seal flipper; also human arm

Taqriasuk person's name

Taqulik dog's name, literally "which has a white spot over its eyes"

tarqaq, pl. **tarqait** leather strap running over the top of a *qajaq* to hold in the hunting equipment

tarquti poker for an oil lamp, often made from an Arctic willow stem

tikkuu onomatopoeia: a firearm going off

tinguit, pl. of **tinguq** liver

tulimaat, pl. of **tulimaaq** mammal rib

tunirjuit, pl. of **tunirjuk** mammal sternum

turqujaat, pl. **turqujaaq** larynx

tuurngaq, pl. **tuurngait** term for a shaman's helping spirit. Used as a name for the devil by some of the first missionaries

U! Uu! onomatopoeia: sound of great satisfaction after eating food

Ua! command to dogs: "Forward!"

Ua! Ua! interjection shouted by a hunter to make a seal dive under water and thereby tire it; also onomatopoeia: sound of vomiting

Uai! interjection to curse dogs or people

uanniq west wind

uati part of the home, to the left and right of the entrance, which adjoins the wall

uirsaq human-looking invisible male lover, incubus

Uit! command to dogs: "Forward!"

Ujararjuaq place name, literally "big slab of rock"

ujjuk bearded seal (*Erignathus barbatus*)

Ukiliriaq dog's name. Used for a dog whose fur has several large patches of different colours (often white and black)

ukpik, pl. **ukpiit** snowy owl (*Nyctea nyctea*)

uliuliniq, pl. **uliuliniit** meat, sinewy fillet from the back of a beluga

ullugummitaaq daily meal

ullutusiq, pl. **ullutusiit** long day, the long days around the summer solstice

ulu woman's half-moon knife

ulunnguat, pl. of **ulunnguaq** xiphoid process of mammals, literally "which resembles a woman's knife (ulu)"

umiarjuaq large boat of the Whites, literally "big boat"

umiqruit, pl. of **umiqruq** seal snout

umm see **uumm**

Ungaa! onomatopoeia: plaintive cry of a human baby or an Arctic hare

ungati side extension of the sleeping platform of the igloo

ungirlaaq laced bag of meat, made here from a piece of beluga skin

uqaujaq, pl. **uqaujait** leaf of an Arctic willow, literally "which resembles a tongue"

uqumangirniq nightmare

uquuqu baby talk mainly for a bird or sea animal

usuujaq *qajaq* bow, literally "which resembles a penis"

usuujaq, pl. **usuujait** homonym of previous word: means "sausage," an imported product

utsulutuq little bone, figurine of a vulva

Uu! onomatopoeia: sound of satisfaction with food being eaten

Uugaq dog's name, in the legend of Luuumaajuq

uujuq, pl. **uujuit** boiled meat

Uujun ukua interjectional phrase: "Here are some pieces of boiled meat"

Uumm! also see **umm!** and **mmm!** Onomatopoeia: sound of satisfaction after eating food

uummatit, pl. of **uummati** heart

Uuppaa! interjection that accompanies effort of lifting, carrying, or pulling something heavy

uuttuq seal stretched out on an ice floe and basking in the sun

ADDITIONAL READING

SELECTED WORKS BY MITIARJUK NAPPAALUK

Nappaaluk, Mitiarjuk. *Qimminuulingajut ilumiutartangit*. Montreal: Kativik School Board, n.d.

———. *Qupirruit*. Montreal: Kativik School Board, 1987

———. *Sanaakkut Piusiviningita unikkausinnguangat*. Edited by Bernard Saladin d'Anglure. Inuksiutiit Allaniagait, no. 4. Quebec City: Association Inuksiutiit Katimajiit, 1984.

———. *Sanaaq*. Transliterated and translated from Inuktitut by Bernard Saladin d'Anglure. Montreal: Stanké, 2002.

———. *Tarrkii piniarningillu*. Montreal: Kativik School Board, 1997.

———. *Tininnimiutaait*. Montreal: Kativik School Board, n.d.

———. *Silaup piusingit inuit nunangani*. Montreal: Kativik School Board, n.d.

SELECTED WORKS BY BERNARD SALADIN D'ANGLURE ON INUIT

Prof. Bernard Saladin d'Anglure has published extensively on Inuit in French. His work is entirely relevant for understanding the ethnographic details in the text of Sanaaq. *Fortunately for the monolingual reader, some of his work has been published in English. This list contains articles available in English along with his major books in French.*

Aupilaarjuk, Mariano, Tulimaaq Aupilaarjuk, Lucassie Nutaraaluk, Rose Iqallijuq, Johanasi Ujarak, Isidore Ijituuq, and Michel Kupaaq. *Interviewing Inuit Elders 4: Cosmology and Shamanism*. Under the direction of Bernard Saladin d'Anglure. Iqaluit: Nunavut Arctic College, 2001.

Saladin d'Anglure, Bernard. "Inuit of Quebec." In *Handbook of North American Indians: Arctic*, edited by David Damas, 476–507. Vol. 5. Washington: Smithsonian Institution, 1984.

———. "Contemporary Inuit of Quebec." In *Handbook of North American Indians: Arctic*, edited by David Damas, 683–88. Vol. 5. Washington: Smithsonian Institution, 1984.

———. "Nanook, Super-Male: The Polar Bear in the Imaginary Space and Social Time of the Inuit of the Canadian Arctic." In *Signifying Animals: Human Meaning in the Natural World*, edited by Roy Willis, 178–95. London: Routledge, 1990.

———. "The Mythology of the Inuit of the Central Arctic." In *Mythologies*, edited by Yves Bonnefoy, 25–32. Chicago: University of Chicago Press, 1991.

———. "The Shaman's Share or Inuit Sexual Communism in the Canadian Central Arctic." *Anthropologica* 35 (1993): 59–103.

———. "From Foetus to Shaman: The Construction of an Inuit Third Sex." In *Amerindian Rebirth: Reincarnation Belief among North American Indians and Inuit*, edited by Antonia C. Mills and Richard Slobodin, 82–106. Toronto: University of Toronto Press, 1994.

———. "Brother Moon, Sister Sun, and the Direction of the World: From Arctic Cosmography to Inuit Cosmology." In *Circumpolar Religion and Ecology: An Anthropology of the North*, edited by Takashi Irimoto and Takako Yamada, 187–212. Tokyo: University of Tokyo Press, 1994.

———. "Shamanism." In *Encyclopedia of Social and Cultural Anthropology*, edited by Alan Barnard and Jonathan Spencer, 504–8. London: Routledge, 1996.

———. "Erotic Dreams, Mystical Kinship and Shamanism." *North Atlantic Studies* 4, 1 and 2 (2001): 5–12.

———. "An Ethnographic Commentary: The Legend of Atȧnarjuat." In *Atanarjuat: The Fast Runner*, edited by Paul Angilirq, Zacharias Kunuk, Herve Paniaq, Pauloosie Qulitalik, and Norman Cohn, 196–208. Montreal: Coach House Books and Isuma Publishing, 2002.

———. "Inuit and Shamanism." In *Atanarjuat: The Fast Runner*, edited by Paul Angilirq, Zacharias Kunuk, Herve Paniaq, Pauloosie Qulitalik, and Norman Cohn, 209–30. Montreal: Coach House Books and Isuma Publishing, 2002.

———. "*Etre et Renaître Inuit: Homme, Femme Ou Chamane*." Paris: Gallimard, 2006.

———. "The Construction of Shamanic Identity aong the Inuit of Nunavut and Nunavik." In *Aboriginality and Governance: A Multidisciplinary Perspective from Quebec*, edited by Gordon Christie, 141–66. Penticton: Theytus Books, 2006.

———. "The Inuit 'Third Gender'." In *Aboriginality and Governance: A Multidisciplinary Perspective from Quebec*, edited by Gordon Christie, 167–78. Penticton: Theytus Books, 2006.

———. "The Whale Hunting among the Inuit of the Canadian Arctic." In *Aboriginality and Governance: A Multidisciplinary Perspective from Quebec*, edited by Gordon Christie, 179–202. Penticton: Theytus Books, 2006.

Saladin d'Anglure, Bernard, and Colin Anderson. "The 'Third Gender' of the Inuit." *Diogenes* 52, 4 (2005): 134–44.

Saladin d'Anglure, Bernard, Richard Baillargeon, Jimmy Innaarulik Mark, and Louis-Jacques Dorais. *La Parole Changée En Pierre: Vie Et Oeuvre De Davidialuk Alasuaq, Artiste Inuit Du Québec Arctique*, Les Cahiers Du Patrimoine 11. Québec: Governement du Québec, Minstere des Affaires culturelles, Direction generale du patrimoine, 1977.

Saladin d'Anglure, Bernard, and Igloolik Isuma Productions. *Au Pays Des Inuit: Un Film, Un Peuple, Une Légende*. Montpellier: Indigène éditions, 2002.

CRITICAL WRITING ON INUIT LITERATURE

Carpenter, Mary. "Stories: 'Skeleton Woman,' 'Woman of the Sea.'" In *Echoing Silence: Essays on Arctic Narrative*, edited by John Moss, 225–30. Ottawa: University of Ottawa Press, 1997.

Coates, Corey. "The First Inuit Autobiography: Text and Context(s)." *The Northern Review* 28 (2008): 261–70.

Gatti, Maurizio, ed. *Littérature amérindienne du Québec: écrits de la langue française*. Montreal: Hurtubise, 2004.

Gedalof [McGrath], Robin. *Paper Stays Put: A Collection of Inuit Writing*. Edmonton: Hurtig Publishers, 1986.

Kennedy, Michael P.J. "Inuit Literature in English: A Chronological Survey." *Canadian Journal of Native Studies* 13, 1 (1993): 31–41.

———. "Southern Exposure: Belated Recognition of a Significant Inuk Writer Artist." *Canadian Journal of Native Studies* 15, 2 (1995): 347–61.

———. "The Sea Goddess Sedna: An Enduring Pan-Arctic Legend from Traditional Orature to the New Narratives of the Late Twentieth Century." In *Echoing Silence: Essays on Arctic Narrative*, edited by John Moss, 211–24. Ottawa: University of Ottawa Press, 1997.

Martin, Keavy. "Arctic Solitude: Mitiarjuk Nappaaluk's *Sanaaq* and the Politics of Translation in Inuit Literature." *Studies in Canadian Literature* 35, 2 (2010): 13–29.

———. *Stories in a New Skin: Approaches to Inuit Literature.* Winnipeg: University of Manitoba Press, 2012.

McGrath, Robin. "Canadian Inuit Literature: The Development of a Tradition." Ottawa: National Museums of Canada, National Museum of Man, 1984.

———. "Images of the Land in Inuit Literature." *Etudes/Inuit/Studies* 9, 2 (1985): 133–39.

———. "Reassessing Traditional Inuit Poetry." *Canadian Literature* 124–125 (1990): 19–28.

———. "Circumventing the Taboos: Inuit Women's Autobiographies." In *Undisciplined Women: Tradition and Culture in Canada*, edited by Pauline Greenhill and D. Tye, 223–33. Montreal and Kingston: McGill-Queen's University Press, 1997.

Neuhaus, Mareike. *"That's Raven Talk": Holophrastic Readings of Contemporary Indigenous Literatures*. Regina: Canadian Plains Research Center Press, 2011.

Petrone, Penny. *Northern Voices: Inuit Writing in English*. Toronto: University of Toronto Press, 1988.

Stott, Jon C. "Spirits in the Snowhouse: The Inuit Angakok (Shaman) in Children's Literature." *Canadian Journal of Native Studies* 5, 2 (1985): 193–200.

———. "Form, Content, and Cultural Values in Three Inuit (Eskimo) Survival Stories." *American Indian Quarterly* 10, 3 (1986): 213–26.

Watson, Christine. "Autobiographical Writing as a Healing Process: Interview with Alice Masak French." *Journal of Indigenous Thought* (2000): 1–11.